D0409695

SPEAKING OF LOVE

SPEAKING OF LOVE

ANGELA YOUNG

BEAUTIFULBOOKS

First published 2007

Beautiful Books Limited
117 Sugden Road,
London SW11 5ED

www.beautiful-books.co.uk

ISBN 9781905636068

9 8 7 6 5 4 3 2 1

Copyright © Angela Young 2007

The right of Angela Young to be identified as the author
of this work has been asserted by her in accordance with the
Copyright, Designs and Patents Act 1988.

All rights reserved. No part of this publication may be
reproduced, stored in or introduced into a retrieval system,
or transmitted, in any form, or by any means (electronic,
mechanical, photocopying, recording or otherwise) without the
prior written permission of the publisher. Any person who does
any unauthorised act in relation to this publication may be
liable to criminal prosecution and civil claims for damages.

Every effort has been made to fulfil requirements with regard to
reproducing copyright material. The author and publisher will be
glad to rectify any omissions at the earliest opportunity.

A catalogue reference for this book is available from
the British Library.

Jacket design by Ian Pickard
Cover painting: 'Grey Laburnum' by Brue Richardson
Printed in Great Britain by T J International

for
BRUE

'You must take care of love;
if not it goes bad.'

a six-year-old girl,
recorded in my grandmother's commonplace book

Part One
Thursday, 27 July, 1996

Iris's story

I have come home, after a long and difficult journey. I travelled alone and it was some time before I realised that I had arrived.

★ ★ ★

I am in Wales to tell my stories.

My bedroom is high in the watchtower of a mediaeval castle and through the window I can see the tiered lawns that cascade down from the castle walls to the Bristol Channel. Pennants flutter from the tops of the striped storytelling tents on the jousting field.

I stood in one of those tents last night. It was cavernous and empty, but I sensed a thousand pairs of eyes and a thousand pairs of ears. I shuffled self-consciously onto the wooden stage and found that my head was too heavy to lift, my voice too reedy to carry.

I had to force myself to breathe and it took me half an hour to find my voice. If that happens on Sunday my storytelling career will be stillborn.

But people tell stories all the time.

When I was in Salem a man told me about a nurse who arrived to take him to the ECT block with an umbrella.

'To keep the snow from my head,' he said and he laughed.

He told me that he and the nurse had walked side by side along the snow-covered path between snow-covered lawns, under the snow-laden trees. He told me he'd seen rabbit prints and deer prints in the snow, and the parallel prints of the patient and the nurse who'd gone before. He told me he'd walked in fresh snow because he wanted to see his own footprints on the way back.

'That's the only important thing,' he said, and he slapped his thigh like an old-fashioned music hall entertainer. 'Footprints.'

Speaking of Love

I don't know what happened to him, but I'll never forget his beautiful smile nor his story, which never made me laugh.

People forget stories too.

I forgot how my mother died. All I could remember was that I had been with her. And when my father refused to talk about her I knew that was my punishment because I had failed to prevent her death.

He threw everything of hers away but I salvaged the hospital bag of her clothes from the dustbin, and I wrapped the heavy *Carousel* records that they used to dance to in my grey school cardigan and hid them in my room. I kept a lavender bag of hers under my pillow and one night I watched, through the bannisters, as my father fed photographs of my mother into the fire. I was too young to understand that he did what he did because he was locked in; all I knew was that I was locked out.

So I lived in my small upstairs room and had conversations with the characters in the books I read until, one winter evening, one of them replied. It said my name, 'Eereece', the way my mother said my name. And then I realised that it was my mother.

'Remember, Eereece, that I shall always love you,' she said, with a smile in her voice. I heard the smile too.

She only came at night, but she came often.

In the morning, when I opened my eyes and realised she wasn't there, an ache would fill my throat until I was sure it would burst open. Even now if I smell burnt dust on an electric heater a lump forms in my throat and reminds me how I used to sit on the floor under the window, by the heater, and close my eyes and long for her to return.

When she came she told me the stories she'd always told me, and sometimes we just talked. But I never asked her how she died because she always seemed so alive.

And then the goblin turned up.

He came when I started to drop things.

I broke one of the *Carousel* records that I'd watched my parents dance to and the spine of my mother's collection of French fairytales split one night when it fell from my hands.

Iris's story

The goblin hissed out, 'Fumble fingers, fumble fingers', every time I dropped something. He lived in a corner of my bedroom. It became The Corner I Was Terrified Of.

One evening, when my mother's lavender and vanilla smell filled my bedroom she told me that the goblin wasn't there. She said he was just a figment of my imagination. So I stood and faced the Corner. I told the goblin he didn't exist. I said I never wanted to hear his voice again. But as I pulled the eiderdown up under my chin I heard him hiss and I saw his long, pale cracked fingers stretch out towards me from the Corner. I heard him lisp, "Syour choice, Iris. 'Scompletely your choice. But if I no longer exist then your mother no longer exists. 'Sup to you Iris. You choose.'

Of course there was no choice. My mother's voice was as precious as my life because it was the only thing of hers that I didn't have to hide from my father. He didn't know I could hear her so he couldn't take her away. He didn't know about the goblin either. I couldn't tell him anything and I knew, deep inside, that all he wanted was for me to disappear.

He used to love the stories my mother told. He was as captivated as I was when she'd suddenly look up from her supper, or her sewing, and ask us if we knew that the best Parisian milliners were the ones who persuaded spiders to spin coloured webs for their embroidery threads. Or that the reason Gustave Eiffel ended up with beautifully latticed girders for his great Tower, instead of the solid ones he'd asked for, was that no one spoke the language of the Eiffelene trolls who'd mined the iron and made the great girders and brought them to Paris from Meurthe-et-Moselle. No one knew how to ask the trolls to stop work, so they hammered and struck at the iron until *they* thought their work was done.

We both knew that several days later she'd tell us a whole story about the milliners and their spiders, or about Gustave and the Eiffelene trolls and I know that my father looked forward to those stories just as much as I did. And I know that he loved my mother, the way he danced with her told me so; and I thought he loved me, but after she died he died too, inside. I realise now that the only way he could cope with her loss was by ignoring anyone or anything that reminded him of her, he could not tolerate them. But all I knew then was that he found me intolerable.

He painted my bitten nails with a pungent, brown liquid at night and pulled white mittens onto my hands and tied them with shiny white ribbons round my wrists. I only survived because I could hear my mother's voice. As long as I could hear her I wasn't alone.

I listened to her stories and I began to tell them to myself, on the way to school. And I often heard her say, 'Just,' (she said it with a soft 'j'), 'Just as long as you see the pictures, Eereece, the words will come.'

Even now, forty-three years later, I still hear my mother's voice, although hers is the only voice I hear now. She reminds me to follow the pictures when I tell a story. And it's always worked. As long as there are pictures in my head, the words come. Even when I see pictures that I've never seen before I know I must follow them.

For weeks now I've watched the pictures from my stories travel beneath my eyelids and, in the evenings, I've given them words while Dick cooks our supper. I've told the stories at my local story-telling club and I've told them to myself on my long walks through Thetford Forest. But now I'm here at the festival and, despite all the pictures and all the words, I am very nervous.

I remind myself that six years ago, at The Abbey, or at Salem years before that, I'd never have dreamt I could do this. I reassure myself that I've come a long way, that I can do it, that I have come home.

* * *

There is a letter that I take with me everywhere. A letter whose words I know by heart.

This is what it says:

> *Mum*
> *It's horrible what I've got to say but I've got to say it.*
> *I can't come and see you ever again. Sorry. Vivie*

PS: This is why.
Seeing you makes it all come back and then I'm completely useless. The only way I can cope is if I don't see you. Sorry. Even when I came with Charles I wasn't much use, was I? I don't know what to do for you, Mum, so I can't see you. I don't know what else to say.
Except sorry.

Dick says I stab myself every time I read her letter. He says the wounds will never heal that way. But it's the only thing of Vivie's that I have, so I keep it.

I should throw it away, but I can't bear to.

It's her thirtieth birthday on Sunday but I haven't seen her for six years. I long to hug her. I long to hear her voice. I long to look at her.

Poor Vivie. She tried to mend me. She tried to make me well. She tried to care for me all by herself, but she was only a child.

She tried to keep people away from me as I had made her promise.

And now she is scarred. I know she is. I can feel it.

I've written to tell her that I know, now, why it all happened and that I know, now, what she tried to do and how impossible it was for her. I've said that I know that no one can mend anyone else, especially not a child, especially not a daughter.

But in the meantime I cannot plan to see her. I can only hope with all my heart that there will come a day when she wants to see me.

And that day will be a fine, fine day when it comes.

If it comes.

Vivie's story

Vivie was talking to herself in the shower. As the water flowed over her body she spoke slowly, as if she was learning lines.

'I've got something to tell you,' she said, as she squeezed shampoo into her hand. 'I've been meaning to tell you ...' but she stopped. She knew it wouldn't work if she began like that because Charles, with his incurable optimism, would smile expectantly and then she'd never be able to tell him the bad news.

So she started again. She soaped her hair and she said, 'I've done a terrible thing. Well, no, not terrible, exactly, but you're not ... you won't like it.' That sounded better. Then he'd sit down and drum his fingers on the kitchen table. He'd look worried and she'd sit beside him and tell him what she'd done.

Vivie let the water rinse the soap from her hair and said, 'I'm sorry, Charles, but I just couldn't go through with it. I got rid – ' but as she stretched up to push her hair back a sharp stabbing pain made her stagger and bend forwards. She pressed her hands into her groin and the water pushed her long hair forwards over her face. Blood ran down the inside of her thigh.

When the pain eased Vivie stood and let the water pour over her face. She wanted the water to hide her tears. There wasn't anyone in the bathroom to see her tears, but Vivie felt as if she was being harshly judged for them, so she hid them.

The judgements, as Vivie called them, had all been harsh recently. On the bus on the way back from the hospital a sudden spitefully disapproving judgement had so shocked Vivie that she'd got off the bus and gone straight to the nearest pub. It had taken several glasses of wine to stop the judgement's insistence that she should not have got rid of the little body that had been growing so innocently inside hers.

Vivie's story

Vivie yanked the towel roughly across her back and tried to get rid of a persistent image of Charles kissing her and opening a bottle of champagne. If she'd kept the baby he would have done that, and he'd have danced his funny little tap dance. He would have hummed his tuneless hum and whistled. He'd have rung everyone he knew and then he'd have said, 'Are you very, very happy, my darling?' over and over again.

Vivie scratched her cheek as she angrily pushed her tears away.

She'd been shocked by her reaction to her pregnancy. She'd felt nothing but an overwhelming despair and the thought of Charles's kindness to her, his patience and his desire to please her made her feel even worse. She knew she didn't deserve him. And she knew she should have told him about the baby.

She tossed her hair back without bothering to finish drying it, threw on the clothes that she'd dropped onto the floor of their bedroom the night before, wedged a thick wad of lavatory paper between her thighs and hurried from the house, slamming the door.

She was going to be extremely late for work.

Matthew's story

The car is about to overheat, I've forgotten to bring any water and there's a siren wailing somewhere and a haze above the cars in the traffic jam in front of me. I'm staring at the architectural mess that is St Thomas's and I'm thinking I might just melt the way the tarmac's melting.

I'm willing the traffic to move not only because I'm going to be late for Dad, but because all this hanging about is giving me time to think about things I've been trying not to think about, viz. Vivie. I've been trying to put her out of my mind since I saw her on Monday. It was a stupid idea to go to the Prom. I wish I hadn't. I wasn't even planning to go after Julia cancelled, but I couldn't concentrate at work.

I stared at the models of the coloured drums we'd dreamed up for the student residences at UeL, imagining them on site, built, occupied, functioning just as we'd planned, overlooking Albert Dock and shimmering with reflected light from the water. I paced the office thinking about the contractors and the schedule and wishing we'd heard whether our bid had been successful. But I couldn't do any useful work and I couldn't stop going over all the work we'd done, even though at that stage in a bid there's nothing practical to be done, so in the end I went to the Prom to distract myself.

If I'd thought about the Prom programme I suppose I might have thought about Vivie because she's always loved that concerto. But I hadn't seen her for years and so when I did see her, on the other side of the arena, it was a shock. I saw her black cap first, and then her hair. The cap was pushed back on her head with the peak flipped up the way she's always worn it, and it struck me that the angle of the peak to her face was precisely the same (one hundred and twenty degrees) as the angle between the inverted rooves and the walls of the UeL residence buildings.

I looked around the Albert Hall for Charles, but I couldn't see him and I realised I didn't want to see him. I tried to cross the arena in the interval but by the time I'd stumbled over several bags and excused my way through knots of people, Vivie had disappeared.

I waited where I'd seen her. She didn't come back so I decided it couldn't have been her, just someone who looked a lot like her, but Vivie's hair is Vivie's hair. I've never seen hair like it on anyone else, except her father, so I stayed where I thought she'd been standing and I waited. I couldn't help wanting to know how she was and at the same time I didn't want to know. I felt the old excitement and the old foreboding while I stared upwards, redesigning the Albert Hall's fantastically ugly flying-saucer baffles, and then Vivie said 'Hello,' as if we'd seen each other just the day before.

The traffic's moving, at last. It was an accident, right outside St Thomas's Hospital. Now I'm moving and there's a breeze, but my shirt's sticking to me and I'm going to have to stop for water for the MG and for me. I'll phone Dad when I'm out of London and the roads are clear. He surely won't be worrying yet.

Vivie kept her eyes closed all the way through the concerto. She swayed slightly as she listened, lost in the music, and it was all I could do to stop myself putting my hand on the curve of her waist. It's ridiculous, it's embarrassing and it's hopeless. But it persists.

It was hot in the Hall and her hair was sticking to her forehead under her cap. She was wearing that cap the day she asked me the question that I flunked. I used to tell myself that if I got a second chance I would answer her differently, but life's not like that. You don't get second chances.

It was a dry day in April and my father kept saying he'd never known such a dry spring. He was busy watering his garden and Iris's garden, walking backwards and forwards under the arch in the beech hedge. Vivie and I were sitting on the flagstones below Iris's kitchen window between the stone urns that Dad had planted with lavender for Iris.

Iris was in The Abbey and Charles was in Iris's cottage somewhere. Vivie and I sat with our backs against the kitchen wall and she was smoking, as usual. Despite the drought it wasn't warm and I was just about to suggest we went back inside when Vivie asked me if I would give her away. Until that moment I had no idea she was getting married and I couldn't think of a thing to say.

I stared at the neat lines on the newly clipped beech hedge that divides Dad's garden from Iris's, and I thought how much lighter her garden was now that Dad had cut her laurel back. I stared up at the white clouds scudding across the wide expanse of blue, but I didn't look at Vivie, nor did I answer her question. When I finally did find the courage to look at her, she was blowing smoke down between her knees and pulling at the skin on her thumb. She bit the skin and she said, without looking at me, 'Well, will you, Matthew?'

Out of the corner of my eye I saw Dad standing under the arch in the beech hedge. He took a step into Iris's garden and then stopped, turned and went back into his garden. I heard the squeak as he turned off the tap and the sound of running water ceased. I said to Vivie, softly in the sudden silence, 'Your father's supposed to give you away. Why don't you ask him?'

She looked up, said, 'No,' and stared at me through her large grey eyes. She pushed the black cap back on her head and said, 'Even if I knew where he was he's so unreliable he'd probably forget. Anyway, I'd like it to be you.'

She smiled then, and the long dimple made that crease in her cheek. We'd both started to whisper.

I said, 'You could ask my father.'

She said, 'I could, but I'd like it to be you, Matthew.' She screwed up her eyelids against the cigarette smoke. She said, 'We'd both like it to be you.' I stared at Iris's laburnum tree in the middle of the lawn, its long green buds were hanging down, it was just about to bloom.

Matthew's story

I said, 'I can't.' I felt sick.

She said, 'Why not?'

I said, 'I can't give you away, Vivie, that's all.'

She ground her cigarette into a flagstone and it left a black mark. She leaned towards me and she said, 'Matthew, why can't you?'

I wanted to put my arms round her. I wanted to pull her to me and kiss her where the freckles gather by her lip but I didn't move, didn't answer her, stopped looking at her. It was she who jumped up, grabbed my wrists and pulled. She is slight and I was sure I'd be able to resist, but she braced herself and her striped scarf fell down between her arms and swayed as she strained to make me stand. She succeeded because she managed to pull me far enough forwards so that either I had to sprawl onto my knees or get up. I got up and she inclined her head away from Iris's cottage. We walked across the lawn, ducking under the laburnum tree, until we stood by the wooden fence at the end of Iris's garden beneath the beeches that were showing the tips of their furled green leaves.

She said, 'Matthew, what is it? Tell me why you can't.' She flung her striped scarf back over her shoulder and fumbled in her pocket for her cigarettes but the gusting wind blew out the matches as she struck them. When she struck the last one I cupped my hands round hers and our foreheads touched.

I said, 'Vivie …'

She said, 'Yes?'

I said, 'I can't. I mean I didn't know you were … I mean …'

Charles shouted 'Vivienne!' and cut me off. We jumped apart and I swung round to see him striding across the flagstones holding up a bottle of wine. His walk was brisk and businesslike and his footsteps thudded across the lawn.

'Vivienne, my darling,' he called out, 'I think the Pouilly-Fumé's the one to go for.'

I glanced back at Vivie who was looking straight at me. Smoke drifted up from the side of her mouth just where the freckles gather, and she picked and bit at the side of her thumb.

I couldn't say, 'Don't marry him, Vivie. For God's sake don't marry him. Marry me.' I just couldn't say it. She would have thought me mad.

I stared at the small brown triangle that makes a section in her left iris. It suddenly looked like a splinter and I wondered, ludicrously, if it hurt her. I wanted to take it out. And then Charles was standing between us, beaming, and holding three glasses out to me, upside down, their stems threaded between his broad fingers. I took the glasses and Charles poured the wine.

He said, 'Settled then, my darling?' but when Vivie didn't answer, he looked at me.

I said, 'Er ... yes. Yes. All settled.'

He said, 'Good. So glad,' and beamed at us again. 'We were both hoping you'd agree, weren't we, my darling? It'll make young Vivienne here very, very happy.'

Vivie took her glass and Charles said, 'To us, then. All three.'

I remember thinking that the wine was too cold, and wondering where Dad had got to, and staring at Charles and thinking, wildly, that a man with so little hair couldn't possibly marry a woman with so much.

Charles handed me the bottle and cupped his large hand round Vivie's elbow. I watched them walking back towards Iris's cottage; I had the impression that he was walking for both of them.

They stopped under Iris's laburnum tree and Charles said, over his shoulder, 'Getting a bit chilly out here, isn't it? Come on in, old chap.'

Vivie held her glass out in front of her, stiffly. Charles raised his glass to me and when they reached the kitchen door he kissed Vivie on the cheek. I stared up at the wide blue dome of the sky. I heard a blackbird sing and I heard my father whistle a reply from his garden. I turned and stared out across Jepson's field and then I heard Dad calling to me.

'Come and be my eyes for me, would you Matthew?' he said. 'I can't see the damned threads.'

When I walked into Dad's garden he handed me a hose connector. I studied it, glad to have something to look at, glad not to have to look at him.

Matthew's story

Dad said, 'There's nothing wrong with it, it's new. But I don't know what I've done with my specs ... Matthew?'

I said, 'Yup ... right ...' and bent over the tap beside him to have a look.

But as I was fixing the connector to the tap Charles burst through the hedge announcing loudly to Dad that he and Vivie were getting married. That I had agreed to give Vivie away. Dad straightened up and said that was splendid news, and I had to go back into Iris's kitchen to celebrate with them. I had no choice.

Vivie was studying something on the dresser in the corner. She looked up and said, 'Listen to this ... this is wonderful,' but she sounded as if she was about to cry. She said, 'It says here ...' she held up a CD, her eyes shining, her lips pressed tightly together, but she didn't say anything else.

Charles said, 'That's your favourite concerto, isn't it, my darling? They used it in that film ... what's it called?'

He looked at Dad.

Dad said, 'Brief Encounter.'

As soon as I could I went back to London, and I never did give Vivie away.

How could I?

Dad did it. I didn't even go to the wedding.

Vivie's story

Vivie sat on the bus and every time she looked at her watch it seemed that another ten minutes had flown by, but the bus still did not move. The driver said he had no idea what the problem was and, as people began to get off the bus, Vivie thought about getting the train from Clapham Junction, but she didn't. She stayed on the bus because she couldn't face taking the underground from Waterloo. She felt dizzy just looking down escalator shafts; she knew she'd have to fight for breath so far below the street. So she sat on the bus, alone, and felt herself judged for a coward. Of course there was enough oxygen on the underground, how did everyone else manage? But Vivie couldn't remember a time when the thought of the underground hadn't panicked her. She got off the bus to smoke a cigarette but she stood close by, with one hand resting on the side of the bus so that the driver couldn't leave without her, and as she smoked she tried to shut out the words in her head, the words that insisted she should tell Charles the truth about the baby.

A couple of seagulls screeched overhead and they reminded Vivie, cruelly, of the day Charles had told her he loved her. No one had ever said, 'I love you,' to her before and she'd felt as if she might explode with happiness. She'd hugged herself tightly to keep it all inside.

Charles had said, 'It might be too soon to say this, Vivienne, but I think I have fallen in love with you.'

She had gasped, and bitten the side of her hand.

'I love you, Vivienne,' he'd said and she'd been unable to stop smiling. She felt like a child who has been repeatedly told that she could not have the white dress she longed for, the dress she'd set her heart on; only to find it on her pillow when she went up to bed.

Vivie's story

Charles had taken her to Lowestoft to prove to her that what happened in her nightmare couldn't happen. She'd been impatient to know what he was going to show her, but he would not be rushed. They'd eaten prawns that tasted of the sea and drunk cold wine that tasted of gooseberries, and she'd been filled with expectation. But he just kept saying that he'd looked it all up, talked to the people who knew, found out everything he needed to know and all she had to do was trust him. He knew what he was doing, he said. And, when he went to collect the permit that would allow them to walk along the docks, she'd watched the seagulls wheel and listened to them cry and found herself wondering if she and Charles would make love that night because, until then, they had not. Until then they'd danced an uneasy dance, kissing each other goodbye awkwardly, hugging each other and finding that their arms collided and Vivie had wondered if he even liked her. But as they walked along the docks and he'd talked about the boat he wished he'd never sold, she caught him looking at her in a way that excited her and made her think that he might become her man. She longed for a man to call 'her man'.

She'd been wearing her favourite black cap that day, and she'd pulled it down over her ears to keep them warm. They'd walked for what seemed like miles along empty, concrete docks. There were no boats at all and it was a cold, grey day. The seagulls wheeled and screeched and, as they walked through a large empty hangar on a damp concrete floor that smelled strongly of fish, their footsteps echoed. Charles told her that the hangar was where the fish were auctioned, but Vivie barely heard him because it wasn't the fish that interested her. All she cared about was what he was planning to show her, what he was taking such a long time to tell her. She was like a child the night before Christmas. She was thrilled that there was a surprise to come, but frightened that it might disappoint her when, at last, it came.

They'd walked out of the hangar back into the cold grey day, and Charles had pointed and said, 'Over there, I think.' He'd squeezed Vivie's arm and held her elbow in that way that made it impossible for her to walk anywhere except where he walked, and then she'd seen a lone fisherman mending a large net, and two or three painted wooden fishing boats bobbing against a dock. She'd seen a cluster of triangular black flags on tall poles flapping in the wind, and she'd seen a row of nets spread out to dry along the dock. Her heartbeat quickened and she broke free from Charles and began to run.

She ran down the dock and asked the fisherman which nets were for which fish? What were they made of? How often did they need mending? How much fish did they hold? But she asked all those questions so that the only one she really wanted to know the answer to wouldn't seem so strange. When she finally asked the fisherman what the smallest possible space that the smallest possible net could fit into was, her heart was hammering in her chest.

Charles had her cap in his hand when he caught up with her. In her excitement Vivie hadn't even noticed that it had blown off. She held onto Charles's arm and nodded at the fisherman to continue. She crammed her cap back onto her head and listened as the fisherman said that the orange net he was mending was for trawling for deep fish and that the green nets laid out on the dock to dry – which were made, Vivie saw, from fine plastic threads – were for soles. He pronounced it 'sools'. He told them the strength of the nets and what catches they held and what they were made of, and then he looked up and asked what that last question was again. And Charles, squeezing Vivie's arm proprietorially, asked whether there was any kind of net, any kind at all, that a man could fit into his pocket.

The fisherman frowned. His face was weather-beaten and his thick hair was white. He wore a navy-blue cable-knit sweater under black waterproofs and there was a gap where one of his front teeth should have been. His eyes were blue, his rubber boots were yellow and after a considerable time he said, 'Only were the pocket the same size of the man ... and I'm never seen that.'

Vivie buried her face in Charles's jacket because she didn't want the fisherman to see her sudden tears. She heard Charles ask the fisherman if the net for the soles, the finest one – the one that, she'd said later, looked as if it had been woven by a spider – was the smallest net, and she heard the fisherman say that it was. But he said that even that one was thirty feet long, and could not ever in the world fit into a man's pocket, 'Even,' he said, 'were there a man with time enough on his hands to try.'

They thanked the fisherman and as they walked back along the dock Vivie'd told Charles that he was the best friend she'd ever had, and he'd suggested a nice, hot cup of tea. When they were sitting in a hotel on the seafront he suggested a shot of whisky in their tea, and the whisky-tea turned into supper and then, halfway through supper Charles had told Vivie that he loved her and her heart had felt as if it might explode.

She hadn't told Charles that she loved him, the words somehow wouldn't form, but she'd said that she'd known something extraordinary, something wonderful was going to happen that day and now it had; and he'd smiled and ordered champagne and they'd drunk to themselves and to love and they'd spent the night together in the hotel in Lowestoft. And, in the morning, Vivie'd told Charles that she loved the way he'd taken so much trouble to show her that her nightmare wasn't possible. She'd said she loved the way he made her feel safe. She'd said he was her rock, her anchor and her breakwater.

The sound of an engine startled Vivie. She looked up and saw that the bus was about to move off. She ground her cigarette into the pavement and climbed back on board the bus and, as it lurched forwards, she heard the seagulls screeching and she remembered that Charles had told her, that day in Lowestoft, that seagulls fly inland when it's rough out at sea. And as she sat on the bus she thought about what she'd known for some time, what her pregnancy had forced her to face: she knew now that she had never loved Charles.

What she'd felt that night in Lowestoft had been an ecstatic gratitude that someone – it could, almost, have been anyone – loved her. Even in the first year of their marriage she had been surprised that what she'd thought of as her love for Charles had faded so fast, but she'd kept telling herself that she did love him.

Now her pregnancy had confronted her, vividly, with the fact that on that night in Lowestoft she had fallen in love with *being* loved, but not with the man who'd told her he loved her.

Matthew's story

The MG's going like a dream and I'm making up for lost time, I'm not going to be late after all. But just as I left London there was an unexpected smattering of rain so I put the hood up for a bit and the sound of the rain on the canvas set me thinking about Vivie, again, dammit.

When the concerto was over the prommers roared and clapped and stamped their approval but Vivie stayed silent and still and it wasn't until the Hall was quiet again, for an encore, that I realised she was crying. I didn't say anything because Vivie – like me – has always hated anyone knowing she's crying, but when the applause broke out after the encore she turned and smiled and ran her finger under her nose. I searched for a handkerchief. I don't know why because I never have a handkerchief on me. And then I held out my arm and offered her my rolled-up shirtsleeve. She made a choking sound, somewhere between a laugh and a sob, unrolled my sleeve and pressed it under her eyes. The pianist took several bows and Vivie turned away from me to applaud him. When she turned back, she stood on tiptoe and spoke straight into my ear.

She said, 'Shut your eyes.'

I felt her warm breath on my ear and her lips rubbing against it.

I said, 'Why?'

She said, 'Just bloody shut your eyes.'

'Okay.'

'Well? What can you hear?'

'Clapping … whistling … stamping. People shouting "Encore!"'

'*Matthew*,' she said. 'What else can you hear?'

'Nothing.'

'When your eyes are shut,' she said, 'clapping sounds like rain.'

And so it does.

As the orchestra left the stage Vivie said, 'Jesus, it's about time I stopped crying every time I hear that.'

I said, 'Why does it make you cry?'

She looked at me, her grey eyes serious and she said, 'You know why, Matthew. I've told you.' She turned and walked quickly towards the edge of the arena and down the stairs. I caught up with her in the serpentine corridors beneath the Albert Hall and we emerged into the hot, still night together.

I said, 'You haven't told me, Vivie ... tell me over a cup of coffee? Or a drink?' I thought she was going to say no, but she said, 'Okay, coffee,' and hurried away down Queen's Gate. I was just going to say how I wished there were more wide, well-proportioned boulevards like this one in London, when I realised Vivie had walked away so quickly that she was already out of earshot.

I shouted after her, 'Slow down, Lightning, what's the hurry?'

She stopped and when I caught up with her she said, 'I told Charles not to wait up, but I can't stay long.'

We went to Dino's, which was packed, but the waiter squeezed us in at the end of a table and Vivie yanked several paper napkins from a chrome box and blew her nose. We ordered cappuccino and glasses of water and Vivie dipped a napkin into her water and wiped the smudges of mascara away. She didn't bother with a mirror and then, suddenly, she was animated. She wanted to know what films, plays and exhibitions I'd been to, what books I'd read, what new music I'd heard, what project I was working on, and how I was. She asked all the questions until I managed to get one in myself.

After we'd ordered more coffee, I said, 'Does it always make you cry?'

She said, 'Yes. And I know I've told you why.'

I said, 'You haven't. I think you were going to, once, but you never did.'

I looked at her, she bit her lip, shrugged and then she said, 'I read it on the back of Mum's CD ... ages ago. He wrote it when he thought he would never write another note.' She stared at me. 'His first symphony got such bad reviews he convinced himself he was the worst composer in the world and he stopped composing. Completely.'

I didn't say anything.

Vivie looked at me. She said, 'I know I've told you,' but when I shook my head she said, 'he went to a shrink who said he thought he could write himself well. And he did. He wrote his way through his nervous breakdown. He bloody wrote his way through it. He wrote that concerto when he thought he would never write another note, when he thought he was the worst composer ... the worst human being in the world.' She stopped again. 'That's why it makes me cry. He had the courage to write it ... when ... oh *bloody* God. Don't you think it's the saddest, bravest thing?'

Vivie's tear-filled eyes were quite beautiful.

I said, 'Yes, I do,' and I thought back to that day I will never forget. She didn't say any of this, then.

She said, 'The music's so full of hope, it just soars, doesn't it?' She tipped her head back and said, 'And I ... damn! This happens every bloody time. Even when I'm only thinking about it.'

I reached across the table for her hand but she was already yanking more napkins from the chrome box. She slammed the box down onto the table, blew her nose hard, and said, 'Sometimes I wish I didn't know that story.'

And I wish the story I do know had turned out differently, I thought. The story where the man doesn't risk telling the woman how he feels about her because he's afraid of what might happen if he does.

Vivie said, 'Doing anything interesting this weekend?'

I said, 'Dad and I are going to the festival.'

Vivie stared at me over the lip of her white enamel cup and her eyes widened. Then she slammed the cup down onto the saucer and coffee slopped onto the table.

She said, 'Jesus! Not Mum's bloody festival?'

I said, 'Yup. I'm driving Dad. What are they like? I've never been to a storytelling festival.'

She started to say something and then she stopped and stood

up. She looked exactly the way she'd looked the day we went to Salem when I'd meant to be her Galahad but ended up just being her Hopeless.

I said, 'Vivie, what's the matter?'

But she just pulled two pound coins from her bag, slammed them down on the table and left Dino's.

I pocketed the Gitanes she'd left behind and stared at the smoke that curled up from the one she'd left in the ashtray. I made no attempt to go after her.

I walked home over Albert Bridge and the white lightbulbs that delineate its catenary curve against the night sky made me smile, despite my jangled nerves. It's the kind of bridge that a knight in one of Iris's stories might have built for his ladylove, if he'd lived in the age of iron. But as I walked over the bridge I told myself that if Vivie rang to apologise for leaving Dino's so abruptly I'd say it would be better if we didn't see each other again. Vivie complicates my life.

I let myself into my house, poured a glass of wine and dialled Julia's number, hoping she'd still be awake.

Iris's story

The air is clear, the sky is a limpid blue and through my window I can see the dark flat tops of two great Scots pines. They lean towards each other as if they're in conversation.

The sharp sweet smell of crushed lavender fills my room – I'm still puzzled by it, I haven't been able to find the lavender bags – and as the Bristol Channel glitters under the sun I stare down at Rose Lawn, the lawn beneath the one that spreads out from the castle walls, and I think that that is where I will tell my stories on Sunday, in the clear, rose-scented, fresh open air.

I was nineteen before I told a story to another human being, but the story I told Kit just bubbled up inside me and demanded to be told. Perhaps it happened because I wasn't in my father's house. Perhaps it happened because I was with Kit, I don't know. All I know is that it happened and after I'd begun I realised I hadn't the faintest idea where I was going. The memory of the way I told that story makes me blush now, but Kit had just said he hated his hair and I loved it and the words just tumbled out.

'The Red-Headed Kings had a Desperate Dilemma,' I said. 'They lived in a cold, northern kingdom where there were only two laws. One law decreed that anyone found in possession of anything red, anything at all, would be punished, severely. The other that Crowns must be worn at all times, even in bed.'

'How were they punished?' said Kit, and he laughed. I stared at him, stupidly. 'If they broke the decrees, the laws?'

'Live burial,' I blurted out, and my hand collided with my coffee mug. Hot coffee spilled all over my hand.

'Live burial?' said Kit, and he grasped hanks of his hair.

'Yes,' I said. 'So if you were red-headed you had to find ways to avoid the punishment.'

Speaking of Love

Kit pushed our red enamel coffee mugs out of the way, took both my hands in his and said, 'Go on. I want to know what happens next.' I winced when he squeezed my burned hand, and I stared at the wooden table top. There didn't seem to be any more words. There were coffee rings and cigarette burn marks on the table, and I was conscious that Kit was silent, that he waited for me to speak, so I stumbled through the story and whenever I think about it now I remember how I felt then.

I remember how serious Kit's grey eyes were when he said 'Go on.' Their expression gave me the courage to keep telling the story as I groped in the dark with no idea what would happen next. I even forgot about the pain in my burned hand as we sat at the table by the window in the Troubadour, which had – and still has – narrow wooden shelves stretched across it, crowded with coloured enamel coffee pots. At the end of the story I thought I would burst with pride because Kit, the poet-performer, applauded me. And then I knew that we were at the very centre of the universe. We were the only two people in the universe, connected by something no one else had ever felt.

Somewhere in the middle of the story I had seen a picture of a young man draped in a grey cloak, on horseback. When I saw him I followed him and then the story began to come to me.

Kit's hair must have bled out all its glorious red by now. It must be pale and speckled with grey, but when I tell the story I call 'Red Head' these days, I always think of him and the way his hair was then. My own hair was short, dark and shiny then, but now it's grey too. Mine, though, is a good solid all-over-white kind of grey that I like, at least I like it when I remember that I'm fifty, not nineteen, although I still blame the ECT – for the colour of my hair, not for my age.

I'd planned exactly how I would look when I spoke to Kit for the first time. I would be irresistible. I would be the only woman in the room he was compelled to talk to. Instead, this happened. He stood at the bottom of the narrow stairwell in the Troubadour and I stood, frozen, at the top. He wasn't meant to be there. Not yet. Not the way I'd imagined it.

Iris's story

He looked up at me and said, 'Man, that is a short skirt,' and my heart somersaulted. He had spoken to me. The poet, the man I most admired in the whole world. But I was dressed in completely the wrong clothes. I wore my stupid tennis skirt and I couldn't speak. All I could think about was the dress I'd planned to wear. The dress that was in my tennis bag. The dress I had made.

'Are you coming to the reading tonight?' he said.

I nodded and then, inexplicably, ran down the stairs straight towards him. He didn't move and the stairwell at the Troubadour is so narrow that I couldn't get past him. I blushed, furiously. I knew my face was as red as the lightbulbs that glowed in looped rows under the tobacco-stained ceiling.

Then I spoke, straight into his chest. 'It's my tennis skirt,' I said and immediately wished I hadn't said a word. I even stood back and lifted my tennis racket slightly, as if to prove my point. Kit moved his arm like a juggler, or a tennis-player about to serve, and he smiled. I looked down to make my hair fall over my face and then I half-squeezed, half-pushed my way past him into the narrow basement passage and the sanctuary of the lavatory. I remember he smelled of cigarettes and something peppery, slightly bitter.

I slammed the door on the cupboard that was the Troubadour's lavatory and I wished I'd had the wit to thank him, in a sophisticated fashion, for his compliment about my skirt. I wished I'd behaved as if I always wore my tennis skirt to poetry readings, as if it was the thing that everyone did. I turned on the tap that stuck out from the brick wall, stuffed the cloth into the plughole, held my hair back and kept my face in the cold water for as long as I could hold my breath. And then I looked at myself in the mirror. My face was still red, scarlet in fact. I looked like an imbecile, an idiot in a tennis skirt. I looked fourteen. I knew he would never take any notice of me. So I decided to leave, and I promised myself I would never, ever come back. But the only way out was through the coffee house upstairs and I knew he would be up there and I couldn't face him again, so I decided to stay in the lavatory until the poetry readings began. But it was the only lavatory in the place and soon enough someone knocked on the door.

Speaking of Love

I said I'd just be a few minutes but, as I said it, I changed my mind. I decided that no one else would see me in my ridiculous tennis skirt. I would leave the cupboard-lavatory the way I had planned to leave it and Kit Marchwood would see me in the dress I'd brought to wear: the daringly short red dress that showed my knees. The dress that my father would have told me to take off immediately, if he'd seen me in it. And so it was that when I emerged, ten minutes later, wrapped in bright, brittle courage – and the red dress – I knew I was a person my father would never recognise, a person he could not even imagine, and that made me feel better.

I stood in the narrow passage and listened to the clatter and chatter in the coffee house above my head and, when the cupboard-lavatory was free again, I made my lips white and my cheeks pale with powder and a green make-up stick that Gail had given me and I blacked up my eyes and when, at last, I stared into the mirror from under my dark fringe, I practically was Mary Quant. And I knew that however much I blushed, it wouldn't show. I lit a cigarette, blew blue smoke towards the mirror, and the fourteen-year-old tennis child vanished.

The first time I went to the Troubadour Gail took me. My father would have stopped me, if he'd known, but the poetry readings were on the same nights as our tennis lessons so I never had to tell him. We sat at the back of the dark basement room and smoked our heads off, and the first time I saw Kit Marchwood was through shafts of smoke-filled yellow light.

I thought he was wonderful. He didn't read his poetry from a book the way all the other poets did, he stood and spoke it and roared it and whispered it and strode about on his long legs and looked his audience in the eye. His hair shone red-gold despite the smoke, and it stood out in wild corkscrews and spirals and curls. His eyes were pale grey and he said that poetry was an active thing, a living, happening thing.

I couldn't take my eyes off him. I'd never seen, or heard, anyone like him in my life.

Vivie's story

Vivie could read physical movement the way other people read words; the smallest gesture told her what a person might do next.

She'd noticed that the neatly dressed woman at the far end of the platform clutched her crumpled plastic bag at an odd angle to her chest. She'd seen that the woman's lips were moving as she stood, by herself, staring out across the tracks. She'd seen the woman turn and begin walking back along the platform and she'd looked away, too late.

She stood, determined not to look back up at the woman, but she heard her footsteps coming closer and by the time the train arrived and the doors had sighed open, the woman was standing beside Vivie and they boarded the train through the same door.

Vivie's heart beat faster as the woman ignored the many empty seats and sat down opposite her. She felt as if she was electrically wired to the woman; she could feel the woman staring at her. She wanted to move, but she was frightened that the woman would say something to her if she did. She noticed that the buttons on the woman's colourful linen jacket had been put through the wrong buttonholes, and when the woman crossed her ankles a shard of fear jolted through Vivie because the woman's neat high-heeled shoes were caked with mud.

Vivie kept her eyelids lowered and hoped that the woman would not speak to her. Ever since they'd sat down she'd been muttering something about holes and the bag she was clutching crackled. And then, suddenly, the woman spoke in a loud voice.

'You've taken it, haven't you?' she said.

Vivie looked up before she could stop herself.

'You've got it, haven't you?' said the woman, exhaling noisily and staring at Vivie.

Speaking of Love

Vivie held her breath and stared into a small black hole full of straggling, uneven teeth. Its darkness was contained by bright red neatly applied lipstick. And then, before she realised what she was doing, Vivie stood up. The woman grabbed at her with a nail-bitten hand; Vivie pulled away and ran for the carriage door.

'You've stolen the hole in my bag,' shouted the woman. 'I knew it was you as soon as I saw you. People like you should be locked up.'

Vivie's heart lurched and she willed the train to reach the next station. She had to get off. Her fingers were curled into her palms and her nails dug into her skin. She felt sick. It was difficult to breathe. When the train stopped Vivie kept her eyes on the platform until the door sighed shut behind her. Then she looked up because she had to be sure that the woman was still on the train, and not standing beside her. Through the window Vivie saw the woman pulling strings of coloured raffia from her crumpled plastic bag and looking at them with a puzzled expression. As the train pulled away the woman wagged her finger at the raffia as if it had done something it shouldn't have done.

Vivie tried to distract herself as she waited on Shadwell station. She rehearsed what she would say to Sara when she got to the office.

'I'm so sorry, I had to go to the doctor. Forgot to tell you. I can stay late tonight if you like.'

She said it several times, under her breath. Then she rehearsed what she'd say in the tobacconist.

'Three packets of Gitanes, please, and a box of matches.'

She said this several times too, but the ordinary words did not anchor her as sometimes they could and, although she knew where she was, although she could see and touch and hear what was happening on the platform as she waited for the next train, the certainty that at any moment the solid, ordinary world would slide away from her terrified her.

Vivie stared hard at the ordinary man in the pale linen suit who looked away when she looked at him. She watched the little girl who held her mother's hand and looked up and asked when the train would come. She heard an ordinary announcement about the time of the next train. She repeated it again and again to herself. But nothing worked. The woman on the train had reminded her of her mother and now images of her mother filled her mind and, always, when the images took root in her mind they terrified Vivie; they overwhelmed her and made her their prisoner.

She saw her mother's white-gloved hands pulling at the yellow laburnum flowers and eating them as if they were grapes. She heard the tinkling of the bells on the ribbons that bound the gloves at her mother's wrists, and she saw the sheet she had tried to wrap round her mother's naked body lying crumpled on the grass. She heard her mother saying, over and over again, 'He's gone. He's gone,' as if she'd lost the last person in the world.

Vivie's heart hammered and she gripped the edges of the metal seat. She felt transparent and self-conscious; she was sure that everyone on the platform was staring at her, knew what was happening to her, could see inside her.

She lit a cigarette and then she stamped her foot and stood up. It infuriated her that she was so powerless to stop the memories and the waves of fear that came with them. It had all happened so long ago, but the memories – and the fear – seemed to become more acute as the years went by, not less. They should be fading, Vivie thought. They should be disappearing. But they weren't. A harsh judgement ruled that she knew exactly why.

A train arrived, the doors opened and Vivie got on. When a passenger looked up at her with a startled, and irritated, expression she realised she was sobbing. She turned away and scrabbled in her bag for a kleenex. She thought, with a hard little laugh, that he probably thought she was mad.

When she got to her office she yanked open the filing cabinet and pulled out the bottle of vodka that she kept at the back, behind the files. She took a swig, and then another and then, as she put it back, a surge of anger swept through her because the cleaners had done what they always did. They had put her desk back by the window despite her repeated requests that they leave it by the wall on the opposite side of her office.

She threw down her bag and began yanking her desk away from the window. When she'd banged it up against the wall she sat down, turned on her PC and typed a memo to personnel. She wrote that seventy-five pounds had gone missing from her desk. She wrote that she realised it hadn't been sensible to leave money on her desk, but it had been under a pile of paper and only someone who'd moved her desk would have seen it. She wrote that she liked her desk to be by the wall because she could concentrate better there. She didn't write that there were days when she was so terrified of the terrible drop down to the ground that she couldn't think.

Vivie printed out the memo, signed it and put it in her out tray and, as she walked down the corridor to get a cup of coffee, she hoped that what she'd written would get the cleaners fired.

Iris's story

When I arrived I very nearly hugged the young woman who showed me to my room. All the way in the car I'd hoped I'd have a room of my own, but I'd never asked. When they booked me for the festival Dick was amazed that I didn't ask about the accommodation, but I couldn't. I didn't want to find out before I got there. I didn't want to know that I had to share a room because if I'd known my mind would have been crowded with possible faces, possible voices, possible torture. So I put it from my mind but now, to my delight, I find myself in a room that could have been a mediaeval princess's bedroom, and it's all my own.

A spiral stone staircase winds up the narrow stone watchtower to a landing where there is only one door to only one room: my room. The thick oak-panelled door has a large iron latch and the walls are solid yellow-grey stone slabs. The windows are stone-mullioned and the floor is made from planks of polished oak. It must be cold in winter, but in the heat of this summer's day my room is deliciously cool.

There is a wooden washstand with a white china bowl and jug on it which I could fill from the bathroom on the floor above if I wanted to, and a white linen hand towel that smells of lavender hangs from the wooden rail. My bed is like a big wooden boat and there are twentieth-century brass brackets that hold lightbulbs that look like candle flames on the walls. An incongruous white plastic light switch sticks out from a slab of stone by the door but, if I half-close my eyes, I can see sconces and candles and a chambermaid with a candle in her hand.

Yesterday I walked in the gardens and stood on Rose Lawn. I thought the lawns below, and their gardens, looked like stages waiting for their players. One garden is full of stone creatures that sit on their haunches on tall stone pedestals; they clutch weathered iron standards whose small iron flags are petrified in a permanent flutter. Red rose bushes grow at their feet as they keep watch over a circular stone seat.

There is a knot-garden full of neat, low box hedges that twist themselves round beds of lavender and herbs, and there is a rose garden where pink and white and red roses – Dick would know their names – twine their way up the columns of seven stone pillars. There is a garden called the Blue Garden which has a stone stage and a timber roof at one end that faces a large, high-walled lawn. The timber roof is almost hidden by a waterfall of wisteria tendrils, but the lawn that I already think of as my lawn, Rose Lawn, is plain and open. Red roses climb the retaining wall to the north and fig trees are pleached along the red brick wall to the east – Dick will love it – and above Rose Lawn the red brick wall continues on the east side until it meets the Great Hall of the castle. Just before the Great Hall there is a stone arch, through which our festival audience will come. In their hordes, I hope.

I haven't decided yet which way I shall face when I tell my stories. I could face the Great Hall of the castle, or I could face the Bristol Channel. If I face the castle the sun will be behind me but so will a six-foot drop. If I face the sea, the almost-sea of the Bristol Channel, the retaining wall will be behind me and it will help throw my voice forwards. But yesterday it was so windy that my words were snatched from me whichever way I faced. I hope there's no wind on Sunday, and no rain either. The forecast says not.

On the west side of Rose Lawn stone steps lead down from the Great Hall to the ancient jousting field where the storytelling tents are pitched but, hidden in the retaining wall on the opposite side, there is a narrow flight of red brick steps that curve down inside a red brick alcove. They also connect Rose Lawn with the lawn below my window. I discovered them quite by accident this morning, hidden behind a creeper and some sedum. I sat on the bottom step for a while, away from the frantic activity of the festival organisers. I leaned against the wall and caught glimpses of the Bristol Channel as it sparkled under the sun. The alcove is a secret, safe comforting place, a place you wouldn't know was there unless you stumbled upon it.

From my window I can see the magnolias and the figs in the gardens, and the red fuchsias and the dark yew trees which have been pruned to look like giant mushrooms. And there is a laburnum tree on the other side of the stone arch. My heart leapt when I saw it and I sat beneath it and stared up into its straw-coloured seedpods that straggled down. I persuaded myself that it was a good sign, that my stories would flow on Sunday because a laburnum tree thrives so close by.

There are great beeches on the jousting field. Their trunks are covered with glossy ivy, and in the corners of the flint steps that lead down to the jousting field pine needles gather and give off their resinous smell. I can just see the tips of the iron standards that the stone creatures hold, and the iron gate that leads to the flint steps. The sky is a brilliant summer blue, the coasts of north Devon and Somerset are smudged by a heat haze and I, for the moment, am deliciously alone in my room, with just my stories for company.

I am so glad my room is my own. I hated the mixed ward at Salem. There was no privacy; even the most intimate things were done in public. There was nowhere you could be private and the staff watched you all the time. But the man in the next bed liked it because he believed our souls had abandoned us at the gates of Salem.

'But, soon,' he said, 'they'll start to miss us. They'll come looking for us and when they come it'll be easier for them if we're all gathered together. Easier for them to find the body they belong to.' He always watched the door when he said this, and he always whispered, quickly, and dribbled as he leaned over the edge of his bed towards me.

'We need to know as much about each other as possible,' he said, and his hand shook as he stretched it towards me. 'Then, when the souls come back, I can tell them, for instance, that you're the one with the mole on your bum, right cheek, and you can tell them I'm

the one with the scar. From my adam's apple to my adam's ...
look see ... here.'

I heard him, but it seemed to me that he spoke from the far side
of a valley. My tongue was too thick and my mind too clouded to
reply, but he probably never noticed because he never stopped.
And he always took all his clothes off when he talked about
the souls.

'And the souls'll be together,' he said, 'which will be nice for
them. They won't be alone when they travel. Like one of those
package tours, only for souls.' He always fell backwards into
instant sleep, with his mouth open, when he stopped his mono-
logue. Sometimes he fell back in mid-sentence, but there were
other times when he couldn't stop at all and then the night-duty
nurses gave him extra meds to shut him up, and sometimes, in his
anxiety about whether the souls would find the right bodies when
they returned, he'd become agitated and refuse to put his pyjamas
back on and the night nurses would forcibly dress him and strap
him down. Then he'd be taken away for a while.

When he came back he was always very pale and less talkative
and he'd say, over and over again, 'I missed mine, didn't I? Came
for me and I wasn't here, didn't he?' And I'd try to tell him that the
souls hadn't come because I couldn't bear his desperate, anxious
expression. But I'll never know if he understood me because I was
unintelligible then.

I longed to be sent wherever he was sent when he talked too
much about the souls. I imagined a bare room with just one bed
where I could be alone, but I could never muster the energy to
behave like him. I wailed, sometimes, in my efforts to speak, but
they didn't take you from the dormitory for that, they just gave
you more meds. The drugs, the meds, were awful. My limbs
shook and jerked, my mind was filled with fog and my tongue felt
as thick as a carpet offcut. I dribbled and I couldn't coordinate my
movements. If I managed to get the spoon from my bowl of cornflakes to my mouth, the milk would dribble down my chin and my
neck in thick white tears.

I tried desperately to communicate through the fog. I tried to say how humiliated I was that I could not feed myself. I tried to say that I hated the way we had to do the most intimate things in front of each other, but I could not make myself understood. I despaired. I thought I would never make myself understood until, one miraculous night, a nurse sat on my bed and listened. She took my hand and looked at me and she waited until I'd managed to communicate my frustration to her. My head and my limbs jerked and many of my words were unintelligible, but she understood. She was younger than the rest and she didn't dole out the meds as if they were smarties. I devoted myself to her, like a faithful dog.

I would take her a mug of tea in the afternoon. I would shuffle across the day room to give it to her and I'd spill most of it on the way, but she never complained, she just thanked me. And then I would sit beside her. I was desolate when she was not on duty. I loved her because she looked at me as if she really cared, and she never tried to shut the man in the next bed up and, if she could stay long enough, if someone else didn't call her away, I would eventually manage to make words that she could understand. She knew that all she had to do was wait, and listen.

Her name was Ruth Carpenter. They weren't supposed to tell us their first names, but she did. And I held on to her name as if I'd caught hold of the last branch before a waterfall. I would repeat her name to myself and her presence calmed me the way a mother's presence calms a child, just because she is in the same room, just because her voice is familiar, just because she hugs you with strong arms. Ruth hugged us even though it was strictly forbidden.

When she was on duty in the day I would shuffle down the ward corridors after her, and I clung to her for protection when it was my turn to go for ECT, which meant she had to take me. When she was on duty at night I slept peacefully, and I would only go to my appointments with the psychiatrist, rare as they were, if she walked across the garden with me and promised to wait for me. That was when we began our conversations, in the garden. Not that I could talk much, to begin with, but at least I knew there was someone who wanted to understand me.

Speaking of Love

It was Ruth who said: 'Just because you hear voices no one else can hear, just because you see people no one else can see, you are no less of a human being. You can tell me what the voices say, if you like. You can tell me who the people are.'

I fell in love with Ruth the way a young schoolgirl falls in love with an older girl. I depended on her. She wasn't like the others who hardly seemed to see us. And she wasn't like Joan, whose face was full of pity when she came to see me and who, often, obviously longed to get away.

It's thanks to Ruth that I'm here at all. Here, or anywhere that isn't a psychiatric institution. It's thanks to her that I managed to grope my way back from hell. Ruth Carpenter saved my life and I shall never forget her.

Matthew's story

I made it to Dad's in good time in the end, but I rang him from the petrol station on the A14 just to let him know where I was.

He said, 'As long as we leave by three o'clock, we'll be fine.'

I said, 'So that means it'll be okay if we leave by four or five.'

He said, 'Don't be so cheeky,' and hung up. I'm thirty-two and Dad still calls me cheeky. It makes me smile, I don't know why.

Now I'm standing on his kitchen doorstep. I've just poured myself a glass of water and I'm watching him. He's sitting under his yellow parasol, with his back to me. There is a bottle of wine in a cooler on the wooden table beside him and a large sheet of paper is spread out on the grass in front of him.

'Matthew?' Dad says, without turning round.

'Me,' I say, and walk out into the garden. 'What's this?'

Dad smiles and holds out his long-fingered hand. I grasp it: the skin is papery, the arthritic lumps prominent. I remember those hands when they were strong and supple, when they gripped spades and saws and showed me how to graft trees, when they held out vegetables covered with earth. I wish he still had those hands.

He looks up at me. 'It's our route,' he says. 'What did you think it was? A wallpaper sample?'

I squat at his feet and see that he's sellotaped at least twelve pages of a road map together. He leans down and picks up the map and begins to fold it carefully along its already chiselled fold-lines. As I help him I remember how Vivie and I sat on the floor trying to fold Dad's maps as neatly as he always did, after we'd found the railway route to Salem.

' ... Matthew?'

'Sorry.'

Speaking of Love

Dad says, 'I was saying that if we leave by two-thirty, we should be able to travel seventy miles, comfortably, this afternoon.' He smiles and the lines radiate from the corners of his eyes. 'Glass of wine?' he says. And then, 'So, what sort of a week has it been?'

He leans back in his deckchair and the ancient canvas creaks.

'All right.'

'Have you heard about the UeL bid?'

'Yes.'

'Well?'

'We won the contract.'

He leans forwards. He says, 'That is a good deal better than "all right", isn't it?'

I say, 'Yes, it is, yes. It's wonderful. Really good news. I've brought the models to show you, they're in the car.'

He gives me a quizzical look, then he smiles.

He says, 'Well done. Well done indeed, Matthew. I shall look forward to seeing the models and we shall celebrate. And now,' he taps the back of my hand with the wooden handle of a kitchen knife, 'we need a lettuce for lunch.'

A blackbird sings as I cut the lettuce and Dad whistles a reply; soon they are whistling a syncopated duet. He's always done that and it almost always makes me laugh. I say, from the vegetable patch, 'So the journey's going to take us two and a half days, is it?'

Dad says, 'If we're quick,' between whistles.

'You'd think we were going to the south of France, Dad, not south-west Wales.'

Dad just carries on whistling.

I say, 'If you had your way, we'd have left last week, on horse-back, or caught the post-chaise.' I put the lettuce down on the table beside the wine cooler.

Dad says, 'Now there's a thought.'

'Dad ... '

The leaves on Iris's laburnum tree rustle and we both look up; Dad pushes himself out of his deckchair, waving away my offer of help.

He says, "To Thetford Forest's very own Scheherazade,' and lifts his glass.

I say, 'To the storytree,' and surprise myself. That was what Vivie used to call the tree.

Dad and I stand, facing the low, immaculately pruned beech hedge, and we drink to Iris, and to her tree: its seedpods hang down, thin and green but not yet completely empty.

Dad says, 'Make a start on the salad, would you?'

And while I do that, Dad makes an omelette with herbs from the garden and then we sit and eat in the cool of the kitchen.

He says, 'I've never understood why you stay down in the Big Smoke. I wouldn't live there if you paid me, not with all that noise and all those fumes.'

I say, 'The Clean Air Act's been in force for forty years, Dad.'

He says, 'I still wouldn't live there.'

I say, 'Kit Marchwood once said you could be anyone, do anything in London.'

Dad looks at me.

'He was the only person who didn't laugh when I said I wanted to be the world's greatest knight. He said it was an ambition worthy of a knight. When I was young I thought that meant you could be a knight in London, because he came from London. Maybe there's a bit of me that still does.'

Dad says, 'Poets tend to encourage dreams,' but he is smiling. 'If your mother had had her way,' he imitates her Edinburgh accent, 'you'd hardly have seen the Marchwoods at all.'

'I know.'

Dad says, still in his best Morningside, 'You can go next door when you've made your bed, tidied your room, done your homework, walked the dogs and asked your father does he need any help in the garden.'

Those conversations always took place at breakfast, at least that's how it seems to me now. Dad would say, 'I'll walk the dogs later, and I don't need any help this morning, thank you.' Then he'd smile into his cereal and I'd say, 'And I can do my homework tonight,' and my mother would say what we all knew she was going to say. 'Artists,' she'd say, nodding in the direction of the party wall, 'are unreliable. They never eat when they should, they don't know the first thing about running a household, and as for the way they spend money,' she'd always look at me then, 'let it be a lesson to you, Matthew. Look after the pennies, that's what I say.' Her final words were always, 'The artistic temperament, Matthew, is not a practical one. Just you remember that.'

Then she'd look to Dad for support, but he'd never look up from his cereal. He was always on my side about going next door, he never once tried to stop me, and when he pointed out that they'd never been late with the rent, that the house was clean and the garden reasonably kept, my mother would say, 'Och well, that's Iris. She's altogether more reliable than him.' Then Dad would say, winking at me, 'So, there is such a thing as a reliable artist then,' and my mother would frown at my father and fire her final salvo. 'What I'm saying, Matthew,' she'd pause for effect, 'is that I don't want you getting it into your wee head that an artistic way of life is either a sensible or a secure one.'

But if I'd just seen Kit Marchwood striding across the green on his long legs that reminded me of a heron's, I would always ask if I could go next door. Before my mother said yes I had to promise not to stay too long, and never, ever, to entertain the idea of becoming an artist.

If it wasn't raining I'd usually find Iris and Vivie sitting under the laburnum tree on a rug. Once when I went Iris said, 'It's the tree's birthday today,' which was surprising to me because I'd never thought about trees having birthdays.

Vivie said, 'It's six. Our storytree's one whole month older than me.'

I jumped up, bowed to the tree and said, 'Happy birthday.' Some of the laburnum blossoms were at my nose level. I thought they smelled like the tea leaves my mother kept in a special tin. I asked where Kit was. I hoped I hadn't missed him.

Vivie said, 'He's still in bed. Lazybones,' and then she asked me to tell 'One of those Nazzerudeen stories,' which was what I was hoping she would say. I'd never met anyone like Vivie's mother.

She told stories without reading them, and I wanted to see if I could do it too. I was very proud that I'd learned some of the Nasrudin stories and I wanted Iris, particularly, to think I told them well.

I told the one about Nasrudin digging a hole in the earth at the entrance to his donkey's stable because the donkey's ears stood too tall and it couldn't walk under the lintel. They both laughed, but it was polite laughter and I knew I hadn't got the story quite right, so I resolved to practise. I'd borrowed a book from the library and I wanted to be able to tell the Nasrudin stories as spontaneously as Iris told her stories. When we were children she could make a story out of thin air. It always seemed to me that she was never lost for words.

On that day Vivie asked for a story about the tree, 'For its birthday.' Immediately Iris said, 'There was once a small and lonely tree who had no friends, no tree-friends with feet in the earth nearby ...' But as soon as she'd begun it started to rain so we went inside, begging Iris to finish the story, but she said that the story was the tree's story and could only be told underneath it. Vivie protested and then Kit burst through the door at the bottom of the stairs and gathered her into his arms. He was barefoot, his nightshirt was crumpled and his red hair wasn't brushed; I always had to brush mine even if I was just going into the garden. He asked what it was that could only be told underneath the storytree, and we told him. He peered through the window and tripped over the jumble of coloured gumboots by the door. My mother always made me leave my gumboots lined up, together.

Kit said, 'Then we'll just have to make an indoor storytree.'

Vivie, wide-eyed and wriggling in his arms, asked, 'How do we do that?'

Kit said, 'We'll need something to keep the rain off, some money for the bus and a large dose of imagination.'

I thought Kit looked like a strange bird as we walked along the road through Thetford Forest. He wore his black peaked cap, his tight black-and-grey striped trousers, no tie – he never wore a tie – and a bin-liner that billowed round his body in the rain. Vivie and I wore our bin-liners over our heads with holes for our faces because Kit had rejected my offer of raincoats and Vivie insisted that we all wear the same thing. She thought the bin-liners were funny and so did I, until we were waiting at the bus stop on the Bury Road and people stared and pointed at us from their cars. I left my bin-liner on the bus.

We bought tins of paint and brushes in John's Paints in the High Street, and Vivie asked, 'Where's it going to be, our storytree?' When she asked the question, she turned her head to look up at her father and collapsed in a fit of giggles because the bin-liner didn't turn with her and her face disappeared behind it.

Kit said, 'We shall meditate on the place when we get back.'

The expression on John's face made me wish I was two million miles away, and then I wished I hadn't wished that.

Vivie said, 'What's meditate?'

Kit said, 'You'll discover,' and then he said, in a loud voice, that it was about time Brandon opened a decent coffee shop. I hung around by the door wishing the people in the shop wouldn't stare at Kit and Vivie as if they'd just arrived from another planet, and I felt like a heel. Kit bought us each a bar of fruit-and-nut chocolate. Vivie made him go back and get one for Iris, and we ate them as we walked home in the rain because there wasn't any money left for the bus. Vivie held her bar of chocolate out so that the rain fell onto it. She said it tasted even more delicious like that. I got soaked without my bin-liner.

When we got home Iris made us sit by the stove and she gave me a long striped jumper of Kit's to wear until my clothes dried out. I never wanted to give it back. We sat cross-legged on the kitchen floor by the stove, closed our eyes and listened to Kit telling us to empty our minds. He said when they were empty a picture of the place where the storytree belonged would arrive in our minds. He said that was meditating.

Neither Vivie nor I were very good at it; Vivie kept shifting and I kept opening my eyes to see if anyone else had opened theirs. Once, Iris winked at me.

Suddenly Vivie said, 'I know,' and Kit's whole body jumped as if he'd had an electric shock.

Vivie said, 'The door at the bottom of the stairs. That's where it should be.'

Kit opened his eyes but he didn't seem to see us.

Vivie said, 'I saw it.'

Kit said, 'Did you see the white light?'

Vivie, wide-eyed, said 'Yes,' but I knew she hadn't.

Kit looked disappointed and Vivie said, 'Well, just a little bit of it I did. But please, can the storytree go there anyway?'

Kit said, 'The door at the bottom of the stairs is a fine place for the storytree,' and Vivie hopped and skipped round the kitchen table clapping her hands, while Iris began to make marks on the door with a cutting tool with a wheel on its end that she fetched from her sewing box. And then she said, 'Matthew, I think you should paint the tree's trunk and branches. You've got an eye for the way things are put together.'

I thought I would burst with pride.

Iris said, 'Think of hands with their fingers stretching upwards, if that helps. That's how I often think of my tree.'

She said that she and Vivie would paint the flowers.

Vivie clapped her hands and Iris pushed Vivie's hair away from her face and kissed her on the cheek. She said, 'Think of hanging lanterns. You know, the kind people used to carry at night.'

Vivie said, 'The kind people carry in fairy tales?'

Iris nodded and she ripped up some more bin-liners and tied them around our necks and we began to paint. I loved painting that tree. I loved the smell of the paint and I loved standing on the chair Kit brought for me so that I could paint the high branches. Kit painted the leaves on after me, and Vivie and Iris painted the yellow blooms. I pretended that Vivie was my sister and Iris and Kit were my real parents. Afterwards we ate buttery crumpets smothered with my mother's blackberry jam, and Iris poured tea for Vivie and me – my mother only ever gave me milk – and then we sat on bright cushions with little mirrors sewn into them beside the painted storytree, and Iris told us the tree story.

Vivie sat on Iris's lap and leaned back and flyaway strands of her red-gold hair got caught in the tree trunk I'd painted. Iris told

Vivie that because the tree's paint was in her hair she was a dryad. Vivie asked what a dryad was and Iris told her, and then I said that the lines her hair had left on the trunk made it look like the bark of a real tree.

Iris smiled and said, 'You're quite right, Matthew, isn't he, Kit?'

Kit said I was a rare knight, and I was glad he didn't know how far away I'd wished myself when we were in Brandon.

Dad says, 'A penny for them.'

I say, 'Next door ... painting the laburnum tree.'

He says, 'Do you still regret it?'

I say, 'What?'

He says, 'Ending up at the Mac and not the Slade?'

I say, 'No,' but we both know that's not entirely true.

Dad pushes himself up from the table, puts his hand on my shoulder and then takes my plate.

I say, 'I'll wash up.'

Dad says, 'No you won't. You'll fetch my suitcase and my camera. I want to take a photograph of you standing beside that beautiful and not entirely practical car of yours.'

Vivie's story

Vivie was trying to write a press release that should have been finished the day before. Sara had given her until five o'clock but the deadline, which usually spurred her on, was making no difference. She stared at her PC and tried to dredge something up, anything, about mountain boots. But the best she could do was hate them. She realised she'd forgotten every word of the company's presentation and she couldn't find their letters or brochures, not even their logo. She tried to remember the atmosphere at the factory, the posters in their design room, the shape and the colours of the boots, but nothing came. All she could remember was a man hurrying across the car park towards the factory, his head down against the rain, his arm around several books. She wrote 'Rugged Boots. Footwear for the Thinking Man,' and deleted it. She banged her keyboard with her fist and heard the muffled hum of the earth movers far below. She wrote, 'JCB-Drivers do it in Rugged Boots,' picked up the keyboard and dropped it back onto her desk. She wrote, 'Who Cares what Anybody wears on their Stupid Feet?' and went to get another cup of coffee.

Vivie came back to her office with three tins of bloody-mary mix and a fresh cup of coffee. She put the tins at the back of her filing cabinet beside the bottle of vodka and she swallowed three aspirins, drank the coffee and tried the press release again. She stood up. She thought a dose of carbohydrate would help. She would get a Danish, and a croissant. But she didn't get past the filing cabinet. She emptied a tin of bloody-mary mix into her empty coffee cup, poured a large slug of vodka into the tin and shook it. But she forgot to put her finger over the opening in the tin and pale red liquid spewed out across her white T-shirt, and over the papers on her desk. She ran down the corridor to the lavatory to clean up.

Speaking of Love

Vivie couldn't shift the stain from her T-shirt, so she put it on back-to-front knowing that her hair would cover it. When she got back to her office she threw white paper towels onto the pale red mess on her desk. She slung the tin into the bin and made another attempt at the press release, but her hands were shaking and there was sweat on her temples. She lit a cigarette and tried to concentrate.

Vivie cobbled together a press release that she knew Sara would hate and took it down the corridor. She put it on Sara's desk with a note saying she didn't think it was quite there yet, but could they talk, and then she went back to her office, shut the door and lit another cigarette. She wondered what time Charles would be back.

She thought about how frighteningly easy it had been to talk to Matthew on Monday night and how she'd almost told him about the baby. She'd turned away quickly as he came towards her and run down the stairs, shocked by the delight she'd felt at seeing him, shocked by the pleasure it gave her to watch him from the bottom of the stairs as he stood, with his thumbs in his pockets, rocking on his feet in that way she knew so well.

And then, when the concerto began she'd concentrated on the pianist's hands and imagined it was Rachmaninov himself playing, Rachmaninov throwing back his head and laughing in triumph because he'd beaten the black dog, beaten the madness that had threatened to silence him and his music. But she'd never once forgotten that Matthew was standing right behind her.

Vivie lit another cigarette and inhaled deeply. She stood up and paced about her office, always keeping away from the long windows and the terrifying drop to the ground far below.

She wished Sara would hurry up.

She wanted to get the press release finished and go home.

Iris's story

A s I practise the story I call 'Red Head' with my back to the rose-covered retaining wall and my eyes on the almost-sea of the Bristol Channel that sparkles under the sun, the young dark-haired Iris I was, all those years ago, smiles down the years at me. She stands in the queue in the basement of the Troubadour with people who smelled of patchouli oil, people who thought it funny when other people stared at their long hair and colourful clothes and thought them delinquent, as my father would have done. That young Iris loved poetry as they did. She wanted to live the kind of life they lived, not the grey, closed, unlived, silent life she lived with her father. That Iris, especially in that red dress that night, was excited. She saw a bright future for herself. She was on the threshold of a new world, a new life as ... a poet's girlfriend, perhaps.

* * *

When the candles were lit the queue in the basement began to move and I scrabbled for the money in my cigarette packet. I held it out to pay at the little table just inside the door, and when I looked up I saw Kit behind the girl who tore the tickets from a pad. A single lightbulb lit them both; his hand was on her shoulder.

'Well, hello again,' he said.

I couldn't look at him. I said, to my feet, 'I decided not to play tennis.' I felt the blush burn my cheeks and hoped it wouldn't penetrate the thick protective mask of green make-up. And then I realised, of course, that Kit Marchwood had a girlfriend. The ticket girl.

'Prefer poets to tennis players, then?' she said, sarcastically.

'Very wise,' said Kit.

I looked up. He'd taken his hand from her shoulder and I saw that his hair shone under the lightbulb. 'Very wise, indeed,' he said and he peered at my feet in their new, pointed, red patent leather shoes. He smiled and I stared into his grey eyes. 'What?' I said, quite inarticulate and quite unable to take my eyes from his.

'Well,' he said, and he smiled, 'you'd have trouble running to the net in those, don't you think?' He held out his hand. 'Kit Marchwood,' he said, as if I didn't know.

'Hello,' I said, and held out my hand. At the same moment the girl gave me my ticket and our three hands collided. But in one fluid movement Kit lifted his hand, bowed theatrically, and gestured at the rows of wooden crates in the gloom.

'Some of the best seats in the house are still available,' he said and I laughed, took my ticket and failed to say another word.

I walked into the room. It was lit by candles that stood in painted flowerpots on shelves and in alcoves. I hoped I wouldn't stumble over a crate, and I wished I'd managed to say something to Kit. But I hadn't. So much for the new Iris and her new life.

I squinted at my ticket and saw Kit's name hand-written on it. I found a crate, sat on it and thought about what I could have said. I could have said how much I loved his poetry. I could have recited some of it to him. I could have been witty about stupid tennis. I could have … and then I felt a hand on my shoulder. I jumped and turned round.

It was Kit. 'Don't panic,' he said, 'I don't bite.'

I giggled.

'I was wondering,' he said, 'would you like a cup of coffee? Afterwards?'

'Where?' I said.

'Shall we say … here?' he said, and he looked up at the ceiling.

'Er – yes. Yes. That would be … yes.' I was afraid I'd shouted.

'I'll come and find you,' he said, and stood up.

My smile was so broad, it hurt. But I had managed not to say, 'Do you really mean me?' Or, 'Are you sure I'm who you think I am, in the dark?' I could have squealed with delight. I could have shimmied. But I didn't. The new Iris was back.

And then the lightbulb by the door clicked off, the candles flickered and, for a moment, I couldn't see Kit. I stared, stupidly, at the place where he had been and then I saw him, as he sidled away between the crates. He raised his hand and smiled at me, and then he turned and walked towards the little stage under the brick arch at the far end of the room.

I barely heard the first poet because I was already upstairs with Kit. I imagined his questions, I invented my replies. I stared at his bony face, at his mass of curly red hair, at his grey eyes. And he smiled back at me and talked, and listened. I was in heaven.

Kit was the last poet on stage that night. He strode onto the little platform and the smoke-filled yellow shafts of light made a halo of his hair. He whispered his first poem fiercely. He was wonderful, and I heard every word. He never once read from a book, nor even from a scrap of paper. He was just him and his poems, his energetic body and his long legs, his pale grey eyes and his wild red hair.

His last poem made me laugh, but I was the first to laugh and I immediately clapped my hand over my mouth. My laughter was loud and he probably hadn't meant to be funny.

He began the poem with his back to us. '*I am no one's,*' he growled, '*And no one shall be mine.*

I am free.

I can be

Whatever I wish.'

He whirled round to face us and suddenly he was a clown, a court jester. I saw a multi-coloured cap on his head. I heard its bells tinkle. He put his palms together and looked up, as if he was about to pray.

'*I am no one's,*' he said, his voice soft but clear,

'*And no one shall be mine.*

I am free

This is me and ...'

He tipped his hands forwards as if he was about to dive. His hair fell down over his face.

'*My life ...*'

He looked up at us, his grey eyes twinkled and willed us, I thought, to laugh.

'*As a fish.*'

I laughed and clapped and then I clapped my hand over my mouth and the silence seemed to go on forever until, eventually, someone else laughed, then more people laughed, and I laughed with them, and Kit dropped his arms and bowed so low that the ends of his curly hair touched the little wooden platform.

It still amazes me when I think about it. Kit was the audience for the first story I ever told to another human being. He was its inspiration, but he was also the man to whom I'd hardly said an intelligent word, at least not until I began the story. And, at times, not even then.

It was a warm May night and the Troubadour's studded wooden door was open. Several people sat outside at tables on the Old Brompton Road and, while I waited for Kit at the table by the window, I felt self-conscious. I was sure the waitresses looked at me with pity because, of course, Kit did this often. Of course, he never turned up. Of course there was a back door, a secret way out, and the girl he'd flattered that night would be left alone. I wanted to leave and when, finally, I did push my chair back I felt sure, I knew, I sensed with every nerve in my body and with the blush that began its inevitable rise up my throat, that I had been seen.

And I had.

The man leaned against a plane tree on the Old Brompton Road. The wooden shelves in the window with their rows of coloured enamel coffee pots bisected his body. A shaft of light from a streetlamp fell directly onto him and he smiled straight at me. He seemed closer than he could possibly have been. I could see that he had a snaggle tooth and dark eyes, and he held a pipe. His hair was dark and brilliantined. He wore a tweed jacket, beige corduroys and a pale, checked viyella shirt. His appearance was old-fashioned, but he was not old and he looked so directly at me that I had to turn away, but even then I could feel his stare. It unnerved me.

Iris's story

I knew he had moved even though I had turned away and then, out of the corner of my eye, I saw his hands hang his tweed jacket over the back of a chair at a table on the street, just the other side of the window. I could have reached out and touched his hands if the glass hadn't been there. They were beautiful hands. They reassured me somehow, and so I looked up. He smiled. I smiled back and, quite suddenly, I felt better. Not so self-conscious, not so obviously alone.

I pulled my chair back in, picked up my mug of coffee and then I heard Kit's voice. I watched him stride towards me on his long legs between the closely packed tables. He sat down opposite me, pushed back the curly red mass of his hair with his hands, ordered some coffee and I wondered why I'd ever doubted that he would turn up.

The man on the other side of the window signalled to a waitress, and then Kit said he was glad I'd laughed.

'For a minute,' he said, 'I didn't think anyone else would.'

'I couldn't help it,' I said. I was glad he'd known it was me.

'Sometimes,' he said, 'people just get too serious about poetry. Sometimes it's just funny, or silly.' His grey eyes seemed blue, just then. 'If I get the chance I'm going to perform that one next week.'

'Is there another reading next week?'

'Not here ... at the Albert Hall. There's a poetry fest. They're calling it holy communion.' He looked at me. 'Don't you think that's funny?'

I didn't understand.

' "Wholly",' he said, 'with a W. And two Ls.'

I laughed, too late, and dug my nails into my palms. I felt stupid. But he talked on about the poetry festival and I don't think he noticed.

'It's amazing. Ginsberg's here and Corso's here ... and Ferlinghetti and Horovitz and Harry Fainlight and Adrian Mitchell. My name's on the list but the organisers say there are two or three hundred who want to read. Still, if there isn't a slot for me, maybe I'll just leap onto the stage and perform anyway. What d'you think?'

'I think you should,' I said.

He narrowed his eyes. 'Come,' he said. 'It's next Wednesday.'

'What time?'

'Evening.'

I noticed a movement on the other side of the window. It was the man. He held the pipe by its bowl in the palm of his hand. He lit it and then he looked at Kit, nodded at him. Kit didn't seem to notice, but I was glad. Glad that he'd seen me with Kit. When I turned back Kit had pulled off his short-sleeved striped jumper. His emerald green shirt was crumpled, his hair even wilder after his jumper had rumpled it.

'I'll have to get ... I'll have to iron my hair.' He ran his nicotine-stained fingers through it.

'Iron your hair?'

He moved constantly, I don't think he was ever completely still.

'Yup. That's how I straighten out this mess of a head.'

'I don't think it's a mess.'

'Try having it on your head. I hate it.'

He was very thin and his bony face was covered with freckles.

'How could you hate it? It's beautiful.' I blushed.

He changed the subject. 'Why do you come here in your tennis disguise?' he said.

'My father thinks I'm ...'

'... playing tennis, I know. But why?'

'Because he wouldn't let me come here ... if he knew.'

'I like that,' said Kit.

I stared at him.

'It makes poetry dangerous ... if you have to tell lies to come here.' He twirled a curly hank of red hair round a long, bony, nicotine-stained finger.

'What else wouldn't he let you do, if he knew? What else is dangerous territory?'

I felt like a child. I wished I hadn't said a word about my father.

'I didn't mean ... he doesn't control my life ... he doesn't know how I live. We hardly ever talk.'

I turned away, embarrassed. I saw the man's hand, and the smoke that curled up from the bowl of his pipe on the other side of the window.

'My father doesn't like people,' I said. 'He often says that. He says people complicate things.'

'How long have you been a prisoner in your father's house?'

I turned back to Kit. I felt as if he'd stabbed me. 'What do you mean? I'm not … he's just … ,' but for the first time in my life I realised how strange my father's words were. Outside his house his words, the words he said so often, sounded distinctly odd.

'How long?' said Kit.

'As long as I can remember,' I said.

Kit ordered more coffee and a drink called Amaretto which smelled like glue. Then he reached across the table and took my hand. His was warm. Mine felt insubstantial, hardly there.

'You should try flying,' he said, but before I could ask what he meant, the ticket girl materialised from nowhere and stood beside him. She put her hand on his shoulder.

'Come on, Kit, let's beat it,' she said.

I stared at her perfect, Jean-Shrimpton knees and I knew he'd leave with her. But he hadn't let go of my hand.

'Not now,' said Kit. He didn't look at her.

The ticket girl waited, but still he didn't look at her. She took her hand off his shoulder.

'Be like that then,' she said, and she flicked her long blonde hair behind her shoulder and left.

Kit winked at me.

'Isn't she your – '

' – I am no one's. And no one shall be mine,' he said.

I said I'd never thought of myself as a prisoner before and Kit said you have to realise you're in prison before you think about escape, and then it was my turn to change the subject. The conversation made me feel shaky, made my hands shake, so I told him I really meant what I'd said about his hair. I said, 'Please don't iron it. It's beautiful.'

'Have to,' he said, seriously. 'It's the grottiest hair around.

Much too curly to be hip, especially now it's long. And I've been thinking about dyeing it ... brown.'

'Brown?' I said. 'You can't. You absolutely can't.'

He stared at me. His grey eyes laughed.

'Why not?'

'Because,' I said, 'of the Desperate Dilemma of the Red-Headed Kings ... who lived in a cold northern kingdom where hair like yours was prized above all else ...'

And I launched into the story.

'Only the poets, the medicine men and the Kings had hair like yours,' I said. 'The unrulier and the redder the hair, the more respected the person. Red hair was a mark of distinction ... in those days.'

As Kit took my hands skeins of his red hair fell down over his forehead.

'Go on,' he said.

He was, almost, still and his grey eyes were fixed on mine. He let go of my hands for a second to pick up his glass and swallow some more Amaretto and then he said, 'I want to know what happens next.'

After that he never once let go of my hands.

I closed my eyes and I heard my mother's voice. 'Just as long as you see the pictures, Eereece,' she said, with her soft French 'j', 'the words will come.'

And I saw the pictures and the words did come.

Kit's eyes encouraged me to keep on when I faltered and sometimes he whispered a question that prompted me, and every time I looked at him, every time I decided, definitely, that it was a ridiculous story and I would stop, his eyes urged me on. And so the story that I now call 'Red Head' was told for the very first time.

When I reached the end, he said, 'How many times have you told that one?'

'None. I made it up just now.'

'Wow.' He leaned back and signalled to the waitress. 'But you've told other stories before?'

'To myself, or to my mother.'

'Two more Amarettos,' he said to the waitress who smiled at him, but he ignored her and smiled at me. 'Well,' he said, 'I think you're a natural.'

'My mother was a natural,' I said. 'She never learned to read well in English so she told me stories instead. She made up stories about stones and trees and birds and hats and trolls and me and, well, anything. Until I went to school I thought everyone told stories the way she did.'

'Some people still do,' said Kit, and lifted his glass.

'It's the way I keep her alive,' I said.

'Perhaps your mother is your muse,' said Kit.

I swallowed some more Amaretto. It made my lips and my fingers sticky. I tried to like it.

'Here's to the first story you've ever told to a living, breathing human being,' said Kit.

On the pavement outside the Troubadour I put out my hand. Kit smiled, took it and pulled me towards him. He leaned down and kissed me and I breathed in his bitter peppery smell and his tobacco smell and the gluey-Amaretto smell.

'Find those wings,' he said, 'try flying.'

He pulled a key from his back pocket. 'Flying'll get you out of prison.' Then he opened a dark blue door beside the Troubadour and was gone.

I could have dreamed it, except that my chin itched from his stubble and, through the window, through the rows of coloured coffee pots on their shelves I saw the waitress pick up our glasses and our red enamel coffee mugs, and I could still taste the Amaretto. And I knew the man with the pipe had been there because there was a lump of smoking tobacco in the ashtray.

I turned and half-walked, half-ran towards the Earls Court Road and I stretched out my arms like a child when she pretends to fly. I thought about stories and I thought about my father's house and I felt, for the first time in my life, that there really might be a place for me in a world that was not my father's world. A real place in a real world that I did not have to invent, a world full of possibilities, a world full of poetry and words, and, perhaps, even a poet.

I hummed Marianne Faithfull's 'This Little Bird' all the way back to my father's house.

Matthew's story

'In about a mile we'll turn north-west,' says Dad, 'onto the Ely Road.' I glance at him, he is holding his glasses up on his forehead and staring at the map. 'Is that enough information?'

I say, 'I know the Ely Road, Dad.'

He says, 'Right you are,' and turns away, letting his glasses drop back down onto his nose. Then he says, 'Oh my word. Stop, please. Stop now.'

'Where?'

'Here ... there.'

'There's nowhere to pull over, Dad.' I hit the heel of my hand hard on the steering wheel as I try to pull onto the verge too quickly and it begins to throb. I say, 'A bit more warning next time, please.'

He says, 'Sorry. But did you see those poppies? They're positively glowing. I'd like to take a photograph. Just for the record.'

I reverse the car along the verge and Dad struggles to open his camera case. He takes a photograph of the poppies, refusing my offer to take it for him, and after that I drive slower and we stop, every so often, for a photograph. He knows this country so well, but he's behaving as if he's never seen it before. He takes pictures of my favourite pink willow-herb and he takes pictures of cow-parsley skeletons; he takes signposts and great expanses of arable land; he even took a couple of photographs as we left Thetford Forest, twisting awkwardly backwards in his seat. He takes a photograph of a great rust-coloured, dying dock with a red admiral perched on top of it and he tries to take some thistledown as it blows past the windscreen.

He hands me his camera and says, 'Be my hands, will you?

Film's finished.' He nods towards his suitcase on the back seat where I discover at least ten rolls of film squirrelled away.

I say, 'Dad, we're only going for the weekend.'

He says, 'Meant to tell you I was planning this,' and he tries to stretch his fingers out straight. 'I want some photographs, for the record, you know. I promised Iris. Well, and I promised myself. Things along the way, things that catch my eye. Things to remember this journey, this weekend, by.'

Dad has always kept photograph albums, scrapbooks, commonplace books, odd bits of information cut from newspapers and notes of his own. He started doing it in hospital, after Dunkirk. He said it helped him make sense of things, afterwards, and since then he's always done it, especially when he travels. His boxes of cuttings used to drive my mother mad; his chief subject is the natural world, but sometimes it's me, I suppose I count as natural, or one of my projects, and recently he and Iris have been compiling a book of strange facts about trees, complete with photographs and drawings. But these photographs, I suspected, were because he wanted a record of this journey for Iris.

He tells me it's the largest storytelling festival she's been booked for. He looks so proud when he tells me.

I put the new film into his camera and give it back to him. He balances it on his knees and we drive on without saying much. When we cross the border into Cambridgeshire and the Fens the flattening and widening of the land make the sky seem several times its natural volume, as if it has become the earth's parachute. We bump over the Ely to London railway line and the steering wheel vibrates under the heel of my hand, making it throb again. Sometimes I wonder if there are splinters of glass still left under the scar, although no doctor has ever found any. But if there are any still in there, they were honourably won.

It was May, it had been raining and Vivie sat opposite me under the arch in the beech hedge that divides our gardens. Drops of rain dripped from the hedge onto us and Vivie hugged her knees. Her hair was pulled tightly back in a ponytail. I'd never seen her hair like that before.

She said, 'He doesn't like walking and he doesn't like talking very much. He doesn't laugh and he's always telling me to "Be still, child".' She looked at me. 'I mean I know I can be a bit, you know, thing ...'

' ... of a pest,' I said. She lunged at me, but only half-heartedly.

'But I'm not "child" ... and he just keeps saying what he hates. So far he hasn't said one thing he likes.'

'We made a mistake, didn't we?'

She bit her lip. 'Yes, we did. At lunch he said ... no, guess what he said.'

'I don't know ... um ... he doesn't like your house.'

'No ... he said he *doesn't like people.*' She rolled her eyes. 'What is there to like if you don't like people?'

We heard voices from Iris's kitchen and Vivie stood up, brushed the earth from the back of her shorts and was gone. She always moved so quickly I'd nicknamed her 'Lightning'.

I went inside and upstairs to finish my homework, but as I passed the window in the passage I saw Iris putting a wooden kitchen chair under the storytree. She was behaving oddly, I thought, as if she couldn't decide where to put the chair. She kept picking it up and moving it, hugging the back of it, putting it down again and staring at it. I stood by the open window, watching her. Vivie's grandfather came out and sat on the chair. He wore a dark suit which looked very odd in their garden, and a thin dark tie. His clothes were quite different from the clothes my father wore even though I guessed they were about the same age. He sat upright in the chair, lit his pipe and opened his paper.

Iris and Vivie brought out a table and a pot of coffee and some cups, and then they sat on the striped rug under the laburnum. The yellow blooms hung down like bobbly yellow icicles, above them.

Vivie knelt beside her grandfather and I heard her say, 'Grandpa, this tree has been our storytree since I was born.'

He didn't look up from his newspaper but she carried on talking. She said, 'And it's a tradition in our family. If you sit under the storytree, you have to tell a story. So,' she put her hand on his knee, 'you're our family, you can tell a story.'

A wisp of smoke rose above her grandfather's newspaper but he didn't put it down.

Vivie said, 'Everyone knows at least one story.' She looked back at Iris who was standing up now, holding her hand out to Vivie. She had an odd expression on her face.

Vivie said, 'I'm sure you know one.'

Iris said, 'Grandpa doesn't like stories, Vivie. Come with me.' Then she took Vivie's arm and pulled her away to the end of their garden; even then Vivie's grandfather didn't put his newspaper down.

When Iris and Vivie came back, Vivie said, 'Sorry, Grandpa, don't worry about telling a story.' Iris smiled vaguely, and wandered away, out of my sight. Vivie said, 'I'll tell you one, instead.'

I suppose if I was trying to read my newspaper and a nine-year-old was pestering me like a wasp buzzing round a jam-pot, I would be irritable too. But I vowed then that when I was an adult, I would never ever do what he did. At first I thought he was just going to ignore her, but then he folded his newspaper, very neatly into quarters, and put it down on the table. He tapped out his pipe against the table leg and put it into his pocket. Then he stood up, put his hands under Vivie's armpits, picked her up and shook her. He said, very loudly, 'That will do, child,' but when Vivie shouted back at him to let go of her, he dropped her and put his hand over her mouth squeezing her cheeks with his fingers, and when she still fought him he pulled a handkerchief from his pocket and started stuffing it into her mouth.

I flew down the stairs and into the kitchen. My mother was standing with her back to the garden door and as I tried to get behind her she caught hold of my arm and said, 'And just where do you think you're going?'

I said, 'Vivie's in trouble. I've got to help her!'

She said, 'Matthew Aldwater, your imagination is running away with you. I want to see you go right back up those stairs and finish your homework.'

Matthew's story

When I refused to move until I knew whether Vivie was all right, my mother said, 'She's coming to tea this afternoon. We'll see just how she is then.'

And so, reluctantly and very slowly, I went back upstairs and, as I stared down into Iris's deserted garden, I hit the window-pane with the heel of my hand, hard, and the glass shattered. My mother had to take me to hospital and, with childish logic, I was triumphant. She had refused to let me help Vivie so my wound was her punishment. I had to have seven stitches and I hoped it hurt her to watch the needle digging into my skin.

By the time we got back from the hospital Vivie's grandfather had left, and soon after that Iris told Vivie that they must not see anyone because, she said, people could be dangerous. She said they must not answer the telephone or the door and she said they would fend for themselves, and that was when I got it all wrong.

Vivie made me promise not to tell anyone what Iris had said and I did try. But I failed to convince my mother that I knew nothing and when, in the end, I told her everything I knew I told her because I felt helpless and because I was sure that my mother, the nurse, would know what to do. But I made a terrible mistake when I told my mother how I felt. I cried out my frustration and my inadequacy and my inability to help Vivie in my mother's arms, but as my mother comforted me and I dried my tears, she was already planning to ring the doctor who committed Iris to Salem.

Perhaps there was no alternative, but when Iris was taken away I blamed myself. The pathetic way I'd blurted out that I didn't think Vivie could cope for much longer still makes me wince, because what I really meant was that I didn't think I could cope for much longer. I told my mother the things Vivie had made me promise not to tell because I wanted to rid myself of the burden of Vivie's belief in me. She was convinced that I would know what to do, that I could stop Iris being taken away, but I didn't and I couldn't.

And so, at twelve years old, I made a frightening discovery. I found out that if you say how you feel you lose control over what happens next. The terrain changes irrevocably and you are lost.

Dad says, 'Matthew? Did you hear me?'

I say, 'Sorry, no I didn't.'

He says, 'Pull over when you can. I want to take a photograph of the Wicken windmill, it looks as if they've finally hoisted the new sails.'

Vivie's story

Vivie's telephone rang and, expecting it to be Sara, she said, 'I'm on my way.' But it was Charles. 'Where to, my darling?' he said, laughing.

'Nowhere,' said Vivie.

'I doubt that,' said Charles. 'If I know my Vivienne she's always hurrying somewhere.'

Vivie bit deeply into the skin by her thumbnail.

'So, how is my angel?' said Charles. 'Been missing her old salt?'

'I'm fine,' said Vivie, her voice muffled by her thumb. 'But I've got a press release to write. I'll ring you later.' She slammed the telephone down and swore. Her thumb bled and, as she wrapped the tomato-juice stained paper towel round it, Sara walked into her office.

'Jesus, Viv,' she said, 'what the hell's happened?

'Oh I ... just bit my thumb.'

'Are you sure?'

'No ... it's um ... tomato juice. As well.' She tried to smile, but failed. 'The press release is on your desk.'

'It's in the bin,' said Sara, 'and this is the very last time I pull you out of the hole you seem so determined to hurl yourself into. It needs a complete rewrite. What were you thinking of? Or not thinking of?'

Vivie followed Sara down the corridor, her heart hammering. Sara began dictating a new press release before they reached her office and Vivie had to run back for a pad and a pen. By the time she sat down Sara's words were flowing so quickly that an image of grass cuttings spewing from a lawnmower filled Vivie's mind.

'Thanks,' said Vivie when, at last, Sara stopped talking. 'I'll type it up.'

Speaking of Love

'Not so fast, Viv,' said Sara. 'I'll give you one last chance, and this is it.' She held out a copy of the *Guardian* and waited for Vivie to take it.

'There's an article in here,' said Sara, putting the tips of her fingers together and looking over the tops of her half-glasses, 'about the revival of storytelling. Oral storytelling. It's a hot topic and I'm sure we could make use of it in our DoE "Remember Your Teacher" press releases. Think about it, will you? I'm thinking "Just Listen". I'm thinking "Listening Works". I'm thinking "O.T.O.S: S.O.S – Our Teachers as Oral Storytellers: Serving Our Schools". But that's not all I'm thinking, Viv. I'm thinking this time you'd better do the thinking. This time you deliver. A.O.T.'

'Yup,' said Vivie, not looking at Sara. 'I owe you a drink.'

'Tonight would be good,' said Sara, unexpectedly. 'It's always good to relax with a colleague.'

Vivie ran back to her office. She didn't let her rage out until she'd shut the door and was sitting in front of her PC. Then she hit the keys so hard that her fingers hurt and she yelled out the words as she typed them. She hated her job. And now Sara wanted her to do the PR for an oral storytelling project, a subject that would constantly remind her of the one person she spent her life trying to forget.

Vivie felt herself judged as a child for her fear of her mother. And she felt herself judged as a coward for failing to tell Charles what she had to tell him. And obviously, the judgement pronounced, she was utterly incompetent at her job.

But when she walked back to Sara's office with the press release she felt a rush of happiness that it was done, and a strong desire for a large dose of the only solution she knew.

Iris's story

I shall tell my stories with my back to the retaining wall. If I tell them with my back to the sea they get lost, and anyway I walk about when I tell my stories and it would be ignominious, to say the least, to disappear backwards over the six-foot drop in the middle of a story.

'There was, once,' I began, as I faced the almost-sea, 'there was once a King who loved his daughter so much that he wanted her to have everything that was his.'

I don't know why I've decided on these stories already, but I know this place has influenced me, even though I know well enough what happens when I tell, these days. I know that often, when I stand in front of an audience, some of the stories I have decided to tell leave my head and others, ones I hadn't thought I'd tell, fill my head. It depends on the place and the audience, but these stories, the stories I used to tell Vivie, seem to fit this magical, mediaeval place. And so, for now, they're the ones I plan to tell, the ones I'll think about and practise. What happens on the day, on Sunday, I'll only know when Sunday comes. But I shall face the Bristol Channel, the almost-sea, and the white sails of the distant boats. I shall stand with my back to the Great Hall of the castle and I shall follow the pictures in my head, and try to remember to breathe.

I rehearsed the story about the princess who made friends with the creatures of the night, the princess who left her father's kingdom, but when I stumbled, when the pictures went from my mind, I was suddenly not sure that anyone would want to hear this story, or any of my stories. I lost my nerve. I thought they were ridiculous, pointless, idiotic fairy stories. I wondered how a fairy story could possibly touch people who live the way we live now?

And then I remembered how much Dick loves these stories,

and how Vivie used to love them. And I made myself follow the pictures and shut out the demons who would kill my voice. I saw the King in his state library. I saw him in his long claret-coloured robe without his crown – he was off duty – I saw him in front of the mullioned windows of his study which are just like the ones in my bedroom in the watchtower, except that there isn't any glass in this King's windows. I saw how he could see right down into his courtyard where his soldiers stood guard, if he turned his head.

'The King wanted his daughter to inherit the ways, the manners, the habits and the customs – not to mention the riches and the territories – of his kingdom, and he looked forward happily to the day when she reached the age of majority, when all that he loved would become hers.

'But the King's daughter, the Princess, was not happy about this arrangement – she did not want what was his – she wanted another life, a different life, a life of her own.'

When I make myself push on through a story I discover, or rediscover, what it has to say to me and then I feel better, then I can believe in the story again. Then I can see its pictures and find the right words. I know this, I know it well, but it's so much easier to run away, to stop, to give up, just in case it doesn't work, this time. Just in case the magic doesn't happen, this time. Just in case it really isn't any good, for all time.

But when I'm not telling stories I feel dead so I have to take these risks to stay alive. I have to risk a story badly told because if I don't, I'll never tell it well. And this place helps and, I remember, Vivie liked it best when I told her stories under our laburnum tree, her tree, the tree she called our storytree. But my garden is small, enclosed and intimate. I have never told stories in such a wide-open place. I hope my voice won't get lost out here.

Twice in my life I had no voice at all. Twice in my life I lost everything: my stories, my life, my voice, my very self. But I have regained these things although a large part of my life, my daughter, is still lost to me. My hand closed over her letter in my pocket, but I forced myself not to take it out and re-read it. Although I hardly need to read it – I know it by heart.

Iris's story

I wish I knew Vivie's childhood by heart, but the ECT scorched my memory. It robbed me of Vivie's childhood. I can no longer remember the way she looked and the things she said. I have lost the whole of her young life except for one precious day, one precious time that escaped the jolts of the ECT's jagged hatred. There is one set of pictures that remain like a tiny oasis in the blasted, burnt-out landscape that is my memory from that time, the barren place where Vivie's childhood should be.

It was a warm day, the laburnum tree's flowers looked like yellow-gold lanterns, and I had just finished telling Vivie 'Red Head', when she asked if the lady-in-waiting married the newly crowned young king.

'I don't know,' I said. 'Perhaps.'

'But you *made* the story. You *must* know what happens.'

'I only know what I have told you,' I said. 'I don't know what happens after the story ends.'

Vivie rolled her eyes and stood up, she must have been seven or eight years old. She did a cartwheel and then she began to walk about. She talked to herself as she went backwards and forwards between the laburnum tree and the wooden fence under the beeches at the end of the garden. She walked fast; Matthew's nickname for her was 'Lightning' because she always did everything at high speed, and she wore her favourite jeans and an old checked shirt of Matthew's. She always preferred his cast-offs to anything I made for her.

She pretended to be the lady-in-waiting in the story and then the young king, and then she was herself. She asked questions of each of them and she was very serious as she invented their answers, and while I watched her I felt such a surge of love for her, for everything about her, for her lean body and her self-absorption, for her inventiveness, for the way she laughed when she pretended she was the young king, for her gloriously wild red-gold hair, for her freckled skin. My whole body ached to hug her and hold her and keep her just the way she was forever.

But I didn't move or say a thing. I just watched her. Eventually she flung herself down on the rug beside me.

'I've got something to tell you,' she said.

'What is it?' I said.

'They told me everything,' she said. 'So now *I* know what happened, even if you don't. I even know what the lady-in-waiting said to the king.'

'Aren't you going to tell me?' I said.

'They told me it was private,' she said, very seriously.

I laughed, but I should have known better.

'It *is* private,' she said. 'And it's not funny.' She crossed her arms and thumped them down against her small body. She turned away from me. She started to cry and she pushed me away when I tried to put my arms round her.

'I'm sorry,' I said. 'I shouldn't have laughed. It isn't funny, you're quite right. I promise I won't ask again. It's none of my business.'

'No it isn't,' she said. 'And I won't *ever* tell.'

But it wasn't long before she turned back to me and I said I was sorry again and she said she might, perhaps, tell me the things they'd all said, one day, and then she giggled and fell towards me on the rug and I was filled with a bitter-sweet love: a selfless love that wanted the world, and all its glories, for my daughter, and a selfish love that wanted her to stay just the way she was, and stay close by, forever.

I wanted time to stop, that afternoon. I wanted to watch Vivie's breathless hundredth cartwheel, feel the warmth of the sun, imagine her future but keep her safe, with me. I wanted never to have to stop my laughter at her jokes. I wanted to keep hold of that sweet, connected feeling, that simple knowledge that this is how it was meant to be, forever.

And then Matthew shambled under the arch in the hedge and told us a story from a book he'd borrowed from the library. It was one of the Holy Fool, Nasrudin's, stories. I'd never heard them until Matthew began to tell them. He told the story very well, except that he couldn't contain his exuberant laughter. He told the story of the Mulla Nasrudin's wife who went to wash the Mulla's long white shirt in a stream but a crow flew down, stole the soap and sat high above the Mulla's wife in a tree, with the soap in his beak, and would not come down.

Eventually the Mulla's wife gave up and she went home with the Mulla's dirty, wet shirt in her hands. She told her husband what had happened. She expected him to be exasperated, but he just smiled at his wife and said, 'Let the crow keep the soap. He needs it more than us. Look at the colour of *his* clothes.'

Matthew loved that book. I think I borrowed it from him once, but I can't remember. And then Vivie challenged Matthew to a cartwheel competition. Matthew was stronger but Vivie was neater. Matthew's cartwheels were all gangly legs and arms and he landed on all fours, but Vivie's were fast and neat as a Catherine wheel and she always landed on her feet, with a little bounce. I judged Matthew the winner for the number he managed to do, but Vivie for the way she did them.

'So we've both won,' said Vivie. 'That's not a proper competition. Both people can't win.'

That day with Vivie made me long for my own mother. I longed for her for myself and I longed for my daughter and my mother to have known each other. I had no idea, then, how I would long for Vivie when she was a grown woman. I had no idea how we would be separated, how she would not be able to bear to see me, because of the way I was. Twice.

Dick has always said that Vivie will come back in her own good time. And just before I came here, to the festival, he said I must let her choose the time and I know he is right, and I know I must, but it is so hard. How can I know if she'll ever want to? I write to her from time to time. My letters are quite sane, quite useless, probably, but I always say that I will answer any questions, tell her anything she wants to know, anything. And sometimes I say I know, now, how frightened she was, particularly the first time, when she was so young. I have told her that I clung to her then because, in my madness, she seemed so sane; the fact that she was a child didn't occur to me, then. But now I wonder if I'll ever be able to forgive myself for the terrible responsibility I heaped onto her young shoulders. Poor Vivie.

Speaking of Love

I have written all this to her and I have tried to explain what I know, now, about myself, but otherwise Dick is right, all I can do is wait. The rest is for her to do, or not to do.

'Just let her come to you,' Dick says. 'That's the best way.'

I wrote to her last week to tell her about the festival. I told her I had been booked to tell my stories on Sunday, her birthday. I said I would love her to come but I know she won't.

I wonder what she does with my letters. Perhaps she doesn't even open them. My father never opened my letters, he returned them unopened. At least Vivie doesn't return mine.

'Iris, can I get you anything?'

The sound of an unfamiliar voice made me jump. It was one of the festival organisers. She squatted, perched like a bird on the edge of the retaining wall above me, her dark hair held back in the purple plastic identity band that's meant to go round her wrist. She held a walkie-talkie to her ear. I said there was nothing I needed and I rolled my yellow identity band round my wrist. You can't take them off, unless you cut them, and you have to show them each time you come into the festival grounds. They look just like hospital identity bands. When I had Vivie, mine was pink, I think. Or was that hers?

The girl stood, smiled and answered the voice that crackled in her ear from the walkie-talkie, and I found myself annoyed, unreasonably, that there weren't any grey hairs in her glossy dark head. She hurried away and I began again on the story that Vivie loved best of all, the story of the princess who only went out at night, the princess who disobeyed her father and made friends with the owls.

There was a gentle hum from the generator on the jousting field below, and steel rang out against steel as the last tent stakes were beaten into the earth.

Vivie's story

Vivie stared at Sara's half-full glass of red wine and wondered how a person could drink so slowly. She still wanted to drink a bucketful, and quickly. She'd made Sara laugh several times, but now she had to say the only really important, serious thing on her mind. The thing she'd been wanting to say all evening, but it seemed unwilling to make itself clear.

Sara fidgeted and Vivie took it for a sign that she wanted another drink. 'I'll get more,' she said and signalled wildly to the waiter with her glass.

'I've had enough,' said Sara, standing up, 'and I think you have too.'

'I've had an abortion, Sar,' said Vivie, suddenly.

'You've already told me,' said Sara. 'And I've told you what I suggest you do.'

'And I haven't told Charles. I need to know what to say. Could you ... ? I know I've got a pen ... somewhere.' Vivie put her glass down, carefully, on the floor beside her and scrabbled in her bag. Then she looked up, 'What was I looking for?' she said.

'A pen,' said Sara, acidly.

'What on earth would I need a pen for?' said Vivie. 'And where's the waiter?'

Vivie lit another cigarette and Sara waved away another cloud of smoke. When the waiter came Sara ordered two large glasses of water and shook her head at him when Vivie ordered more wine.

'I don't think so, Viv,' she said.

'I hate being called Viv,' said Vivie. 'And what makes you the bloody expert? Stop telling me what to do.'

Vivie searched for her glass, saw it on the floor, kicked it over as she reached for it and swore. Then she stood up and wove her way towards the bar. When she turned, holding a tray with two large glasses of water on it and one large glass of red wine, she couldn't remember where she'd been sitting and she couldn't see Sara. She shrugged, looked around and caught the eye of a man in a pale linen suit in the corner, and then she tripped. The glasses of water went flying but, by a miracle of determination, Vivie caught her glass of red wine and the man laughed.

Vivie spotted her handbag on a sofa and stumbled towards it. There was a large piece of paper on the table. Vivie read her name. And then she read, 'See you at the presentation tomorrow.' She stuffed the paper into her bag, sat down and gulped the wine. Then she got up and staggered over to sit with the man in the pale linen suit because he'd laughed.

When Vivie eventually left the wine bar it was late and she had to wait a long time for the train and then for the night bus. Her head lolled against the bus window and she very nearly missed her stop and when she asked, in the all-night chemist, for sleeping pills, slurring her words and saying that she'd left her prescription at home, the pharmacist said he had none in stock. He said he would order them and she could pick them up the next day.

Vivie shrugged, swore and wove her way along Charles's street. She tried to steady her walk and when she stood outside Charles's house – she'd never thought of it as their house – she rearranged her face into a suitably sober expression.

And then she rang the doorbell because, for some reason that she could not fathom, she'd found it impossible to make her key fit the lock.

A judgement that she only ever thought of herself broke the surface of the alcohol sea and made Vivie gasp.

Iris's story

The man who'd stared at me outside the Troubadour leaned against the wall of the shop. My heart skipped a beat and I crossed the road quickly towards him. I suddenly had an urge to tell him I was Kit's girlfriend, but I didn't because, when I said it in my head, it sounded ridiculous. The man and I hadn't even met, after all. And I hadn't seen Kit again, either.

I unlocked the shop, turned off the alarm, wound up the metal grilles, turned on the lights and watched the bolts of material begin to glow. I loved the way they did that, under the lights. But, all the time, I knew the man watched me even though I didn't look round and I talked like a mad thing as I opened the shop. I told him how I loved the way the lights made the colours of the materials come alive every morning. I told him how I loved the way the materials felt: slippery satin, soft tweed, rough linen, stiff taffeta. And I told him how, sometimes, I breathed in the smells of the materials. I told him the way they smelled comforted me.

But it was all nervous chatter and when I turned round he just leant against the doorjamb and puffed on his pipe. He looked as if he hadn't heard a word I'd said. I asked him, hesitantly because I didn't want to offend him, not to smoke, because the materials absorb smells. He smiled – his smile was deliciously crooked – half-turned, bent one knee and tapped out his pipe against the heel of his shoe. He put the pipe into his pocket and turned back to me, hands out, palms in my direction and he smiled, as if to say 'No pipe, no smoke.' As he walked across the shop with one hand held out, I wondered if he'd ever set his pocket on fire.

'Dexter's the name,' he said. 'John Dexter. I have been meaning to do this for a long time.' And he looked down at me. I took his hand and stared at it. It was a truly beautiful hand. The fingers were long with squared-off fingertips and neat nails. There was a prominent pale grey vein that snaked its way across the back of his hand and the skin was smooth and uniformly pale. It really was a beautiful hand.

'But first, about the other night,' he said, 'it was never my intention to interrupt ... anything.' He smiled.

I blushed and wished I could think of something to say, but I couldn't. Anyway I couldn't remember that he'd interrupted anything.

'I have seen you several times at poetry readings,' he said. 'I should have said something to you sooner. But judging by the other night, I would say I have missed my chance.' He looked at me. He waited for me to say something, but I didn't.

'I thought so,' he said. 'Well, never mind. Perhaps we could be friends?' He smiled his crooked smile, showed his snaggle tooth. 'Would that suit you, old girl?'

'I'm not an "old girl",' I said, but I smiled. I couldn't not smile at him.

'Simply a figure of speech,' said John Dexter. His voice was deep, with a slight crack in it.

'Friends?' he said, and he squeezed my hand.

'Friends,' I said.

When he left he said he'd be back soon, and I wondered what it would be like to be friends with John Dexter. I'd never had a man-friend before. I watched him walk away, watched him take his pipe out of his pocket, watched the pipe smoke trail over his shoulder, but he never once looked back. And then he turned the corner and was gone.

I saw Kit the next day.

I had just measured out several yards of green linen for a customer in a Courrèges minidress when I saw him outside my father's house, which was diagonally opposite the shop. He jigged up and down on the pavement and his red corkscrew curls bobbed wildly. I don't think I even made an excuse to the customer, I just dropped the heavy scissors and ran into the street.

'Kit!' I yelled, as if he might disappear if I didn't shout. 'Kit!'

He spun round, screwed up his eyelids and stared across the

road. I wondered if he was short-sighted. 'What are you doing here?' I said, my voice far too loud as I crossed the road.

'Looking for you, of course,' he said.

'How did you know where to come?' I said, and my voice shook as I stood in front of him.

'I followed you home,' he said, and he put his hand on my arm.

'But you ... outside the Troubadour you just disappeared into ...'

'Into my flat. Then I came out again and followed you.'

'Why didn't you catch up with me? Why didn't you say something?'

'Because you ... because I didn't want to frighten you ... and I wanted to make sure you got home safely. Well, that and,' he looked straight at me, 'I wanted to know where you lived.'

'You're making it up,' I said.

'Nope. You were singing. Well, humming.'

'What was I humming?'

'Marianne Faithfull. "This Little Bird".' He hummed it.

I stared at him. I'd thought about the Troubadour. I'd imagined myself with my finger on the bell beside the blue door to Kit's flat. I'd imagined Kit with his hand on the door, at the bottom of the stairs, Kit delighted to see me. But every time I imagined that, I also imagined the girl with the Jean-Shrimpton knees at the door and I never knew what to say to her. For all I knew it was her flat, and anyway I wanted Kit to want to see me. I wanted him to come and find me. It never occurred to me that he didn't know where I lived.

'You could have rung me,' I said.

'No, I couldn't,' said Kit, and he smiled.

'Why not?'

'Because it's difficult to ring a person who hasn't got a name.'

'Didn't I –'

' – no, you didn't.'

'It's Iris,' I said, and the blush began to rise, 'Iris Stone.'

'Well, hello, Iris Stone,' said Kit, and he leant down so that his face was very close to mine. 'Remember the poetry fest, Iris Stone? It's tonight, Iris Stone. Will you come?'

'Yes I will,' I said. 'Yes, I'd love to.'

We looked at each other.

'And see,' said Kit, 'no sign of an iron.'

He pulled a handful of his hair down until it was straight. When he let it go it coiled back up, at least three inches. 'But I may need intravenous injections of a particular story … until I am completely cured.'

I laughed. I wanted to touch him, but I didn't.

'I finish work in half an hour,' I said as we crossed the road back to the shop.

'Come with me now,' he said, and I did. I almost forgot to lock up. I don't know what happened to the customer.

'Do you always wear that dress?' he said as he reached for my hand when we crossed the Cromwell Road.

'Not exactly always,' I said. 'But it reminds me of the poetry reading – it reminds me of last week.'

'I'm flattered,' he said. 'And I like it.' His hair bobbed and jigged as he walked.

'Are you going to read, I mean perform, tonight?'

'Hope so. Don't know. There are still hundreds who want to.'

It was a glorious warm evening and when we reached the Albert Hall there were people on the steps. They talked, they smoked, they laughed and they leaned against each other; and there was a long queue. The man in front of us wore a black leather jacket with 'Poets for Pot' painted on it in white letters, and women handed out flowers to everyone in the queue. They said, 'Poets for Peace', and 'Poets on Peace Alert', and one of them gave me a red rose and Kit a yellow and white iris. He bowed to me with a flourish, kissed the iris and gave it to me. I gave him my rose.

We passed a group of Americans on the steps. They talked angrily about Viet Nam.

'I've heard Mitchell's poem is about the war,' said Kit. He rolled a cigarette with one hand, and smiled at me. 'It'll be the best day of my life if I end up on stage with these luminaries.' He flicked up the top of his steel lighter, lit his cigarette and inhaled deeply.

'You will,' I said. 'I have a feeling you will.'

Inside the Albert Hall people smoked and drank, talked and laughed quietly in their seats. Some of them held up their flowers, several wore dark glasses. My seat was in the front row, by the stage, which was wooden and circular with seats ranged all around it. The choir stalls and the gigantic organ pipes faced me and the air smelled pungent, sweet and heady. Kit sat in front of me, on the edge of the low wooden stage. He rolled yet another cigarette, only this time he crumbled something that looked like dark Demerara sugar on top of the tobacco. Then he lit it, leaned forwards, held it out to me.

'Want some?'

I hesitated just too long and he smiled. 'It's all right,' he said. 'There's a first time for everyone.'

I blushed.

'Inhale and then swallow,' said Kit. 'Keep it down for as long as you can ... makes for a better high.'

The festival took forever to get started but I don't think anyone noticed. I certainly didn't. We were all bathed in a haze of good-will and laughter, and dope; we felt that poetry really could make a difference, that it might even make peace. And the Hall was full. People leaned over the railings high up in the circular gallery under the dome and when one of them turned sideways something flashed, and I saw a pipe and a small flame that flickered and I knew it was John Dexter. He turned back, his pipe in his mouth, and looked down and nodded at me. I lifted my yellow and white iris and he raised two fingers in the peace sign. And then, at last, the readings began.

Of all of them the one that touched me the most was the one by Adrian Mitchell. He didn't look much like my idea of a poet, he wore a tie and a button-down shirt and his hair was short, but his poem was magnificent and he performed it with a quiet passion, by turns softly angry and fiercely sad.

Speaking of Love

'I was run over by the truth one day,' he said,
'Ever since the accident I've walked this way.
So stick my legs in plaster,
*Tell me **lies** about Viet Nam.'*

He glanced at the sheet of paper in his hand.

'Heard the alarm clock screaming with pain,
Couldn't find myself so I went back to sleep again.'

There was a murmur of laughter and then an expectant silence.

'So fill my ears with silver
Stick my legs in plaster
*Tell me **lies** about Viet Nam.'*

The Hall was absolutely still.

'Every time I shut my eyes all I see is flames.
Made a marble phone book, carved all the names.
So coat my eyes with butter
Fill my ears with silver
Stick my legs in plaster
*Tell me **lies** about Viet Nam.'*

Suddenly I was in tears. I leaned towards Kit.

'I smell something burning, hope it's just my brains,
They're only dropping peppermints and daisy-chains
So stuff my nose with garlic
Coat my eyes with butter
Fill my ears with silver
Stick my legs in plaster
*Tell me **lies** about Vietnam.'*

Iris's story

I clung to Kit. My tears seeped into his sleeve.

> *'Where were you at the time of the crime?*
> *Down by the Cenotaph drinking slime*
> *So chain my tongue with whisky*
> *Stuff my nose with garlic*
> *Coat my eyes with butter*
> *Fill my ears with silver*
> *Stick my legs in plaster*
> *Tell me **lies** about Vietnam.'*

I looked up and through my tears I saw the great grey organ pipes that reared up behind the poet.

> *'You put your bombers in, you put your conscience out*
> *You take the human being and you twist it all about.'*

And I stared and stared at the organ pipes but they were no longer organ pipes. They had become great grey cone-nosed missiles of mass destruction, head down in their silos, primed and ready to be released. To kill and to maim. To bomb and to burn. To shred people's bodies and make their blood run.

I was frightened. I gripped Kit's shoulder. I tried to change the missiles back into organ pipes but they wouldn't be changed. I tried to get the blood-stained bodies out of my mind but they wouldn't go.

> *'So scrub my skin with women*
> *Chain my tongue with whisky,*
> *Stuff my nose with garlic*
> *Coat my eyes with butter*
> *Fill my ears with silver*
> *Stick my legs in plaster*
> ***Tell me lies about Viet Nam.'***

The Hall was silent for a long time, as if we collectively held our breath, and then there was an explosion of applause. People threw their flowers at Adrian's feet and shouted for more, but he just bowed and the organiser leapt up to the microphone and said, 'What we need now is a mood shift, man ...' and before he could introduce the next poet Kit was at his side and the organiser handed him the microphone saying, 'I think the mood shifter's just dropped in. Or dropped something.'

Kit slid the microphone back into its cradle and stretched his arms out wide, palms to the audience.

'Look,' he said, 'no words.'

The audience laughed and Kit launched into a longer, funnier version of his fish poem and then he performed a poem about how difficult it is to find words, any words, when you wake up in a strange girl's bed, with no idea what her name is, no idea where you are, and no idea where you were when you met. The audience loved him and applauded loudly and then the organiser clapped him on the back and Kit left the stage. His grey eyes shone when he sat back down in front of me. He turned to face the stage immediately and I leaned forwards, put my hands on his shoulders and kissed the back of his curly red head. He put his hands over mine and I was surprised to find that they shook. My own hands sometimes shake when I'm excited or when I'm nervous, so I don't know why I was surprised that his shook, but I was.

And then I laughed hysterically, with relief, because the missiles had gone, the images of the blood-stained bodies had gone, the fear had disappeared and so had my tears.

And I realised I was very, very, very hungry.

Vivie's story

Vivie ran down a wooden pier, yelling. She yelled because she had to make her voice heard above the wind and the rain. She wore a thin summer dress.

A tall figure stood at the end of the pier with his back to her. He was so tall that he seemed to Vivie to be a giant. He wore a dark belted raincoat that flapped and smacked around his rippling trouser-legs and a black trilby that never once threatened to blow from his head. Vivie tried to stop herself yelling at the giant because she knew what would happen in this, her recurring nightmare. But she never could stop herself yelling.

'I was only telling a story,' she yelled down the pier. 'Just a story. Don't you tell stories in your family?'

The wind always poured down her throat after she said that. It filled her lungs and she swallowed and gulped and felt as if her lungs would explode. She had to stop running and she gasped and couldn't speak any more and that was when the giant turned round. It always happened then.

He strode towards her and grabbed her under her arms and lifted her up. He shook and shook and shook her and she became a floppy doll in his hands. And as he shook her the words she knew she mustn't speak started to tumble out. They fell from her mouth, in her dream, in small crenellated pieces of coloured plastic. They landed and bounced on the wet wooden boards of the pier and the giant's feet crushed them as he carried Vivie backwards. Her feet dangled and her ribs hurt and then the giant slammed her down on the wooden boards and her transparent plastic sandals slipped. She felt as if she'd jumped off a high wall and forgotten to bend her knees. The giant pulled a dry sponge from his pocket and stuffed it into her mouth. She knew she would choke on the words that were piling up in the back of her throat; she struggled to get the sponge out of her mouth. But in the struggle she slipped and fell onto the wet wooden boards and, whatever she did after that, she could never move.

The giant walked away from her, backwards, never taking his dark eyes off her. His trilby stayed on despite the wind and his wispy grey hair flew up from under the brim. She wished she could turn and run, but she could not move. Her knees were frozen onto the wet boards and her arms were pinned to her sides. She felt the words building up and beginning to block the back of her throat. She knew she was going to die.

The giant stopped when he got to the end of the pier, automatically, without looking round. He always knew when he'd reached the end. Then he put his hand into his raincoat pocket and pulled out something that spilled and spilled and never stopped spilling from his pocket.

Vivie had had the dream so many times that she knew what was coming, but every time she hoped that the giant would pull something different from his pocket, something she might like. But, as always in the dream, he pulled out a large orange net.

The giant pulled and pulled and pulled the net from his pocket and it spooled down into a bumpy orange pile on the pier beside him. When there was nothing left in his pocket he began to whirl the net over his head like a lasso. It looked like a gigantic orange cloud and it hissed and snaked through the air towards Vivie who knew that this was her last chance to get up and run. But she never could move and the net billowed out and landed on her, heavily, hurting her through her thin, wet dress, pinning her to the slippery wooden boards of the pier.

This time the net stank of fish and Vivie saw that there were bits of fish stuck in the net: heads and tails and innards. In her terror, Vivie wet herself and, from her frozen position under the net, she heard the giant's footsteps boom, boom, booming down the pier. She saw the turn-ups on his dark trousers. She saw his shiny brown shoes and his silky black socks. Then she saw his hands on his knees, his reddened fingers, and his face, exactly level with her face, black-red with rage. All this she saw through the knotty, fishy orange net that pinned her to the slippery wooden boards of the pier. And then the giant shouted louder than the wind and the rain. He shouted judgements. He judged that Vivie spoke out of turn and that she was selfish. He shouted that she must never, ever say what she'd said to him again and that she was not the only pebble on the beach. *Not the only pebble on the beach.* Vivie could see the shiny red insides of his mouth, his red uvula, his tobacco-stained teeth. She squeezed her eyelids shut. She knew she was going to die and the wet in her knickers was stone cold. She wished she could block her ears against the giant's words but she could not move her arms and the knots in the net dug into her, hurting her everywhere.

And then, suddenly, there was no sound at all. The rain and the wind stopped and Vivie felt the warmth of the sun on her back. She sat up quite easily. She spat out the dry sponge and all the words that had been stuck in the back of her throat streamed from her mouth. She watched the small crenellated pieces of coloured plastic bounce on the miraculously dry wooden boards. And when this happened she was always free. The net was beside her and she stood up and, in the sunlight, the net was no longer heavy nor full of knots, no longer orange but a light, almost translucent green that glittered with raindrops, like something a spider might have made. Vivie left it behind her in a tangled bundle and walked away.

But always, as she walked away, she knew that she should have collected pebbles from the beach and put them into the net and dropped it over the end of the pier and watched it sink. Always she knew this, in her recurring nightmare, and always it was too late. Because once she had begun to walk away down the wooden pier, she could never turn back.

In her dream Vivie moaned and this time, as she stood at the end of the pier in the sunshine, Vivie told herself that she must remember the pebbles next time. Because if she could sink the net next time she had the dream she could, she was sure, stop the dream forever.

Iris's story

We couldn't find anywhere to buy food when we left the Albert Hall, and I was so hungry.

'It's the dope,' said Kit, and he laughed. 'There's some food at my flat.'

I imagined a cheddar and tomato sandwich as we ran up the stairs to his flat. We were high on the poems we'd heard, high on Kit's performance, high on life and each other. I'd never felt so alive.

Kit shoved records and books and mugs and ashtrays and clothes into a corner. We sat on brightly-coloured cushions with little pieces of mirror sewn into them, and there was no sign of the girl with the Jean-Shrimpton knees.

The food was a packet of Ritz crackers; a tin of sardines that Kit had to open with a screwdriver that he hit with his shoe because he couldn't find, or didn't own, a tin opener; a hunk of old, cracked cheddar – the only thing I'd been right about – and a bottle of Chianti in a raffia basket. It was delicious.

Kit poured the wine into a jug, stuck a candle into the wine bottle, and we talked and talked and talked and talked and he played Bob Dylan's *Bringing It All Back Home* over and over again. He said Dylan was the king of poets and he said the song 'She Belongs To Me' was for me. He said I was an artist. I said he was. He said we both were.

And then Kit came and sat beside me on my bright cushion and he kissed me. And we drank the last of the wine and he kissed me again, and he undid the long zip at the back of my red dress and then, somehow, the Ritz-cracker crumbs found their way under my back. They scratched my skin and we tried to brush them away, but they wouldn't go. Kit made jokes about cookies that crumbled and backs that got scratched and things that took the biscuit, and we dissolved into laughter and into each other. And then, quite suddenly, I heard my own laughter as if it came from someone beside me and I saw several pairs of coloured plastic gumboots in a shaft of sunlight by a door. There were yellow boots and red boots, blue boots and green boots all piled up haphazardly, luminous and bright.

I opened my eyes. I could feel Kit's heart and I smelled the nicotine and the wine on his breath. I smelled his peculiar, bitter peppery smell and I told him about the pairs of gumboots and he laughed. His body relaxed sideways against mine. His stubbly chin scratched my shoulder.

'So, Miss Ritz-cracker,' he said, and he made a fist and held it to my mouth like a microphone, 'would you care to comment on sex and gumboots? Is there, would you say, a colour that particularly excites you?'

'Red,' I said. 'Definitely, definitely red.'

He kissed me, rolled over and reached for his tobacco and cigarette papers.

'What do you see?' I said.

'Never seen a thing,' he said. 'But I'm hoping it's contagious.'

He handed me the cigarette.

'It's never – that's never happened before,' I said.

'Never?' he pushed himself up, leaned on his elbow.

'No. Never.'

A patch of freckles spread their way along his cheekbone, as if they'd been blown there through a straw.

He pulled the striped rug down from the sofa and threw it over us and we stared up at the ceiling. It was dark blue, and there were silver stars and crescent moons stuck onto it and a bare lightbulb that hung from a frayed, plaited cord.

'Gumboots,' he said, and blew a thin line of smoke from the corner of his mouth. 'Groovy,' he said.

I smiled to myself all the way home and, as I walked past South Kensington underground station, the sun rose and the white houses turned an unbelievable shade of pink.

RED HEAD

*L*ong ago, in a cold, grey, northern kingdom, there lived a King who wore his crown all the time, even in bed. In that kingdom the regal right to rule was proclaimed by the wearing of a crown. Without a crown upon his head a man could not be proclaimed king nor, without a crown upon her head, could a woman be proclaimed queen.

In that same kingdom it was well known that red was the source of all evil. The law decreed fires and all red stuffs illegal, and a mixture of water and chalk was applied to red lips and red cheeks, for they too were illegal. And for those who were born with red hair, these were bad times indeed. They shaved their heads, and their faces, daily, and the hill-women of the kingdom, who had long fingernails and the disposition for such things, were employed to pluck out stubborn red eyelashes.

Anyone discovered in possession of anything red, whether human or mineral, animal or vegetable, was immediately sentenced to death by live burial.

At the first sign that the leaves on the kingdom's many trees were about to turn red, great grey blankets were carried up long thin ladders and spread over the trees until every red leaf had fallen to the ground and crumpled and become a harmless brown. The people were ordered to turn their faces from sunrises and sunsets, and the hill-women were kept busy making potions that disguised the colour of the blood that leaked from the people's wounds, from time to time.

Now, the King of this kingdom had a jealous wife and a good son. He also had a terrible secret. Every morning

86

Red Head

of every day it was necessary for the King's barber to shave and oil the King's head and face, and that of his son. And every morning of every day it was necessary for one of the hill-women to pluck stubborn eyelashes from the royal eyelids. For both the King and his son had abundant fiery red hair which, if left to its own devices, would have sprouted in red tufts and spikes and tangled itself into red curls all over their royal heads and bodies. In a kingdom that punished, by live burial, those discovered in possession of anything red, this was indeed a terrible secret.

And, as if that wasn't enough, the King had another difficulty. It is not easy to keep a crown upon a smooth, well-oiled scalp at all times, so the King sent for the royal goldsmith who said that he understood his Majesty's difficulty precisely and suggested that the kingdom's only crown should be melted down. The royal goldsmith explained to the King that with one third of the gold he would make a special, light crown for the King with two particular attachments that would fix the crown to the sides of the well-oiled royal scalp. A crown which, because of its lightness, his Majesty might even forget that he wore, from time to time. 'And with the other two thirds of the gold,' said the royal goldsmith, with a deep bow, 'his Majesty the King will find himself that much the richer.'

And so it was that the royal goldsmith delighted the King and the plan was executed, and the King subsequently divided the molten gold that had made him richer equally among the hill-women and his barber, in gratitude for their tireless service and for their faithful silence about the terrible royal secret.

But one morning, when the King was in a hurry to attend to the affairs of his kingdom, he failed to unfold the particular attachments that fixed his crown to the sides of his scalp and so it was that when he hurried out of his apartments he did not notice that his new, light crown slipped backwards, slid down the train of his long silk robe, rolled away behind him along the carpeted corridor and through the open door of his jealous wife's apartment. It settled, finally, under her bed.

The King's jealous wife, whose hair had a greenish tinge, was constantly on the watch for a chance to expose her husband's redness to the kingdom so that she might be crowned Queen one day and so, on that morning, she could not believe her luck. She snatched up the crown and tried it on. But crowns with particular attachments made for well-oiled scalps can never fit heads covered with hair and so, in a fury, the jealous wife flung the King's crown into her closet and locked the door.

Late that evening the King remarked that his courtiers had shown him an extraordinary lack of respect all day. The King's wife merely stared at the King's head and the King discovered, as his hands flew to his head, that he wore no crown.

'Why did no one tell me?' said the King, mortified.

His jealous wife made no answer, but the King ordered that no one should sleep until the crown was found. He woke the court, who woke the kingdom, with orders to begin a Great Crown Hunt. For in that kingdom the regal right to rule was proclaimed by the wearing of a crown. Without a crown upon his head a man could not be proclaimed king nor, without a crown upon her head, could a woman be proclaimed queen. By the next evening, when there were no reports that the crown had been found, the King was in a very agitated state. And by the next morning, when the King's barber asked him, politely, several times, to keep still, the King simply could not and so it was that the King's barber drew blood from the King's head and the King, who until that day had known that his blood was blue, saw that his blood was red.

Red Head

The King stared, horrified, into the mirror, and watched the colour of the source of all evil pour down his face. He called a halt to the Great Crown Hunt, refused all the hill-women's bandages, medicines and advice and died, filled with the terrible knowledge that his own blood was the colour of the source of all that was evil.

The King's good son and heir, the king-in-waiting, thought the thing to do first, in such dreadful circumstances, was to ask the people of the cold, grey, northern kingdom if they would resume the Great Crown Hunt. He would think about the redness of his blood later. The people agreed to resume the Great Crown Hunt and were about to set off, when the jealous widow persuaded her son that it would be for the best if he joined the Great Crown Hunt himself.

'After all,' she said, 'you know exactly what the lost crown looks like.'

And so it was that the king-in-waiting and the people of the cold, grey, northern kingdom resumed the Great Crown Hunt. They travelled to every part of the kingdom on foot; they travelled beyond the kingdom by boat, and they vowed that they would not call a halt to the Great Crown Hunt until the crown, without which the king-in-waiting could not be proclaimed king, was found.

The only people who did not join the Great Crown Hunt were those whom the jealous widow had ordered to stay behind: the hill-women, the barber, the royal goldsmith and the one lady-in-waiting at whom the king-in-waiting had begun to gaze far too often and for far too long.

'There is a task which I wish you to undertake,' said the jealous widow to those who remained behind, 'in return for which you may have unlimited access to the castle's pantries.'

Tempted by food for which they would not have to forage, those who remained behind agreed to the task before they knew what it was. This made the jealous widow smile behind her hand.

'The first part of the task,' she said, 'is to return to the crown what belongs to the crown.' She stared at the hill-women and at the barber.

'The second part of the task is to receive and deliver what belongs to the crown.' She glared at the lady-in-waiting at whom the king-in-waiting had begun to gaze far too often and for far too long.

'And the third and final part of the task is to combine,' here she stared at the royal goldsmith, 'what belongs to the crown with the crown, and to deliver it to me.'

The jealous widow unlocked her closet and brought out the King's lost crown with a flourish.

'You will not breathe a word of this to the Crown Hunters,' she said to the assembled, gasping company, 'on pain of the most severe punishment in the kingdom which, as you all know, is live burial.'

Because they had no desire to die, at least not by live burial, the hill-women gathered up their share of the molten gold – the golden nuggets with which they had weighted the hems of their skirts – and handed them to the lady-in-waiting; the barber handed the lady-in-waiting a large pair of golden scissors, and the lady-in-waiting handed all this gold, and the dead King's lost crown, to the royal goldsmith, who set to work.

The royal goldsmith spent more than a year in his attempts to mould the precious metal as the jealous widow had requested, and eventually, to his great relief, he succeeded. He set his creation on a purple cushion and carried it to her.

'I cannot wear this!' shouted the jealous widow as soon as she saw what the royal goldsmith had made. 'Have you lost your MIND? This crown is RED!'

The royal goldsmith had struggled so hard and so long with the precious metal – which had seemed to him to be truly resistant to his attempts to mould it as the jealous widow had commanded – that he had not noticed its growing redness. But now he had to admit that it was a crown of reddened gold that sat on the purple cushion in front of the jealous widow.

'How could you do this?' said the jealous widow. 'I need a crown that will proclaim me Queen!'

'I can only think, your majesty,' said the royal goldsmith in a state of terrible confusion, 'that, by some process that even I, the royal goldsmith, cannot understand, the gold has acquired redness.'

'I can see THAT!' retorted the jealous widow and she summoned the lady-in-waiting at whom the king-in-waiting had begun to gaze far too often and for far too long. The jealous widow ordered the lady-in-waiting to throw the red-gold crown, the kingdom's only crown, into the river that ran beneath the castle. Immediately.

The young lady-in-waiting went to do what the jealous widow required of her, but she went with a heavy heart for it seemed to her that even if this crown was red, it was still the young king-in-waiting's birthright and she did not wish to throw that birthright into the river from which nothing had ever been known to surface. So, as she stood on the riverbank with the red-gold crown in her hands, she hesitated and in her hesitation in that dank and muddy darkness, she slipped, and the red-gold crown fell from her hands as she reached out to save herself from the river. And so it was that the young lady-in-waiting heard the splash, and knew that the red-gold crown had fallen into the dark river from which nothing had ever been known to surface.

And so it was that the seasons turned and the Great Crown Hunt continued; and the jealous widow sickened and died of the green bile that ate away at her heart. And because the Great Crown Hunt continued there were not enough people left in the kingdom to cover the trees with great grey blankets when the autumn came, and the leaves on the trees turned red for all to see. But the lady-in-waiting noticed that nothing evil occurred. She noticed that when the hill-women gathered their herbs they hitched up their skirts and a brilliant red silk showed underneath. She noticed that the barber's beard grew full and red and that the royal goldsmith wore red-gold rings on his once ringless fingers and when, for the first time in her life, the lady-in-waiting watched the red sun set, still nothing evil occurred.

But the lady-in-waiting did not talk about these things. She kept them secret in her heart because she wanted to be sure. And then came the day, yet another year later, when word reached the cold grey northern kingdom that the Great Crown Hunters were on their way home.

The young lady-in-waiting stood on the drawbridge to greet the king-in-waiting and his band of Crown Hunters. But it was a sad, sorry, kingless, crownless, cold grey band of hunters who trudged across the drawbridge draped in the hooded grey cloaks that kept out the cold winds of the kingdom. And it was an even sadder, sorrier young lady-in-waiting who informed the king-in-waiting of the jealous widow's death. She was just about to tell him the sorriest news of all, the news of the loss of the red-gold crown, when her attention was caught by something that the Great Crown Hunters must have been too exhausted to see for themselves.

The lady-in-waiting saw patches of red all about them. As they shuffled past her, beneath the grey portcullis, the lady-in-waiting saw that their lips were red and so were their cheeks; their hands were red and so were their noses; some of them had red eyebrows, red eyelashes and red beards, and wisps of something distinctly red curled out from beneath the grey hoods of several of their cloaks.

The young lady-in-waiting also saw, as she stared about her, that the leaves on the trees had once more turned red. But what she noticed above all was that, despite all these patches of red, despite their deeply held belief that red was the source of all evil, even despite the fact that there was no crown for the king-in-waiting, nothing evil nor bad had occurred. Absolutely nothing at all.

The lady-in-waiting collected herself and ran after the king-in-waiting and as she ran her cheeks reddened, but she did not apply the chalk and water mixture that she kept in her pocket. When she caught up with him the lady-in-waiting whispered something into the king-in-waiting's ear and he threw back his head and laughed. Exactly what the lady-in-waiting whispered no one has ever known, but as the king-in-waiting laughed the hood of his grey cloak fell back, a shaft of sunlight broke through the grey clouds and the hair that covered the king-in-waiting's head was seen by all to be a glorious red red-gold.

The lady-in-waiting and all the Crown Hunters gasped. They stared at the king-in-waiting. They stared at his head of abundant, thick, spiky, curly, shiny red-gold hair and slowly, one by one, they began to smile. The king-in-waiting's hair in all its glorious red-goldness looked exactly like a crown. A rather unruly crown, they agreed, but a crown nonetheless.

Gradually, timidly to begin with, the Great Crown Hunters pulled back their own grey hoods and those with red hair stared at each other and then at their young king-in-waiting who simply smiled back at them.

A mirror set in a red-gold frame was brought for the young king-in-waiting and, as he looked at his head of red-gold hair, he wondered how it had ever come to pass that such a head of hair, such a colour, such a crowning glory, could possibly have been believed to be the source of all that was evil.

And so it was that the king-in-waiting's Great Crown Hunters declared, with one voice, that they had found what they had been looking for, at last. They had found a crown for the king-in-waiting's head, a crown which, by its very nature, could not be lost, at least not until such time as a natural successor was old enough to succeed him. They proclaimed that the king-in-waiting now had the regal right to rule.

And so it was that, for the kingdom's celebrations, fires were lit once more and red wine was drunk, and ever since then lips have remained red in that kingdom, and red hair has been prized for its rarity, royal connections and many other things besides. Red leaves are never covered with grey blankets and nothing evil has ever happened as a result.

And, while the kingdom celebrated, the newly crowned King of the newly reddened kingdom gazed at the lady-in-waiting who had made him laugh, and at whom he had often gazed for far too long according to his jealous mother. And as he gazed at her she untied the large white scarf with which she had always, until that day, bound her hair so carefully.

The newly crowned King watched a torrent of royally red-gold hair cascade over the lady-in-waiting's shoulders and down her back, and then he threw back his own royally red head and together they laughed and then they sang and then they danced until, when they turned together, they saw the magnificent red sun rise.

Part Two
Friday, 28 July, 1996

Vivie's story

Vivie tore the duvet off and scrambled out of bed. She banged her arm against the door and swore. She tried to remember how she'd got home, and she wished she could remember what she'd said to Sara.

She screwed up her eyelids against the sunlight and then stumbled into the shower. She let the water pour over her face and the words she would say in the chemist as soon as she could get there ran through her head. 'Alka Seltzer, please and my sleeping pills.'

And then she remembered that the chemist had said he hadn't got any sleeping pills. And then she remembered the man in the wine bar. And then she remembered that Charles was back.

She grabbed a towel and called to him, but he didn't answer. She ran back to the bedroom, threw off the towel and yanked the cupboard door open. She turned, catching her elbow on the door and saw Charles standing in the passage.

'You must have had your nightmare last night, my darling,' he said. 'You shouted in your sleep.' His voice sounded odd.

'My God, Charles, I thought you'd gone,' said Vivie, staring at him. He walked into the room and perched on the end of their bed. He looked very odd, too, Vivie thought. She leaned down to kiss him, felt dizzy and stood up again quickly. Then she realised he'd turned his face away and her heart lurched. He'd never done that before.

'Sorry if I woke you up,' she said, regaining her balance. 'Did I shout all the usual stuff?'

'You said, "I was only having a baby. Just a baby",' said Charles. 'You kept saying that.'

'I was only telling a story, you mean? Just a story. That's what I shout … in the nightmare.'

'No,' said Charles and he looked at her steadily. 'You said, "Baby".'
'Did I?'
'Yes, Vivienne,' he said. 'You did.'
Vivie began to shake.
Charles looked as if he was leaning in to a very steep slope and trying to stop himself sliding down it. Vivie turned away, trying to control her tears, but she couldn't. She crumpled to the floor.
Charles didn't move from the end of the bed. Vivie shivered, her hands grew wet from her tears and her nose ran; she kneeled naked on the floor but Charles stayed exactly where he was on the bed. Through her fingers Vivie saw his neatly shod feet shifting on the carpet.
'So,' said Charles, 'since it's true about the baby, I can only assume that the rest is true, too.'
Vivie looked up. 'What "rest"?' she said, pulling a kleenex from the box on the dressing table. She stared at Charles. He really did look odd, as if he'd swallowed something he wished he hadn't. He didn't answer.
'I'm so sorry about the baby,' Vivie blurted out. 'I should have told you ... should have asked you ... well, at least told you. But I just couldn't face it ... not the way I've been feeling.'
'I don't see what asking me's got to do with it,' said Charles, pushing himself awkwardly up off the bed.
Vivie couldn't take in what Charles was saying. She longed for some Alka Seltzer, or at least some water, or a strong cup of coffee to help her concentrate.
'And precisely how have you been feeling, Vivienne?' he said, standing by the door.
'Hungover,' she said, matter-of-factly. 'And sad and fright-ened,' she said, surprising herself.
'And that would be because?' said Charles.
'Charles, please, stop it. Speak as if it's you speaking.'
'Why have you been feeling frightened and sad, Vivienne?'
'Because I've lost our baby and because – '
' – You haven't lost "our" baby any more than you've lost your nightmare,' said Charles. '"Our" baby is, obviously, growing

healthily in your womb.' He glared at her and Vivie gasped. She
had never seen his eyes so ice cold. She stood up and put her hand
on his arm, but he moved it away.

'Get dressed,' he said.

Vivie grabbed her kimono and tried to tie the sash, but her
hands were shaking so much that she gave up.

'And my name, Vivienne,' said Charles, staring at a patch of floor
under the window, 'is not Matthew.' He said the words slowly, as
if he was practising words in a language he did not speak.

'What do you mean?' said Vivie. 'Charles, what on earth do
you mean?'

'Exactly what I said,' said Charles. 'My name is not Matthew.'
This time he said it quickly and then he left the bedroom.

Vivie heard his hurried footsteps on the stairs and then she
heard the door slam. She was too shocked to move, let alone to
call after him.

Iris's story

I saw the silhouette, my father's dark shape, through the frosted glass panels in the dining-room door. I saw him put his hands on the arms of his wooden chair, and push himself up. I saw him move towards the door on the other side of the glass. I saw the outline of his pipe and I wondered why he'd lit it so early in the morning. I stood on the bottom step. I held tightly to the newel post, frozen in the pale light that came through the doors.

I watched the gilt handle move downwards. I heard the familiar click and squeak as the door opened. And then my father stood in the doorway. He wore his dressing gown, but even in his dressing gown my father looked dressed. I realised that his pipe was not lit, but he kept it clenched between his teeth as he spoke.

'I shall now telephone the police,' he said.

'Why?' I said. I looked at my hand. It shook.

'Because they will need my permission to call off the search.'

'But I was with Gail – '

' – to lie is unattractive, Iris, very unattractive indeed.'

He walked past me, so close that I could have touched him. I watched the back of his red-and-brown paisley silk dressing gown as he walked into the sitting room, towards his desk. I sat on the stairs. I stared at the dead fire through the bannisters. I heard the telephone bell ring as my father dialled the numbers and I heard the dial circle back after each number. I could see one claret-coloured pyjama leg, one black leather slipper, and the hem of his dressing gown. I heard him ask for the Duty Sergeant.

I saw the shaft of sunlight that fell diagonally across his back.

I heard him thank the Sergeant and apologise, curtly, for the time he'd caused him to waste. He said that, yes, I had returned and that, no, I had come to no harm. I heard the clack the receiver made as he put it back onto its cradle. And then my father walked past me, upstairs, his hands in his dressing-gown pockets. The hem of his dressing gown brushed my arm.

When I got to my room I couldn't sleep.

Then I heard the goblin hiss, 'Fumble fingers, fumble fingers,' from the corner in my bedroom and I felt as frightened as the child I had once been. But now the fear had substance and it was dark. I felt it close in on me. I felt it push down on me and make my heart beat too fast.

My father was at breakfast before me. He wore his dark suit, as usual, a dark tie and a white shirt, as if he still dressed to mourn my mother. Even now I find it difficult to picture him in any other clothes, except his dressing gown.

'I think it's about time I met the young man,' he said, as if he meant he thought it was about time he shot the 'young man'.

He'd made toast, coffee and boiled eggs. The same breakfast he made every single day. My hand shook when I poured the coffee. I spilled some. I dropped my toast.

'It is customary to meet one's future son-in-law, at least once,' he said, 'before the wedding.'

My heart thudded and I sat down. I didn't look at him when I spoke. I couldn't. 'I'm sorry I lied last night,' I said. 'But what I did isn't a crime and I never meant you to be worried. I should have thought. I'm sorry I didn't. I should have rung you.'

The goblin whispered from the stairs behind me. 'Fumble fingers, fumble fingers,' he hissed, and the air grew cold. I'd never heard the goblin outside my bedroom before. And then I felt the dark pressure against my back. It pushed me forwards, pushed me down. I gripped the edge of the table, tried to make my arms strong against it.

'Can you hear – ?'

' – I shall place an announcement in the *Times* after we have met.'

'What?'

'Actions have consequences, Iris, as you should know.'

My father stood up and left the room. I heard him walk up the stairs. I heard him come back down. I heard him open the front door, and then close it behind him. The lock made a very precise little click.

'This'll put fire in your veins,' said Kit, as he handed me a tumbler of red wine. It was nine o'clock in the morning.

We sat very close together on his bright mirrored cushions and I imagined the wine as it flowed through my veins. I thought of it as sap; I thought of myself as a tree. I tried to sit up straight and stretch my arms, but the pressure was too strong and I crumpled back down.

And then, as if he instinctively knew what I needed, Kit knelt in front of me, took the glass out of my hand and put the heels of his hands on my shoulders and pushed backwards. It helped. I felt I could resist the dark pressure behind me, with his help.

'I didn't know where to go,' I said.

'It's all right, babe,' said Kit. 'It's cool.' And he rocked me from side to side and the pressure eased. And then he put me to bed and when I woke a sodium street lamp lit the room and it glowed, eerily. Kit stood, naked, beside the bed. I stared at his long, lean, freckled body in the orange light.

'What time is it?'

'Me getting into bed with you time.'

'Seriously.'

'Seriously.'

Later, downstairs in the Troubadour, Kit said, 'I don't mind meeting the old codger, if that's what he wants. Might be a gas.'

'You haven't been listening,' I said, but I couldn't stop the smile that broke across my face as I tried, and failed, to picture my father as a 'gas'.

'He's going to put an advertisement in the *Times*.'

'For what?'

'I mean an announcement.'

'It's nothing to do with him.' Kit laughed. 'Nothing at all.'

'He thinks it is.'

'Well, he can't do it.'

'What if he just does?'

'What will he say? Mr Stone is *pleased*,' Kit raised his eyebrows and I looked at his pale eyelashes, so pale they were almost white. 'No, Mr Stone is *delighted* to announce the engagement of his daughter, Iris Stone, to ...' he spread his hands, shrugged. 'Pick-a-name. Any-old-name. He-doesn't-even-know-my-name.'

Kit swallowed some Amaretto. 'He hasn't got enough information. It'll be an announcement without half the words.' He looked at me and his grey eyes laughed. 'But I'll still come and meet him, if you like,' he said.

And so he did.

He wore a purple crushed velvet suit, no tie and an emerald green shirt. His hair was wilder and more glorious than ever. My father sat in his wing-chair with one leg neatly crossed over the other. He wore his dark suit, his tightly tied dark tie and his white shirt. And he smoked his pipe, of course.

'What do you do?' he said.

'I am a poet,' said Kit.

'No, I mean what precisely is it that you do? For a living?'

'I write poetry, and I perform it.' Kit leapt out of his chair and the sherry spilled from his glass.

'That is your job?' said my father, incredulous.

'I don't think of it as a job,' said Kit, 'it's more a way of life. But if what you mean is what can I offer your daughter,' he put his glass down and opened his arms wide the way he does when he speaks his poetry, 'I can offer her laughter and poetry, an untidy flat, rented, and anything and everything else that the gods, in their abundant wisdom, may decide to provide.'

Kit bowed so low that his hair fell forwards and hung down from the nape of his neck to the floor. His hands stuck out behind him as if he was about to dive, or fly, and I looked sideways, through my hair, at my father who raised an eyebrow and said, 'Obviously you are not serious.'

'Completely,' said Kit, and downed the rest of his sherry.

At lunch Kit refused to be silent. He said how delicious the roast beef and the Yorkshire pudding were, and how he could live on nothing but my horseradish sauce for days – it's mostly whipped cream – and how it's very difficult to find a word that rhymes with meringues, and then he said, 'Iris told me your wife used to tell stories. It obviously runs in the family. Which of Iris's stories – '

But my father was already halfway out of the room.

Kit stared at me. 'What the hell did I say?'

'You broke the rules. Sorry. I meant to tell you.'

'Well, what the hell are the rules?' said Kit. He pushed his chair back and stood up. He was very angry.

'Stories are forbidden in this house,' I said.

'This is a madhouse.'

'My father will not talk about my mother. He leaves the room if her name is mentioned and her stories are forbidden territory. She is forbidden territory.'

'The man's a madman, and a bloody rude madman. How the hell have you managed to survive here? Why haven't you flown?'

I didn't know I was going to pack, I just found myself in my room.

I heard footsteps on the stairs, several times. Each time I stood absolutely still in my room. Each time I realised that I had imagined the footsteps but, each time, I waited until I was sure my father wasn't about to open my bedroom door. Then I tiptoed between my cupboard and my bed and continued to pack my things.

I dropped things, and my hands shook. I heard the goblin whispering, 'Fumble fingers, fumble fingers,' from the corner. I felt the dark pressure push down against my back. I had to steady myself several times and I had to tell myself that I could leave it all behind, in this house, in this room. That I could run from it.

I packed my red dress and my red shoes. I packed John Lennon's *In His Own Write*. I packed Marianne Faithfull's album and the one unbroken *Carousel* record, still wrapped inside my old grey school cardigan. I packed a pair of jeans, a Biba hat and a long purple dress. I packed some gold and purple beads and my make-up. My hands shook when I scooped as much underwear as they would hold from the drawer, and I packed my mother's book of French fairy tales with its broken spine. As I closed the cupboard door I saw the canvas bag with the hospital's name sewn into it on the top shelf, the bag that held my mother's clothes, and I pulled it down and took it with me too. And then I said, 'Goodbye,' to my room and everything in it. I even said 'Goodbye,' to the Corner.

I left a note for my father that said, 'I am safe. Please don't send the police after me.' And I left my keys on top of the note in the beaten brass dish on the hall table. The last thing I saw in my father's house was the dining-room table. It was a messy still life of left-over lunch. And then we walked out.

Kit carried my suitcase. I carried the canvas hospital bag over my shoulder. Neither of us said anything. It was so simple.

I didn't realise that I'd hardly breathed, or that I walked on tiptoe until Kit mimicked me, at the corner, under a plane tree. He looked like a monstrous caricature of a burglar with his finger to his lips, and his exaggerated bent-kneed, tiptoed strides.

I laughed, but it was a hollow laugh.

We left my things in the Kenco Coffee House on the King's Road, and then we walked to Battersea Park. The thing I remember most about that day was how green everything was. The lawn in Burton Court was emerald and the leaves of the plane trees were a polished, oiled, mossy green. The limes were a pale, translucent green and the ivy climbing up a red brick house in Cheyne Walk was jade flecked with pale yellow-green. The Thames was an opaque grey-green.

We walked along Albert Embankment and past Cadogan Pier. We watched a woman and a young girl feed bread to the seagulls the way my mother and I used to. We walked over Albert Bridge and into Battersea Park and all the time I expected Kit not to be there the next time I looked.

But every time I looked he was beside me; his long legs strode confidently along, his curly red hair blew around his freckled, bony face. It wasn't until we leaned on the stone embankment wall in Battersea Park and stared down into the grey-green Thames that I realised I couldn't feel my hands.

It was a warm day in June, but my hands were quite numb.

Matthew's story

We spent the night in Flitwick. We'd meant to go a bit further but Dad took a fancy to a hotel we passed so, even though we'd planned to stay in B&Bs, he said we'd stay in the hotel if they had rooms. Now we're having breakfast in a high-ceilinged Georgian dining-room with three windows looking south over a croquet lawn. Dad was up early and he's already been round the walled vegetable garden and the herb garden and I wouldn't be surprised if he hasn't asked who's responsible for their trees.

His sellotaped map is spread out beside him on the table and he's looking at me over the tops of his half-glasses and saying, as if he knows exactly what I'm thinking, 'They've got their own bees too, Matthew. They've said I can have a dekko before we go.'

My father managed to grow all the vegetables we ever needed on his small patch and, with Iris's help, he still does. He thinks the fad, as he calls it, for organic food is very funny because, as he says, 'They could save themselves the expense. Dig a vegetable patch.'

I remember the smells most: the wet earth when we dug the potatoes up, the sweet carrots in their cool sand box in Dad's shed, the mellow honeyed scent the apples gave out from their slatted wooden shelves and the musky smell of the beans on their poles.

I saw Vivie standing under the poles once, in the middle of the night. I opened the window and Vivie whispered, 'Thank goodness it's you, not Auntie Joan.' She had her mother's apron on over her nightdress and she put a handful of beans into the pocket. Then she bent down and started sawing at a cabbage stalk. Her hair kept falling over her face and she had to keep stopping and pushing it back. She went into Dad's shed and came out with a

Matthew's story

handful of carrots and then she stepped over the lavender bushes and walked up the lawn towards me, rubbing a carrot against her mother's apron and biting at it, as if her behaviour was perfectly normal.

I said, 'Vivie, what on earth are you doing?'

She hissed, 'If you think I'm stealing, I'm not. I mean we'll buy some and pay you back ... it's just that we're ... a bit hungry. But we're fine.'

I said, 'Dad would give it to you Vivie, you know that. You don't need to take it ... especially not in the middle of the night.'

Vivie rolled her eyes. 'Do you think I'm stupid, or what? I know it's the middle of the night. But Mum doesn't want to see anyone so we're fending for ourselves. Remember? I told you,' and she turned and ran away under the arch in the beech hedge between our gardens. I followed her as quickly as I could, in my pyjamas, but by the time I got to their kitchen door it was locked. I knocked on the window until Vivie had to look up. She shook her head, but I just kept on standing there until she had to open the door. She hissed, 'Please go away.'

'I want to know if you're all right. What you're doing is weird.'

'We're fine. I've already told you. Fine.'

Vivie glanced towards the painted laburnum tree on the door at the bottom of the stairs. She said, 'She's coming. PLEASE GO!' and she turned away from me so quickly that the ends of her hair whipped across my face and then I heard the stairs creaking. Vivie whispered, 'Go,' again, and pushed me back through the door and turned the key. I went back through the beech arch but I didn't go into our cottage, I stood by the gap where the hedge doesn't quite touch the party wall and stared into their kitchen.

Iris was wearing what looked like a sheet and sitting opposite Vivie. Vivie had her back to me. I saw Vivie break the carrots into pieces, tear up the cabbage and the beans and then push them across the table in a pile, but Iris didn't touch them so Vivie got up and stood beside her mother and began to break the raw vegetables into even smaller pieces and put them into her mother's mouth.

Speaking of Love

I stood there and wished I'd stopped Vivie writing to her grandfather, wished I'd never helped her open his letter in the first place. But Vivie had said, 'How can I forget I've got a grandfather now I know I've got one, like normal people? I'm going to write to him,' and she'd scribbled the address on a piece of paper and stuffed it into the pocket of her jeans while I slid the letter we should never have opened back into its envelope, re-sealed it as best I could and put it back on the high shelf above the stove.

She said, 'I'm going to invite him here. For a surprise for Mum.'

I said I thought that was a really bad idea. I said there might be a reason why Iris hadn't told Vivie she had a grandfather, why she hadn't opened his letter. I said maybe they didn't get on, or something, but Vivie just said, 'Maybe they don't. But he says he wants to meet me so he must want to see her too. It'll make things better, I know it will. She's been so sad about Dad and stuff,' she bit her lip again, 'and so have I.'

I'd been sad too, but I didn't say so.

Vivie said, 'I'm going to pick some flowers for her,' and as she ran out she almost collided with her mother under the beech arch, hugged her and ran off. Iris didn't seem to notice that I was in her kitchen, nor did she seem to hear me when I said I'd just come to ask Vivie to go for a walk.

Dad says, 'Most satisfactory.'

I look up from my toast and watch him pushing his glasses up onto his forehead.

He says, 'When you reach my age you'll find that small things please you very much, and this pleases me.'

He was tracing yesterday's route on his map with his forefinger. He says, 'We turned left and then right to cross the Newmarket to Ely Road, we drove straight over the Cambridge to Ely road, then there was that *bridge* over the Bury to Huntingdon road,' – he looks up – 'that's the A14 to you. Then we drove straight across the Cambridge to St Neots road, but *under* the A1 – I grant you there's no longer any other name for that road – and now we're about to perform the coup de grâce of the journey so far,' he smiles at me and the lines radiate out from the corners of his eyes, 'we shall take an *unnumbered* road on a bridge *over* the M1.' He laughs, tries to pull his fingers straight and then sips his tea. 'I thought of a good word for it last night.'

'What? The M1?'

He says, 'No ... it occurred to me that this way of travelling is rather like darning, only considerably more rewarding.'

His crooked fingers hold his toast and guide his knife to spread the honey and he says, 'Darning is exactly the word for this careful negotiation of the minor roads. This shunning of the motorways makes the journey an end in itself. Although,' he smiles, 'I am very much looking forward to the destination.'

Vivie persuaded me to come to the station with her to meet her grandfather and we sat on a newly painted green wooden seat. Well *I* sat, she was too excited to sit and she danced about in front of me while her hair flew about her face so that she had to hold it back with one hand. But when Vivie talks she uses her hands so she had to keep letting go of her hair and it kept flying around her face.

She said, 'What do you think he'll be like?' And, before I had a chance to answer, 'Do you think he'll be really old?' And then, 'Do you think Mum will be really, really pleased?' And then, 'Matthew, stop being such a Misery. It's going to be wonderful, like meeting your favourite long-lost father, I mean grandfather, in a fairy tale.'

The train pulled in and several people got off, but there was only one man wearing a dark suit and a dark hat. He had a very old-fashioned brown suitcase with a white cardboard label tied to the handle. Vivie tore towards him and kept saying, 'Grandpa? Are you Grandpa?'

He said, 'If you are Vivienne,' and looked down at her as she jigged about. There was a pipe clamped between his teeth but he still managed to speak. Vivie grabbed his hand as if she'd always known him and tried to pull him along the platform. He said, 'Slow down, please. My legs are somewhat older than yours.'

Then he said, 'Where is your mother?' Vivie said, 'She doesn't know you're coming. It's a surprise. This is Matthew.'

I held out my hand but he didn't take it, and he didn't answer any of Vivie's questions on the way home in the taxi which made me very nervous. He reminded me of my maths teacher who hardly spoke, and sounded cross when he did. He behaved as if you weren't there and made you nervous of asking him anything. I was really anxious but Vivie just kept talking, leaning forwards and holding onto the back of her grandfather's seat and describing everything to him. She told him how close we were getting, how he would love their cottage, that this was the road through the Thetford Forest where no buses came, that I was her best friend and lived in the cottage next door, and when we arrived she leapt out of the taxi almost before it had stopped, still talking. She called out to her mother, pushing their front door open.

'There's a surprise outside, Mum! Come and see!'

Iris came out, holding some yellow material, and Vivie pointed and hopped about. Iris dropped the yellow material and put her hand across her mouth. She stared at Vivie's grandfather as he lifted his dark hat. Vivie looked from her mother to her grandfather and then Iris walked slowly towards her father and hugged him. He was holding his hat in one hand and his suitcase in the other, so he couldn't really hug her back.

She said to Vivie, 'I knew you were up to something Vivie Marchwood, but I never guessed ... this.'

They went into their cottage and I wasn't sure whether I was supposed to follow or not, so I just hung about until Vivie came darting out again and grabbed my hand. She said, 'See?', pulling me inside. 'Mum's really really pleased.'

Dad says, 'And so today, we shall darn our way through three counties,' he was looking at me over his linen napkin. 'There's a laburnum tunnel, Voss's Laburnum, in the Friary Gardens at Malmesbury which I would very much like to see. Malmesbury's exactly one hundred miles away. It will make the perfect place to stop, tonight.'

Matthew's story

I say, 'Even I know that laburnums don't flower at this time of year, Dad,' but he just smiles and says, 'It's not the flowers that concern me. I want to see how they have trained the trees and what sort of frame they have used. I'm contemplating making a laburnum tunnel – just a small one – for Iris.'

Vivie's story

Vivie walked along the street carrying a bag from the chemist and a bag from the corner shop. She looked like a person who she'd find frightening; a person whose eye she'd try not to catch, a person she'd find herself unable to tear her eyes from. She'd pulled a creased blue T-shirt over her faded blue and green parrot kimono; her legs were bare, the laces of her trainers trailed along the pavement and she was talking to herself.

She was rehearsing what she would say to Sara when she rang in sick. She couldn't face work, she couldn't face the presentation and, more to the point, she couldn't face Sara because she still couldn't remember what she'd said the night before.

Vivie kept her head down as she walked so that her hair fell across her face. It made her feel inconspicuous because her view of the world was veiled but, to anyone else, Vivie's long, curly, unruly red hair was her most visible attribute. It made her stand out.

In ordinary – unhungover – circumstances Vivie's sensitivity to other people would have alerted her to the man behind her who stopped abruptly when she turned, suddenly, to pick up the baguette that had fallen out of her bag. But on this particular morning her sensitivity was dulled by her hangover and all she could think about was Charles's outburst. She'd tried to ring him, but his secretary had said he was unavailable all morning. To her only, she thought. She felt as if he'd dropped an emotional sandbag on her head. He'd never spoken to her so unkindly before.

She shuddered despite the warmth of the sun, crossed the road and juggled her bags so that she could pull the key from the pocket in her kimono. Then she hurried into the kitchen, anticipating the bitter, fizzing, purifying Alka Seltzer and the reviving coffee as she pulled a hunk off the baguette. She filled the coffee machine, dissolved several Alka Seltzer in a large tumbler of water, added

Vivie's story

some vitamin C, swallowed it with some aspirins, put the Rachmaninov concerto on automatic repeat, finished the baguette and went upstairs.

She swallowed several gulps of coffee, thought about trying to get hold of Charles again before she rang Sara, but knew she couldn't put off talking to Sara any longer. She dialled her direct line. She'd decided she'd sound more convincing if she actually was lying on her back in bed. Then she realised she couldn't even remember what time the presentation was supposed to be. She lost her nerve and was reaching over to put the receiver down when she heard Sara's voice say, 'Sara Vickers,' so she took a deep breath, lay back, felt sick and said, 'Hi, Sara. I can't believe it, today of all days, but I feel like hell. I can't come in. Could we do the presentation on Monday?'

Rachmaninov blasted up the stairs and Vivie shot out of bed to shut the bedroom door, dragging the telephone across the floor behind her. Then she lay back on the bed, feeling dizzy. Sara was shouting.

'Do you have any idea what time it is?' she said. 'The presentation's bloody over. Finished. Done. Where the hell were you?'

'Ill,' said Vivie, feeling weak.

'Hungover more like,' said Sara. 'Well, I've had it, Viv Marchwood. You think the whole bloody world revolves around you, but it doesn't. No client in their right mind would tolerate your idea of service. You don't give service, you give SFA. I've covered for you. I've written your press releases for you. I've stood by you, but you can't be bloody bothered to pull your weight, can you? I've had it, Viv. I've had e-bloody-nough. Consider yourself on notice from today.'

Vivie slumped back against the pillows. Her heart was pounding and the words, 'I've had e-bloody-nough,' ran through her head on endless repeat. She dropped the telephone receiver, hugged the pillow and stared through the window at the fluttering leaves on the cherry tree: their green translucence shone against the bright blue sky, and it struck Vivie that the worst days of her life had always been filled with brilliant sunshine.

Iris's story

L ast night I sat with a group of storytellers in a pub. It was warm and the tobacco plants in the window-box filled the night air with their musky scent. We swapped versions of stories and told jokes and hoped for fine weather and large audiences at the festival.

I felt at home. I always feel at home with storytellers. I belong where stories and storytellers belong but when one of the storytellers, the one who sat next to me, lifted his glass and said 'How do you make God laugh, Iris?' I laughed apprehensively because I wasn't sure I would like whatever it was that made God laugh.

'How do you make God laugh?' I said.

'Tell him your plans,' said the storyteller and he threw back his head and laughed.

I laughed too, but bitterly.

I can't stop the desire to plan. I want to know what will happen next. I want to know when ... if ever ... I'll see Vivie again.

I feel powerless against my desire to predict what will happen. I don't know how to stop the need to keep a place, a sense, a time or a person sacred, just as it is, just as they are, for ever. Perhaps, one day, I will discover.

There have been days when I wanted the world to stand still. One of those days was a day when the sky was at its bluest because the grey of winter was imminent, when the reds and yellows, russets and golds of the leaves made the sky's blue poignant. It was a day when our clothes held the sun's warmth, smelled of the sun's warmth, but it was really only warm in the car, or inside, or if we huddled together.

We'd driven, in a borrowed white Triumph Herald, to Norfolk. Kit wanted to hear the sea, wanted to get away from what he called the 'Dead Zone', the grey London pavements, the grey people, the grey skies. He wanted to find a beach, he said, and yell at the sea. And as we drove north-east the clouds cleared and we left the grey world behind.

'We could live in a beach hut,' Kit said. 'What d'you think?'

We ended up on Hunstanton beach. We walked along the beach, wrapped in the striped rug from his sofa, and eventually we scrambled up through the tall thin grass on the low dunes and found shelter in a sandy dip below a row of painted beach huts. We chose the one we would live in for its colour – royal-blue with a yellow door, yellow eaves and window-sills – and we sat on its blue wooden steps. I peeled a strip of paint away from the edge of one of the steps while Kit tried the door which was, of course, locked. But he, with the sleight of hand of a conjuror, found a key from behind my ear and beckoned me to follow him. He led me down the steps. He held the invisible key high in his hand and he said there'd be another way in, at the back, but, when he saw that there was no door at the back he shrugged with the exaggerated movements of a clown, spread the striped rug on the ground and lay flat on his back.

I lay beside him and listened to the rhythmic susurrus of the waves; listened to him as he described how we would build our own beach hut with a back *and* a front door; listened to him as I stared up at the brilliant blue sky. And then we turned to each other, held each other, pressed our bodies so tightly together that, as Kit said, not even a leaf could have fitted between us, and we made love on the rug in the sand.

And then we ate chicken and lettuce sandwiches, drank bottles of Guinness and watched the clouds scud across the sky. Kit smoked and I told him a story about three Victorian women whose mobile bathing hut our beach hut had once been. I showed Kit the marks the wheels had left against the painted timbers. I said the women had refused to wear the clothes that Victorian polite society insisted they should wear to swim in the sea. I said the women wanted to feel the water against their skin so they covered their bodies with royal-blue and yellow pigments and then they swam, painted to look as though they wore the required costumes, but actually quite naked. They stayed in the sea for a long time because the way the water felt against their skin delighted them, but they stayed so long that the pigments bled away into the sea and so it was that, forever afterwards, they could not leave the water.

'Aha!' said Kit. 'The true meaning of the word mermaid is, at last, revealed.' He sat up and put on a mock-serious expression. 'Mermaids are maidens condemned forever to murmur ... about being stuck out at sea.'

On the way home we took a shortcut and got lost near the Norfolk-Suffolk border. We found ourselves in the Thetford Forest, in a village called St Agnes Redemere. The red-yellow sun was low in the sky and there were seven trees on the small green. Their leaves were like starfish, or stretched-out fingers, and they glowed pink and pale red. I asked Kit to stop the car so that I could stand underneath the trees; I'd never seen leaves that colour before.

A man leant on a spade outside a cottage on the other side of the green. I pulled a red-pink leaf from one of the trees and then we walked across the green, beneath the trees, and Kit asked the man if he could tell us the way back to the A11. The man's eyes were a pale version of the sky, his arms were brown and sinewy. He told us that we had to drive out through the Forest in the opposite direction from the way we'd come, and then I asked if he knew what the trees on the green were called.

'Indeed I do,' he said. 'They're yellow buckeyes, *Aesculus flava*. One of the finest and most neglected horse chestnuts these islands possess.' He smiled and delicate lines fanned out from the corners of his eyes up towards his temples. 'I know because I helped put them there, after the war. They're grafted onto *Aesculus hippocastanum*, the common chestnut. You can tell, from the ordinary leaves that grow below the graft.'

'They're beautiful,' I said.

'They're the elegant, red-headed cousins of the more ordinary chestnut,' he said. 'At least they are at this time of year.'

A large woman came out of the cottage. She wore an apron.

Iris's story

She was younger than the man, mousey-haired and she carried a small boy on her hip. She held out a mug of tea to the man. The man took the tea and the woman set the boy down on the grass. The boy had dark brown curly hair and dark eyes and he began to pull himself up; he held onto the man's trouser leg. The man winced, bent down and moved the boy to his other leg.

'That one will make a stronger support, young man,' he said, then he turned back to us and asked where we'd come from.

'London,' said Kit. 'But we're looking for somewhere … else.'

'London has never been a good place to bring up a family, has it?' said the man who was, I guessed, about the same age as my father.

I shook my head, blushed.

'Would you like a cup of tea?' the large woman asked. 'I've just made a pot.'

And so we had tea with Dick and Joan Aldwater and before we left we'd agreed to rent the cottage next to theirs for a year. Kit had never told me he wanted to move out of London, and I couldn't imagine him at home anywhere except in his chaotic flat above the Troubadour.

'Like the old man said,' he said. 'Carpe diem.'

I don't know why I didn't tell Kit that I knew I'd conceived that afternoon, but I didn't. Sometimes I was too much in awe of him to think that he had ordinary human desires, like me. I thought of him as the superior, elegant, red-headed form of humanity. I was just the ordinary cousin. And I wasn't sure if he saw himself as a father, or me as the mother of his child. We'd never talked about it.

On the way home I thought about John Dexter. I hadn't seen him since the poetry festival, in May, and I wondered why I hadn't seen him, wondered if I'd done something to offend him.

Vivie's story

Vivie opened her eyes and, for a moment, couldn't think what day of the week it was or what time it was. She stared at the yellow light that managed to glow brightly, even through Charles's thick, double-interlined curtains, and she scrabbled about for the source of a high-pitched whining sound. When she realised it was coming from the telephone receiver she banged it back into its cradle. Then she heard Rachmaninov, playing away downstairs, oblivious to everything.

Vivie's headache had receded, but her mouth was still as dry as if she'd filled it with cigarette ash and her heart was still beating too fast. She wondered if Charles had tried to ring while she'd been asleep. She remembered how he always used to interrupt meetings when she rang. She thought about getting dressed and going to his office but she realised that she didn't want whatever was happening between them to happen in public.

She felt untethered, frightened and transparent. She didn't understand what Charles thought she'd done, but she felt guilty because of the things she had done. And now she'd lost the job he'd found for her. She wanted to talk to Charles. But she wanted to talk to the Charles who made her feel safe, not the ice-man he'd suddenly become. The Charles who made her feel safe knew how to stop the awful, untethered feelings.

Vivie thought how good a bloody mary would taste; how it would cure her hangover, and she threw the duvet back.

As she walked down the stairs she felt the beginnings of the most frightening feeling of all, the one where she couldn't feel her edges, the one where she began to fragment. She bit hard into the skin of her hand – it always helped – and tried to make herself breathe slowly. She made a strong bloody mary, picked up the telephone and dialled Charles's number but when his secretary said he was still unavailable she surprised herself by yelling.

Her breath came in short gasps and she yelled that it was an emergency, that she *must* speak to Charles, now. That she didn't know what she would do if she didn't speak to him. By the time she heard his voice she was finding it very difficult to breathe.

'Can you come home?' she panted. 'Please Charles? I – I don't know what's happening. But I'm ... that sliding-off-the-edge feeling's back.'

'Stop behaving like a child,' said Charles, his voice icy. 'And Vivienne,' said Charles, calling her by the name that only he used, 'I think it's time you came clean about what's been going on, don't you?'

Vivie concentrated on breathing. She rubbed her hand over her chest. She managed to say, 'I'm just ... it's just ... I'm feeling the way I feel after I've seen Mum. Only I haven't seen her. I – '

' – If you haven't got the guts to tell me,' said Charles, 'then it seems that I shall have to tell you. I came home on Monday night.'

Vivie heard him swallow.

'I was too late for the Prom, but I came to collect you. I thought we'd have dinner.'

Vivie bit hard into her hand.

'I am not a complete idiot, Vivienne, so please stop treating me as if I were. I saw you and Matthew.'

'Oh my God, Charles, please,' said Vivie. 'I didn't even know he was going to be there. He was just there and I bumped into him and I was going to tell you, I just forgot. I forgot all about it. I was going to tell you.' Her words tumbled out in a guilt-strewn stream. 'I'm sorry, Charles. I should have told you about Matthew and I should have told you about the baby,' she sat down heavily on a kitchen chair, 'but I lost my nerve. I'm a coward. I'm so sorry. Now you know.'

Charles didn't speak but she could hear his breathing.

'Now you know I'm a coward, I mean. And Matthew was just there,' she said. 'I didn't know he was going to be there. It was nothing. We just had a cup of coffee. I haven't seen him for ages.

I haven't seen him since we got married.'

'You mean *I* haven't seen him since we got married,' said Charles. 'Well now I know why. I'll stay with Robert tonight. I need to get to grips with this.'

'There's nothing to get to grips with,' said Vivie, desperately, 'nothing happened. It's nothing.'

But Charles had already hung up.

Vivie stood, shakily, and made herself another bloody mary. Then she walked down the passage into the sitting room and Sara's phrase, 'E-bloody-nough,' began to ring in her ears.

She stamped around the sitting room in time to the concerto, and then she began to laugh, hysterically. And then she shouted, 'E-bloody-nough. E-bloody-nough. I've – had – e-bloody-nough,' and she jerked her head up and down and her long red hair flew and the bloody mary spilled.

Iris's story

And so we moved in next door to the Aldwaters, their black labradors and their dark-eyed, dark-haired little boy. I loved our cottage. It was my safe haven, my retreat, my four safe walls. And it was full of light.

When I woke up on Christmas morning the first thing I heard was the soft sound of a bell. When I opened my eyes I saw two points of light and something that moved. When I sat up I saw a brass angel which turned, slowly, round and round. It flew above two red candles. The angel was propelled, apparently, by nothing at all. The tips of its wide wings glinted and made a brass bell ring as it turned.

Kit's face was behind the angel. He smiled at me, his hair as wild as it always was in the morning. A crazy, red halo.

'Magic, don't you think?' he said. 'Happy Christmas.'

We'd agreed to give each other one present, and whatever it was had to cost less than ten shillings. We'd promised we wouldn't buy anything else. Not even a tree. We didn't have the money.

Kit sat on the bed. He'd opened the curtains and I could see the tops of the bare black branches of the yellow buckeyes against the grey sky. I pulled the blankets up to my nose.

'It's a beautiful present,' I said, through the bedclothes. 'Yours is downstairs.'

'What is it?' said Kit, and he gave me my dressing gown. His grey eyes shone the way they did when he was about to perform a poem. I hoped he'd like my present. I'd made him a John Lennon hat, like the one I'd seen him borrow from a fellow poet in the Troubadour. He hadn't wanted to give it back.

I threw back the covers, shivered, hurried into my socks and slippers, pulled on my nightie and a sweater, and then wrapped my dressing gown tightly round me. Outside, the village green sparkled with frost and a pair of bird's footprints, a parallel path of arrows, marched between the trunks of the yellow buckeyes towards the lane at the top of the green.

Kit wound his striped woollen scarf several times round his neck, tied his hair back with a piece of blue string and put on two pairs of socks. Our cottage had no central heating.

When we were downstairs, huddled by the stove, I gave Kit his present. He immediately put it on and he wore it all day. He even went to bed with it on.

'Now,' he said, 'close your eyes,' and he took my hand.

He led me away from the warm stove. I heard him open the door into the sitting room, the room where I made my hats, felt the cold air and immediately smelled the tree.

'Don't open your eyes until I tell you,' he said.

He let go of my hand and I breathed in the resinous smell, and an image of my father, upright and rigid in his wing-backed chair, and quite alone, suddenly filled my head. I saw him tap out his pipe against the chimney breast, I saw him stare straight ahead at the net curtains that smelled of London dirt. I saw him without a Christmas tree, without anyone, and I wished I'd sent him a present. But he'd returned all my letters, unopened, and so I'd decided not to send him anything for Christmas. I'd wanted to hurt him. But, as I stood with my eyes closed, I wanted to cry for him. No one else would have sent him anything, either, I knew. I wished he wasn't alone. I wished he'd understand. I wished he'd been a father to me the way Dick was a father to Matthew.

I put my hands on my belly and promised my daughter – I was sure she was a daughter – that nothing like this would ever happen to her. I promised her that her parents would never refuse to see her, never return her letters unopened, always talk to her, listen to her no matter what happened. It never occurred to me, then, that there might come a day when my own daughter would not want to see me, when she would not answer my letters.

'You can open your eyes,' said Kit.

A small Christmas tree, lit with looped strings of coloured lights and hung with oddly-shaped balls of yellow and orange crêpe paper, stood in the corner by the window. At the top was a sign which said, 'Partridge', and then an arrow that pointed downwards, and in between the yellow and orange crêpe paper balls there were white paper cut-outs of birds and people. The birds were attached to each other by their beaks or their tails, the people by their hands and feet.

'On the first day of Christmas,' Kit sang, 'I gave to my true love, a partridge in a Christmas tree.'

'When did you do all this?' I said.

'Slowly,' he said. 'In bits. On the second day of Christmas – '

' – but we said – '

' – I know what we said, but I stopped agreeing with us.' He began to sing again. 'On the third day of Christmas I gave to my true love, three speckled hens and a po-o-o-o-o-oem.'

I stood in front of the little tree and touched the figures and the birds, and then I saw that Kit had written something on the back of a large cut-out bird. I took it off the tree.

'Is this the partridge?'

'It is the partridge and the partridge's poem.' He looked at me. 'But I haven't finished the song, yet.'

'Sorry.'

Kit sang me his version of 'A Partridge in a Pear Tree', which was all about us, and about the paper cut-outs he'd made and the poems he'd written, and then he sat beside me while I read the longest of the poems. It was about an apprentice wing-maker called Perdix whose teacher grew jealous because his pupil was obviously about to outshine him, and so the master wing-maker told the apprentice that they must test their wings from the highest hill outside Athens. But before the apprentice could strap his wings to his body his jealous teacher pushed him, and he fell.

A goddess, Athena, saw the apprentice's fall and she changed him into a bird, to save him. But the wings on the apprentice-bird weren't large enough to slow the speed of his great fall, so Athena caught him. And when she caught him she fell in love with him and carried him up to heaven with her where, it is said, they still live.

I held out the bird-shaped piece of paper to Kit.

'Will you read it to me?'

He waved the paper away and I thought he had suddenly decided to go back into the kitchen where it was much warmer, but then he turned, dramatically, and began the poem, by heart.

I sat with my back to the tree, breathed in its resinous smell and watched him, and listened. His grey long-johns had holes in the knees but the parrots on his blue and green kimono glowed. The blue string that held his hair back unravelled as he performed and hung down beneath his new black cap, which he'd pulled low over his eyes.

I was enchanted.

I hugged myself to keep warm, rubbed my hands, and then I put my hands over my belly, closed my eyes, thought about our daughter and flew with Perdix and Athena.

I had forgotten all about my father.

Vivie's story

Vivie stood looking through the bedroom window. She was still wearing her blue and green kimono with its faded parrot pattern. She had a large glass of fizzy water in her hand and she was watching a man in a pale linen suit leaning idly against the garden wall of the house opposite, smoking.

When he turned and looked up, directly at her, Vivie backed into the room. His gaze was frighteningly direct and his face was, vaguely, familiar. And then she remembered. He was the man she'd thrown her drink at the night before. She could only remember her fury and the red wine staining his jacket. Her heart began to thud. Had he been there all morning? Had he followed her home the night before? She didn't even know who he was.

Vivie flung herself onto the bed and, as she did so, two pigeons flew past the window. She stared at them as they landed on the roof of the house opposite. She saw them attempting to keep their balance as they mated on the apex of the roof and then she saw the plant that grew from the gutter beneath them. A plant like that had grown from the window-sill of her flat on Battersea Park Road and, even in her bleakest times, it had made her smile because it was, she thought, such a brave plant. It had abundant foliage and bushy purple flowers but it had no water supply, no earth, petrol fumes suffocated it and yet it grew; it even managed to be beautiful.

Vivie tried to remember the name of the plant, in an attempt to take her mind off the man outside in the street. She had asked Dick, once, but all she could remember was that he'd said butterflies loved it. And, thinking about Dick, Vivie began to cry. She thought about how kind he had always been to her, how she'd longed for a father just like him, someone who was always there, always interested, always ready to listen.

Speaking of Love

Dick was a person whose inside was the same as his outside.

Vivie thought he might even understand what had happened to Charles. But above all she knew he'd listen because he always had.

She leaned over the side of the bed and picked up the telephone.

Matthew's story

The sun is high in the summer-blue sky and a patchwork of green and gold fields stretches away below us. The few wispy clouds move very slowly across the sky, as if the heat has exhausted them, and we are parked in a lay-by at the very top of a hill.

The roof is down and when we were moving the breeze cooled us, but sitting still on the top of this hill it is hot. Dad is wearing his collapsing straw hat which has stray pieces of straw sticking out at all angles, and part of the brim is missing at the back. The lines on the back of his neck remind me of small fissures in rock, and the heat of the sun makes me wish I could persuade him to buy a new hat and throw the old one out, but he won't.

He is making spidery black ticks on the map on his knees and he says, without looking up, 'Darning is a marvellous way to travel, don't you think? It yields such glorious things, such memorable things, such quirks.'

We are just outside Aylesbury and we've been over the M1 and under the A5 and Dad says, 'This'll go into the book of the journey,' and smiles at me. 'When you travel like this there is time to look, time to see things properly, like the old petrol pumps we saw just now. You'd never have seen those on a motorway and, wasn't it marvellous, none of that impersonal self-service business. And did you see the name of the street?' But he doesn't give me time to answer. 'Blackbird Street. And did you see the signs in Woburn for an oyster festival and local wild plaice? There's no sea near Woburn that I know of, but perhaps there was a sea there once, an inland sea, like the Caspian Sea. Perhaps that's why Woburn Sands are called Woburn Sands ... because they were, once, the sands beside the Woburnian Sea.'

He is unstoppable. He says, 'The M40's coming up so we'll go over it,' he makes a horizontal S-bend in the air with his hand, 'and then under the A34. Marvellous, quite marvellous.' He pulls his glasses down from his forehead and stares at the fields spread out below us. He says, 'England in high summer ... emotions at high tide ... who said that?'

I say, 'I think it's one of Kit's.'

He laughs, 'Good heavens,' he says, 'so it is. How could I have forgotten?' He gives me the map and asks me to fold it so that the next page of our route is uppermost, and then he reaches into the glove compartment for his camera and says, 'Be my hands, will you?'

As he hands his camera to me Vivie's Gitanes fall out of the glove compartment. Dad glances at me and I say, 'They're not mine,' and, incredibly, I start blushing. I can't remember when I last blushed and it gets worse as I try to suppress it. I turn away from Dad and ask him what he wants me to take a photograph of, but he couldn't have heard me because he doesn't answer. I tell myself that he couldn't know the cigarettes were Vivie's and the blush begins to subside.

Dad says, 'It needs a new film. And the catches are so fiddly.'

I change the film and add the exposed one to the steadily growing collection in the corner of his suitcase on the back seat, and then I say, 'I haven't taken up smoking Dad, they're Vivie's.'

I get out of the car and go round to the other side to help him out, and then we stand looking down at the valley of green and gold fields, and he doesn't ask me why I've got a packet of Vivie's cigarettes in my car, but I wonder what on earth made me tell him they were hers.

Then he says, as he pushes his battered straw hat back on his head, 'If there's anything on your mind, Matthew, anything at all, you only have to say, you know.'

I feel ridiculous, and I say there isn't anything on my mind, absolutely nothing at all.

Iris's story

The only part of my brain that remained active while I was pregnant, and for some time afterwards, was the part that made stories. So I invented stories for my unborn daughter and told them to her by the kitchen stove and when spring came, and early summer, I told them to her in the garden.

When I was seven months pregnant, Dick brought me the tree. He knocked on the kitchen window and held up a tall, leafy plant in a black pot.

Kit was in London. He'd gone to organise another poetry festival, but I didn't want to leave home, didn't want to go back to his chaotic flat. I loved our cottage. I loved everything about it. I loved the way the sound of the rain against the windows made me feel safe. I loved the sense of security and the warmth the thick stone walls gave me and I loved the smell of the fire in the room where I made my hats. And when the sun shone I liked to sit outside, to drink tea with Joan Aldwater and watch Matthew run backwards and forwards between Dick's vegetable patch and their kitchen door. I loved the way he squatted and stared so seriously at the beech hedge that divided our gardens. He poked sticks into it for hours. And I liked to walk on the village green underneath the yellow buckeyes with their delicate, spread-out five-fingered leaves. I liked to experiment with the things I cooked, and I liked to make my hats. I didn't want to go too far from home. I liked the fact that I had a home. The four walls of our cottage held all that was important to me, they held my whole world.

And I had begun to make a little money. I'd been commissioned to make hats for a wedding in the village and I had several other commissions. I talked to my long-dead French milliner-grandmother as I worked. I felt her look down on me and help me when I got stuck with a design. I loved that time. I liked the luxury of my afternoon rest. I liked to read, and I liked to stop and look up from my book and invent a story and to dream and to stare at the rain from the warmth of my kitchen where I sat, wrapped in Kit's striped rug by the stove.

On the day Dick turned up with the tree the rain had stopped, briefly, but drops fell from the ledge above the kitchen door onto his head and onto the plant he held.

'I've grafted several of these,' he said. 'I thought you might like one.'

'What is it?'

'Laburnum. It will flower next year. Yellow flowers.'

'Yellow's my favourite colour.'

'I know.'

He smiled at me, my generous next-door neighbour who never complained when we were late with the rent, who treated us as if we were his own family, and whose quiet affinity with the trees he tended touched me. He seemed to think of everyone else before he thought of himself. Sometimes he winced and limped because of the scraps of shrapnel that they never could get out of his leg, and when I saw the pain register on his face I tried to imagine him in battle, and I failed every time. I could not picture him killing a greenfly, let alone another human being.

He held out the tree, the laburnum. 'Where would you like it?' he said.

I pushed myself up from my chair, pulled the rug round me and walked towards him, belly first.

'What does it look like when it's grown?'

'Like this, only bigger,' he said, and laughed. 'But it's not a big tree. The branches grow at a forty-five degree angle to the bole,' he balanced the pot on one knee and stretched out his arm to show what he meant, 'and the leaves are longish, trifoliate, oval. The flowers bloom at this time of year and they're yellow, as I said.' He looked at me through his pale blue eyes. 'Deciduous,' he said, as an afterthought. 'Or,' he said, 'if you prefer, I could give you chapter and verse, in Latin.'

I shook my head, smiled and said it was his garden so he should choose where the tree went.

'While you pay the rent the garden is yours,' he said.

'Then I'd like your advice,' I said.

'Well, you could do with something in the middle of the lawn.'

I breathed in the fresh smells after the rain, the sweetness of the grass, the slightly bitter smell that drifted up from the flag-stones, the fresh, rain-washed air. There were dark grey clouds in the west, but there was a small patch of bright blue sky over our heads. A blackbird sang and Dick whistled back to it while I put on my shiny red gumboots. I had to sit down to put them on and I had to wait to get my breath back while Dick walked out across the damp lawn.

'Here?' said Dick, and he turned back to me.

'How tall will it grow?'

'About twenty, twenty-five feet.'

I nodded. 'There, then.' And I walked towards him.

'I'll fetch my spade,' he said.

Dick put the pot down and disappeared through the arch in the beech hedge. When he came back I offered to help but he said, 'Not in your condition,' and began to dig.

He stopped to rub his back, looked at the tall laurel that divides the Old School House garden from my garden and said he'd meant to cut it back.

'Before the school was closed, the schoolmaster kept it under control, but I've rather let it go. You'd never know there was a gate buried in there, would you?'

'Where?' I said.

'Under all that laurel,' said Dick. 'Your cottage was the school-master's. Nice fellow. Pity he retired.'

'Pity the school's closed,' I said. 'It would've been perfect for this little one, and for Matthew, wouldn't it?'

'It would,' said Dick and he started to dig again.

I stood by him. And then I helped him stamp down the wet, rich earth at the base of the tree that barely reached my non-existent waist.

'One thing,' he said, when he'd finished, 'laburnums are

poisonous, especially the seeds. So you watch your little one in the summer. Collect the pods when they fall and search the ground for the seeds. They're black.'

'I will,' I said, and rubbed my belly. 'I'll make sure she's safe.'

At exactly that moment my daughter kicked. Actually it felt more as if she'd stretched out her arm and swept the back of her hand across the whole of the inside of my womb. I put one hand out towards Dick who dropped his spade and steadied me.

'All right?' he said.

'Yes,' I said. 'Yes. I think she's just signalled her approval.'

Dick smiled, rubbed his leg, and said he'd found some stone urns for the lavender he'd promised me. He said he'd bring them over on the weekend. Then he pulled the hose through the arch in the hedge between our gardens and watered the tree. My tree. My laburnum tree.

'So, it's a girl is it?' he said.

'Just a feeling,' I said.

'Joan knew Matthew was Matthew,' he said. 'She was as sure about him as I am about what will grow from a seed.'

He went back into their garden, turned off the tap, came back and wound the hose over his shoulder and under his sunburned elbow. He nodded at the laburnum.

'Some people call them lantern trees,' he said. 'You'll see why when the flowers come, next year.'

'Thank you for my tree, Dick,' I said, 'I know it will be beautiful.'

Then, suddenly, it was cold. Dark grey clouds slid across the sun and there was a tremendous clap of thunder. 'Needn't have bothered with the watering,' said Dick, as he disappeared through the hedge.

I walked quickly back into my kitchen, shut the door and put my hands on my belly. I told my unborn daughter not to worry about the rumble and rage of the thunder. I told her I had my hands over her ears. I told her she was quite safe with me.

Vivie's story

Vivie listened to the telephone ring and ring and ring until, after she'd counted more than thirty rings, an answering machine with a barely audible message cut in. Vivie heard, through hisses and crackles, 'Aldwater here. Leave a message, thanks,' and then the tape began to spool and hiss, waiting, patiently, for Vivie to speak.

Vivie knew just where that telephone was. She pictured the heavy cream-coloured instrument and its dial. She saw it in its place on top of the big boxy answering machine on the table by the stairs.

'It's Vivie,' she said. 'Could you ring me, please?' And she hung up and lay back on the bed, in Charles's house, in London, but she wasn't there. She was in St Agnes Redemere on the day when Auntie Joan had rung the doctor from that telephone. The day when Matthew had just stood, uselessly, holding out a loaf of bread and some apples and saying, 'It smells funny in here.'

'What a stupid thing to say,' she'd shouted at him. 'You're no help.' And he'd looked frightened.

That day Vivie had concentrated so hard on the mugs and the teabags that she hadn't noticed the lid on the kettle was rattling. Auntie Joan took the kettle off the boil and Vivie never did make tea. That day she told herself over and over again that they were fine, just fine, that they were fending for themselves and they didn't need anyone else.

She'd been sure, that day, that Matthew would know what to do, but he hadn't known at all. And that day her mother had looked at her with that sideways-under-her-eyelids look and said, 'He says I must be wary of you, Lily. He says you will try to poison my food.' And Vivie had stared at the yellow laburnum petals that stuck to her mother's bottom lip.

Speaking of Love

The doctor had come that day and Matthew had run away and her mother had kept saying, 'Fumble fingers, fumble fingers, fumble fingers,' in a sad, lost voice that even Vivie had never heard before. The little bells on the ribbons on her white gloves had tinkled every time she moved and Vivie – who'd managed until then – no longer knew what to do. That day she'd broken her faithful promise to her mother because she couldn't cope any more. That day her mother had kept asking her to play and play and play the ancient 78 rpm record of a song that, until that day, she'd loved:

> *'If I loved you,*
> *Time and again I would try to say*
> *All I'd want you to know ...'*

On that day the gramophone needle had scratched and bounced on the old shellac record in the kitchen, and Vivie had watched her mother dance with the doctor.

On that day Vivie saw her mother dressed in clothes she had never seen before. She'd put on an old-fashioned yellow silk dress with a full skirt and a narrow waist. She wore a short yellow jacket and long yellow gloves up to her elbows, and she had pinned a little yellow hat to the side of her head with yellow netting that came down over her eyes. And Vivie had noticed that the buttons on her neat little jacket had been put through the wrong button-holes.

On that day Vivie had turned away and stared out through the kitchen window at the laburnum tree, so that no one would see her tears. And then she'd tried, for one last time, to get her mother to understand – in frantic sign language – that the doctor was a doctor and not a dancing partner. But her mother had just swept past her, waving her away and saying, 'One day you'll learn to move your arms gracefully, Lily. Not like that.'

Her mother's hair had stuck out crazily beneath the little yellow hat and the hairs in one of her eyebrows seemed to have been combed backwards. Her make-up looked as if she'd put it on in the dark, and a tiny yellow handbag swung from her gloved arm. Vivie wondered what such a small handbag could possibly hold.

Vivie's story

And it was on that day that Vivie understood that even if people sounded ordinary, even if they looked ordinary, safe even, on the outside, like the doctor, they weren't. She found out that people she trusted, like Auntie Joan, were unpredictable and unreliable. She had already discovered from her mother that what people showed you on the outside was quite different from what was going on on the inside, and now she knew that a day came when all the inside stuff spilled out.

Vivie watched the unordinary doctor dance her mother into her hat-making room and she watched him open the front door with his hand behind his back, dancing all the time. She watched him dance her mother across the lane and across the green under the seven trees in wide, sweeping arcs, as if it was the most normal thing in the world. She watched her mother turn her head and hold her elbows out as they swept past, as if she, Vivie, was a member of a judging panel at a perfectly normal dancing competition. Except that her mother's high-heeled yellow shoes were caked with mud.

On that day Vivie discovered that the difference between what was normal and what wasn't, wasn't always obvious. When she heard Auntie Joan's dog van engine start up, it sounded exactly the same as it did when she took the dogs for a walk, or drove them all to the sea for a day. But the doctor was dancing with her mother on the green and people had gathered and were staring.

Vivie's mother's mad insides were showing on the outside for all to see, but the people stared as if their own insides were quite normal, as if they'd never do what Vivie's mother was doing. But Vivie knew better, from that day on. She knew that anyone who thought they had a normal inside didn't know much. Vivie knew you had to be on your guard because you never knew when your own insides – or anyone else's insides – might spill out.

Vivie lay on Charles's bed trying to stop the stream of memories. They terrified her as much as they had when she was ten, and the certain knowledge that madness lurked inside everyone, whatever they said, frightened her just as much as it had then.

Vivie was exhausted by a lifetime of standing guard against an enemy she couldn't even see.

And now even Charles, her anchor and her breakwater, even he had showed her that madness swilled inside him, that his apparent sanity and rock-like dependability had been nothing but a mask, after all.

Vivie knew herself judged for a fool.

Matthew's story

We're in another hotel, but this time it's Tudor, all low oak beams and over-worked stone and plaster and the UeL models on the table between Dad and me stand out in direct contrast. The simplicity of their steel construction, the wave-form rooves of the academic buildings and the brightly painted, cylindrical student residence buildings all please me, whereas this claustrophobic oak-beamed dining room doesn't.

I have been telling Dad how the buildings will shimmer with light reflected from the water in Albert Dock, and how we conceived the main academic building as a silver and white cliff and the coloured student residences as if they were bathing huts – hugely exaggerated, of course, but still bathing huts. I've been telling him how the wave-form rooves contrast with the inverted rooves of the student residences and as I describe it all I want to get out from under the low, bowed ceiling of the hotel's restaurant where the golden evening light can hardly find its way in through the small leaded windows.

I say that too and Dad says, 'Hmmm ... but I don't suppose they would have been thinking about light and space, those Tudor carpenters and plasterers, now would they? Warmth would have been more important to them.'

I say, 'I know, but even so it makes me feel I should be smaller, as if I should take up less space. I don't like feeling like that.'

Dad says, 'Your buildings are beautiful, Matthew, you deserve the contract. They're entirely original and they do put me in mind of holidays by the sea. Marvellous. Marvellous. I am very proud of you.' He looks at me and I am embarrassed to see tears in his eyes.

He says, 'When shall I stand in front of them and say, "My son was responsible for all this"?'

'1999 ... as long as everything goes according to plan.'

He looks disappointed and I say, 'That's quick, Dad.'

'It may be quick ... for buildings,' he picks up one of the drum-shaped residence models, a yellow one, and balances it on his palm, 'But I am not a young man.'

I say, 'It's only three years away, Dad.'

We'd already drunk some champagne to celebrate the contract, and we are drinking red wine now and waiting for sea-bass for me and steak for him, all the things, as he'd said when we ordered, that he is not supposed to eat or drink but that he loves. He puts the model down and says, 'There's something I have been meaning to tell you, something I should have told you some time ago, Matthew.'

The waitress arrives at exactly that moment so he stops, but I think I know what he is going to say. When the waitress goes, he says, 'I've had a dicky heart for some time, Matthew. The doctor says I could go on for a good while yet, but he also says it might fail me sooner than ... well sooner than ...' He waves his arm and I stare at his gnarled fingers.

I say, 'What about pacemakers or implants, or whatever they're called?'

He says, 'They're all possible, but I don't like the idea of being run by a machine.' He rests his bent hand on the table and I almost reach across to touch it, but I don't.

He says, 'And anyway, I may have several more good years in me.' He taps his heart. 'But I wanted you to know, just ... in case. I should have told you before.'

The blood is running from the steak on his plate and I have a tremendous urge to find a solution, to save him, to become the knight who rides to his rescue with a miraculous cure.

He simply says, 'It's all right, Matthew. Even if I die tomorrow, I'll have had a pretty good innings, you know. It's all right.'

When I was twelve my head was full of King Arthur and the Knights of the Round Table. My favourite was Sir Galahad, the 'best knight of the world'. I saw myself as Vivie's Galahad. I was going to save her from all the dreadful things that were happening. I was going to be noble and courageous and help her find a way to stop Iris behaving so weirdly.

I would be her knight; I would wear her favour.

I hid half a loaf of bread and some apples in the poacher's pockets of my waterproof jacket and sat under their laburnum tree, waiting for Vivie to come down. Her bedroom curtains were drawn even though it was late morning. As I waited I wondered how Iris would be and I tried to think how I'd be if my mother behaved the way Iris had been behaving. I didn't think I'd have been anything like as calm and practical as Vivie was. I thought I'd have been terrified.

I'd memorised another of the stories from the book of stories about the Holy Fool, Nasrudin. They always made Iris and Vivie laugh and I thought it might help. I wondered if Sir Galahad had ever tried to make the damsels he rescued laugh; I thought it would have made him an even better Knight.

A light came on in their kitchen and I saw Vivie at the stove. I scrambled to my feet and knocked on the window but Vivie mouthed 'Go away.'

I held up the bread and apples and she stared. Then she opened the door, said 'Thank you,' and burst into tears. I hugged her but I couldn't think what to say or do and when Iris came down, naked and madder than ever, I ran away.

I was Sir Hopeless, not Sir Galahad.

Iris's story

The storytelling festival has begun.

The night is warm and starry and I've just walked from the camping ground all the way down to the jousting field. I wanted to see what it was like to arrive at the festival the way the audience will arrive.

I saw the Bristol Channel as it glinted under the moon.

I saw the lights from the Devon and Somerset coasts that twinkled across the water.

I heard people talk about the storytellers they had come to hear and about the perfect summer night.

I walked between trees strung with coloured lights.

I walked between vertical banners that marked the way down across the fields to the castle. I heard the banners flap against the poles and read the words 'Beyond the Border', painted above dragons and castles, kings and knights, damsels and princesses and mythical beasts.

I heard a fiddle play a jig. I heard the pipes join in. I heard people clap and whoop. I smelled ash woodsmoke. I looked up at the castle and down at its grassy moat. I saw the moon, a gibbous moon, high above the battlements. I walked through the stone arch and scrunched along the gravel path beside the tall leaded windows of the Great Hall of the castle. I crossed the lawn above Rose Lawn, my lawn.

I looked up at my bedroom window, high in the stone watchtower, and then I walked down the stone steps and through the little iron gate. I walked down the flint steps between the pines to the jousting field and the scent of the pines mingled with something headier, jasmine perhaps, or honeysuckle, from one of the gardens, and I heard more music and excited voices and I saw coloured lights, apparently suspended magically in mid-air, through the pines. When I reached the bottom of the stone steps, when I walked out onto the jousting field, I saw red, yellow and orange Chinese lanterns strung between two great beeches. They bobbed and swayed and lit the way towards the striped storytelling tents on the long flat jousting field. Flares marked the way when the trees, and so the Chinese lanterns, ran out.

I could hear the fiddle and the pipes clearly, and I saw elongated shadows behind the striped canvas of the main storytelling tent. I went inside and climbed the steps to a seat at the back of a high, raked set of benches. There was a buzz of anticipation and I heard a tinkling sound. When the man in front of me turned I saw small silver bells attached to the red and blue pipe cleaners that twisted up from the front of his hat.

I laughed as the bells rippled out their soft silvery sound, and I closed my eyes and the pictures from the story that Vivie loved best of all, the story that haunted me in the twilight time between Salem and The Abbey, filled my mind. I saw the lonely princess who found the courage to live her life the way she wanted to live it.

There are bells in that story.

NIGHT AND DAY

*T*here was, once, a King who loved his daughter so much that he wanted to give her everything that was his. She would inherit the ways, the manners, the habits and the customs – not to mention the riches and the territories – of his kingdom, and he looked forward happily to the day when she reached the age of majority, when all that he loved would become hers.

But the King's daughter, the Princess, was not happy about this arrangement. She knew of her father's desires and she knew that his great love for her – not to mention his great generosity – should make her happy. But it did not. She did not want what was his. She thought of her inheritance as a terrible burden, a heavy weight from which happiness could not come. She had known happiness, once, when she was just seven years old. At that time her mother, the Queen, had spoken words that the Princess and the Queen's attendants had never heard before: words that had made the Princess's soul sing and her blood hum and, as she listened to her mother's words the Princess had felt truly alive for the first time. She had glimpsed another kind of life, a life of her own.

But she had not felt that way since that day because, soon after the Princess heard the Queen speak those words, the Queen died, and the King never again allowed the dead Queen's words to be spoken by anyone, not even the Princess herself.

The Princess cried for the loss of her mother, and for the loss of the words that had made her soul sing and her blood hum and given her a glimpse of a life of her own. And the Princess noticed that her father did not cry.

Night and Day

The Princess tried desperately to remember her mother's words and, eventually, her exasperated father took her to a meeting of the Emergency Judiciary so that she should hear what would happen to anyone who attempted to speak the late Queen's words. And so it was that the Princess sat on a faldstool below the Emergency Judiciary and even further below her father, the King, and heard this, from the Elder Judge.

'It is decreed,' he said, 'that whosoever shall be heard to speak the late Queen's words shall be punished by the King's own hand. No quarter shall be given. No mitigating circumstance shall be considered. The King has leave to punish the guilty party as he sees fit. The Queen's words shall nevermore be heard in this kingdom.'

The young Princess cried when she heard this and, again, she saw that her father did not. The Princess watched her father touch a jewelled scabbard that lay against his breast, and she watched while he, and the members of the Emergency Judiciary, signed a great parchment with the new Law written upon it. The seven-year-old Princess watched the King stamp his seal – which was shaped like a great sun – into the molten golden wax and all the while she cried and noticed that he did not.

And so it was that the Princess grew up full of grief because she could not remember the words that had made her soul sing and her blood hum, the words that had made her feel truly alive and given her a glimpse of a life of her own. And as her unhappiness grew the Princess weakened until she began to fall asleep constantly and, by the time she was twelve, the King's anger knew no bounds because the Princess slept all day long.

The King summoned his Physician and demanded an explanation.

'I can find nothing wrong with the Princess,' said the King's Physician. 'Therefore there is nothing that I can treat.'

Speaking of Love

'If there is nothing wrong with her,' said the King, 'why, pray, does she sleep all day? Night is the proper time for sleep.'

'It could be, your Majesty,' said the King's Physician, as he attempted to judge the King's mood, 'it could be that the Princess takes after her mother, the late, much-lamented Queen.'

The King made no answer, but he touched the jewelled scabbard that lay against his breast.

'It could be,' said the King's Physician, but he hesitated for he could see that the King's jaw muscle twitched violently, 'it could be,' he said, and he took a deep breath, 'that the Princess dislikes the day.'

Again the King made no answer, but his Physician noted the way the Royal shoulders hunched, the way the muscles in the Royal neck tightened and the way the Royal fingers closed around the jewelled scabbard that lay against the Royal breast.

'It is not unknown in your kingdom,' continued the Physician, perhaps unwisely, 'to dislike the day. I have seen this Tendency in a fair few of your subjects ... over the past five years.'

At these words the King whirled from the window, drew a golden dagger from the jewelled scabbard and held it high. 'You know perfectly well,' he said, 'that the words you have just spoken refer to the words that are expressly forbidden in my kingdom.'

The King's Physician gathered up his robe and said, as he walked quickly backwards towards the library door, 'The Tendency exists, your Majesty, whether or not the words that describe it are spoken.' And with that he fled the kingdom in fear for his life.

But the Physician's words would not leave the King's head. The King wondered whether his daughter, the Princess, really did dislike the day. He wondered whether she slept all day, as her mother, the Queen had done

144

before her, so that she might be awake *at night? He wondered whether she was a traitor to his kingdom just as her mother, the Queen, had been.*

The King ordered night watches to be kept outside the Princess's apartments and, at the same time, he ordered one of his woodmen to cut hundreds of slivers of ash, fourteen of which he stored, each week, in the small pouch on the outside of the jewelled scabbard that lay against his breast.

On the first night of the watch outside the Princess's apartments high up in the belltower, the watchman distinctly heard whispered words and the sounds of footsteps. But he knew that the Princess went nowhere, for the door to her apartments never once opened, so he moved his chair closer to the door and tried to understand the whispered words. But the words that he heard were in a language he had never heard, so the watchman woke the King because he knew he would never be able to give the King an accurate report of a conversation in a language that he could not understand.

The King leapt from his bed and flew up the stone steps that spiralled inside the belltower to his daughter's apartments, and burst into her bedroom. He watched his daughter walk round her room with her eyes closed. He watched her hands move in front of her as if she searched for something, and he watched her lips move. The King heard his daughter whisper the forbidden words, the words that his Queen had spoken before she died. The King's heart raced with rage, but he realised that his daughter walked in her sleep and talked in her sleep, so he decided that there was no need to punish her as the Law required. Instead, he gripped his daughter by her arms and held them, most cruelly, behind her back while he shouted for what was necessary.

The Princess opened her eyes and began to cry. And, once again, she noticed that her father did not.

Speaking of Love

The King shouted for white ribbon, small silver bells and scissors.

The King shouted for white silk, and leaden pails full of water.

And the anger in the King's voice ensured that the things he shouted for were brought at breakneck speed. When everything that the King had shouted for was delivered, he dismissed the night watchman and cancelled all further night watches outside his daughter's apartments.

Then the King ordered his daughter to cut the white ribbon into four lengths and to thread each length through the silver circle at the top of each of the four silver bells. He made her take the leaden pails full of water and place them at intervals around her bed, and then he stopped her mouth with the white silk, and tied one of the four white ribbons threaded with one of the four silver bells round each ankle and each wrist. And the King said, 'If you attempt to walk in your sleep again you will stumble against the pails, and I shall hear the bells. If you attempt to talk in your sleep again, the white silk will begin to choke you and I shall hear you. And so it shall be, every night, until you cease to walk, and talk, in your sleep. Until you learn to love that which I love.'

And so it was that the King slept, every night, in a wooden chair outside his daughter's apartments, at the top of the stone steps that spiralled up to the belltower. Occasionally he would wake and touch the jewelled scabbard that lay against his breast, and pray that he would never have cause to use the golden dagger against the daughter he loved more than anything, or anyone, in the world.

Whenever the King heard the silver bells he would open his daughter's bedroom door and lead her back to bed so that she would stop sleep-walking. And whenever he heard her choke because of her attempts to speak the forbidden words in her sleep, he would pull the white silk back from her throat so that she did not choke. And every morning the King took two slivers of ash from the small pouch on his jewelled scabbard and wedged them between his daughter's eyelids. He told his daughter – when she cried from the pain – that he did all this because of his great love for her. All he wanted was for her to follow in his footsteps, to be like him, to love the things that he loved: the ways, the manners, the habits and the customs – not to mention the riches and the territories – of his kingdom.

The Princess forced herself to stay awake in the day because her father, the King, wished it so, until the day came when he ceased to wedge the slivers of ash between her eyelids and the noises ceased to come from the Princess's bedroom at night. The Princess slept at night once more and the King stopped his vigils outside her apartments at the top of the spiral stone steps in the belltower.

The King was delighted that, at last, his daughter had learned to love that which he loved, and he looked forward with increasing happiness to the day when she would reach her majority, the day when she would inherit all that he loved.

But all was not as it seemed to the King for each night when the King believed his daughter slept, she would wake and leave her bed. And, as she did so, a silvery Night-Spirit would fly through the open casement and blow on the silver bells to silence them, untie the white ribbons, soundlessly move the pails of water away from the Princess's bed and fly with the Princess cradled in his wings through the casement and down to the courtyard. The Night-Spirit would lead the Princess to the queendom where the Princess remembered and spoke the words that had made her soul sing and her blood hum. The words that had given her a glimpse of a life of her own. The words that were forbidden in the kingdom that her father

intended her to inherit when she reached her majority.
The only words that made her feel truly alive.

And the King, her father, was none the wiser ... until
the night before his daughter reached her majority.

On the eve of that great day, the King saw his daughter
sleep-walking across the courtyard in the moonlight with a
silvery figure at her side. She walked with her arms stretched
out in front of her as if she searched for something.

The King would never have seen his sleep-walking
daughter had he not stayed up to read state papers in
his library much later than usual. He did not want to
have to read such papers on the day of the celebrations
for his daughter's majority and so it was that the King
saw that the Princess's lips moved, and he knew that she
was sleep-talking and that the words she spoke in her
sleep were the forbidden words, the words that belonged
to her mother's queendom. The King knew this because
the Princess looked as happy as she had looked on the
only day in her life when he had witnessed her hear the
Queen speak those words, when she had been but seven
years old.

The King saw all this and anger filled his head and
set his thoughts to race. Anger filled his heart and set
his blood to pump. Anger caused him to pull the golden
dagger free from the jewelled scabbard that hung against
his breast and he flew from his library. The King's anger
lent his legs great speed and soon he was close behind
the Princess and the silvery figure, the Night-Spirit, who
travelled by her side. But just as he strode abreast of his
daughter, they arrived at a clearing in the forest.

The King stopped on the edge of the clearing and
watched the welcome the silvery Night-Spirits and snowy
Owl-Elders gave to his daughter. They clearly knew her
well. He watched the Princess sleep-walk into the very
centre of their circle and, when she turned, the King
saw that her eyes were still closed and her hands were

still stretched out in front of her as if she searched for something.

The King heard the words his daughter spoke in her sleep, the forbidden words, and he felt a rage that exceeded by several hundredfold any rage he had felt before. A rage that blocked the words from his mind and caused him to stride out into the clearing and hold the golden dagger high. The King shouted so that his daughter woke from her sleep. And as she opened her eyes, her words, and the silvery Night-Spirits and the snowy Owl-Elders, all disappeared.

'You are my *daughter,' shouted the King. 'This is* not *your territory.'*

The Princess looked at her father and then she looked at the empty places where she knew her companions had been. But instead of sadness at their disappearance, the Princess felt something she had never felt before.

The King advanced towards his daughter. He held the golden dagger high, but the Princess stopped him in his tracks with her voice.

'YOU,' she said, and her eyes flashed, 'would deprive me of all that I love, of all that makes my soul sing and my blood hum. You would deprive me of everything that makes me happy. You would deprive me of my very life. WHY is it your pleasure so to deprive me? WHY?'

'Your happiness is all I have ever wanted,' said the King, and his voice quivered with an unaccustomed emotion. 'At the stroke of midnight ... all that I love will be yours.'

'But I do not love all that you love,' said the Princess. 'This is ... was ... what I love.' And the Princess spread her arms wide. 'You would forbid what I love because, you say, you love me so much. And you would forbid me to speak of what I love because, you say, you love me so much. But I cannot find love in what you would have me do.'

Speaking of Love

The King's voice faltered as he said, 'I do not know how else to show you how much I love you.'

'Love me for myself,' said the Princess, stretching out her hands. 'And let me love that which I love.'

The King could not speak because all the time his daughter, the Princess, had spoken she had reminded him, forcibly, of his long-dead wife, the Queen, and the way she had spoken those self-same words so many moons ago. He could not hold back his tears, nor could he speak for the lump in his throat.

And then, for the first time since he had forbidden them, the King allowed the Queen's words to sing in his head. He heard her words describe the beauty of the queendom that he had forbidden her to live in when she so wished. He heard the words that spoke of the need for a night queendom and a day kingdom. He heard the words that told of the Queen's sadness when the queendom's snowdrops and the kingdom's celandines had ceased to grow together. And the King remembered how his Queen had died with those last words on her lips, and his tears poured down his cheeks and splashed onto the grass in the clearing.

The Princess's anger subsided as she saw her father's tears for the very first time. She walked towards him and she held out her hands and the King let the golden dagger fall, and he let his daughter take his hands in hers. And when they looked down they saw that snowdrops and celandines had begun to spring up beside each other in the places where the King's tears had fallen, and the Princess closed her eyes with relief and began to speak the forbidden words once more and, as she did so, the Chief of the Owl-Elders reappeared in his place, and the Norn of the silvery Night-Spirits reappeared in hers. And when the King's tears finally ceased, the Norn of the Night-Spirits spoke. She said, 'Good King of the day kingdom, we thank you for shedding the necessary tears.'

Night and Day

The Norn of the Night-Spirits and the Chief of the Owl-Elders rejoiced and spoke the forbidden words many times over and, as they spoke the words, midnight struck in a belltower on the far side of the clearing and the Princess was crowned Queen of the night queendom, witnessed by the Owl-Elders and the Night-Spirits; witnessed by the King of the day kingdom himself.

And so it was that the King returned to his day kingdom with its ways, manners, habits and customs – not to mention its riches, its territories and the words of its language – and the Princess became Queen of the night queendom and restored all its ways, manners, habits and customs – not to mention its riches, its territories and the words of its language.

And ever since then the silvery Night-Spirits have wandered freely in their territory and the Owl-Elders, with their beaks like half moons, have spoken the words which are no longer forbidden. And at twilight, the time when it is neither night nor day, those who live in the day kingdom and those who live in the night queendom come together and wander in each other's territories, and find that they can speak in each other's languages quite freely and just as they will.

Part Three
Saturday, 29 July, 1996

Matthew's story

We are having breakfast in the oak-beamed, low-ceilinged, claustrophobic dining room. The sun is trying to make an impression but it only manages a few streaks through the heavily leaded windows.

I say, 'Are you sure you're all right to walk there, to the gardens, Dad?'

But he immediately replies, 'I can do exactly what I did yesterday, and the day before that, and all the days before all those days. I forbid you to treat me as if I had suddenly become an invalid, Matthew. If it had occurred to me that you would, I would have kept quiet.'

I say, 'Sorry, Dad,' and we leave the hotel and walk towards the ruined Friary with its massive, Norman, carved stone porch, and the arches of its triforia that elegantly frame patches of summer-blue sky. The Friary seems to me to be waiting for a kind hand to restore it, or at least a kind imagination to picture it the way it once was. I touch the warm grey stone as we walk by. We are on our way to see the laburnum tunnel in the Friary House Gardens.

Dad says, 'The first King of all England is supposed to be buried here, but they say his grave is empty.' He looks at me, 'And they say,' he smiles, 'that a monk called Elmer made himself wings and launched himself from the tower of the Friary ... in the days when it still had a tower.'

I say, 'Who are *they*?'

Dad says, 'The waitress, at breakfast, before you came down.'

I say, 'What happened to him? The monk?'

Dad says, 'He crashed. But he flew two hundred yards before he crashed, which isn't at all bad for the eleventh century, is it?'

I say, 'It's not bad for a winged man in any century. We're not built for flying.'

Speaking of Love

Dad laughs, and we walk on past the Friary and into the Friary House Gardens and Dad introduces himself to a woman who sits behind a table set out on the gravel, in the sunshine. She has long dark hair and she wears yellow: a yellow shirt tied in a knot at her waist, yellow shorts and yellow canvas shoes.

She says, 'You've come to see the laburnum tunnel, isn't that right?' and Dad nods, obviously pleased that he is expected.

The dark-haired woman walks with us across the gardens and when Dad says what an abundant garden it is, she laughs and says monks' bones have been buried here for two thousand years and they feed the earth well. We walk up an incline and stand at one end of the laburnum tunnel; the seedpods straggling down above our heads are the colour of ripe corn and it is cool and green and shady.

The woman says, 'I love laburnum blooms, don't you? I always think they smell fragrant, like the leaves of jasmine tea.'

Dad smiles, looks at me and says, 'My son thinks so too,' and while they discuss what age the trees should be when they're planted, how they should be trained, what sort of frame to use and how long it takes for the laburnum trees to reach the apex of the arched frame, I wander away along the tunnel, remembering how the delicate scent of the laburnum flowers surrounded me as I sat under Iris's tree waiting for Vivie.

But on the day when Iris said, 'Someone's been stealing the stories, Matthew, there just aren't any stories left,' I had no idea what to say because it seemed to me that Iris and I had stopped speaking the same language. So I just sat there, helplessly, and Vivie hissed, 'I hate you. You're no help at all.' She punched me but her punch wasn't a real punch and there were tears streaming down her face, so I grabbed her and held onto her tightly. It was the only thing I could think of to do and it must have been the right thing because she didn't struggle, but as we watched Iris walk across the lawn and offer some laburnum flowers to the laurel hedge I wished there was *something* I could do to stop the madness that was seeping into all our lives.

Matthew's story

I reach the end of the tunnel and when I turn round I see Dad walking slowly towards me. The woman has gone, and when Dad reaches me he takes my hands in his and I feel their bony, arthritic unevenness. I don't take my hands away from his. He says, 'What is it, Matthew? What's up? Something's been distracting you, worrying at you, ever since we left.'

I say, 'It's nothing.'

He doesn't say anything.

I say, 'It's just that ... well I've been thinking I never was any use to Vivie when Iris broke down.'

Dad looks surprised. He says, 'What makes you think about that now?'

I take my hands from his and look away. I think he knows that I haven't said what's really on my mind, but he lets it go.

I say, 'I don't seem to be able to forget. I mean ...' I turn to face him. I say, 'Actually, Dad, it's not just that. Not really that at all.'

Dad says, 'Thought so,' and he waits. He puts his arthritic hands on my arms and after a while, when I haven't said anything he says, 'It wouldn't be a woman, would it?' I don't say anything and he says, 'Julia?'

Again I don't answer and he says, 'Not Julia, then. Have I met her?' I nod, but I mean to shake my head. I want to end the conversation before the tears that are dangerously close overwhelm me.

He says, 'Have you known her for a long time?' And I hear myself say, 'All my life, Dad, all my life.'

When I look at Dad I see that his pale blue eyes are shining and the wrinkles below his eyes are glistening; he doesn't seem to be trying to hold back his tears and I think that's what does it.

He says, 'It's Vivie, isn't it?' and before I realise what's happening my father has put his arms round me and I am crying like a child. And then, suddenly, I am not in his arms at all but standing at the far end of the laburnum tunnel looking back towards us and watching us embrace in the long, shady tunnel. I turn away, embarrassed, but wherever I look the two men, my father and I, remain in my line of sight, remain audibly comforting each other, in a garden open to the public, in the middle of England.

And then I feel my father's arms around me once more and I say, into the top of his shoulder, 'But it's hopeless, Dad. I missed my chance years ago and even if I hadn't, even if I'd found the courage to tell her I loved her then, she'd have turned me down. Why would she want a man like me when there are men like Charles in the world?'

Dad just waits.

I say, 'I think she knows I meant to tell her ... something ... which makes it even worse, because now she knows what a coward I am. But I've never been any use to Vivie. Never could be. So it's for the best.'

I straighten up and look at Dad and sniff, which for some reason makes us both smile.

Dad says, 'Usefulness, as far as I know, has never had much to do with love and besides, you did try to help her when you were children. You were heroic. You put your whole heart into what you did.'

I say, foolishly, 'You didn't think so then,' as if I was still twelve years old and he smiles and says, 'Of course we didn't. We did what all parents do when they're worried, when they don't know where their children are. We were angry, and we were frightened ... but that was a lifetime ago.'

I say, 'The thing is, Dad, I saw her last Monday at a Prom and it happened all over again. I wanted to say what I never said when she asked me to give her away, but I didn't because it's pointless ... hopeless ... pathetic. And anyway she's married.'

Dad just nods.

I say, 'I've hardly seen her. I thought I'd managed to forget her.'

Dad hugs me again and this time I stay right with him and I hug him back.

He says, 'You've always had a steadfast heart, Matthew. Perhaps it's time you let it speak.'

I say, 'I don't see how I can.'

He says, 'I know.'

I say, 'I wish she wasn't married.'

He says, 'I know,' and he rubs my arms with his hands, and then stands back.

A blackbird sings, but Dad doesn't whistle his usual reply, he just looks at me. And then he says, 'I know,' again.

I say, 'Stop saying you know. It doesn't help.'

And Dad says, 'I know, Matthew, I know.'

Iris's story

There were shouts and whoops and calls outside my watch-tower window. I looked out and saw men and women dressed in striped tights, coloured belted tunics and conical caps. They stood on each other's shoulders and juggled firesticks. They made a human pyramid on Rose Lawn. They faced the almost-sea of the Bristol Channel, just as I will when I tell my stories, tomorrow. They wobbled dramatically, arms outstretched, and they called over their shoulders to anyone who walked under the stone arch that divides this festival from the rest of the world.

The human pyramid blew out fire and juggled coloured balls. It played musical instruments and juggled them, too, and when Rose Lawn was full of people a shrill pipe whistled wildly and then there was silence.

The woman at the top of the pyramid tucked the wooden pipe under her arm, pulled off her cap, made a low bow and said, 'Welcome to the world's greatest – ' and then she stopped, put her hand to her ear in a dramatic gesture and turned her head. She leaned out dangerously from the top of the human pyramid and waited. She made a great show of toppling, almost falling, but when a child's voice called out, 'Storytelling Festival!' all the members of the human pyramid echoed the child's words and the woman at the top of the pyramid straightened up and tossed her conical cap into the air, caught it and put it back on. I could see the muscles in the backs of her calves and thighs working hard to keep her steady.

'And you are going to have – ?' It was another voice from the human pyramid. Another ear turned dramatically towards the audience. Another body that leaned out dangerously and appeared, almost, to fall.

Iris's story

'Ice cream,' said another child's voice. And the voices from the human pyramid echoed the child's words and kept saying 'And?' and the audience called back to the acrobats who leaned out and twisted and wobbled from their pyramid, and made rhymes and jokes with the words that the audience called out. And I pushed my window wide open and when the next member of the human pyramid called out 'And?' I called down, 'Stories!' and the woman who stood at the top of the pyramid reached backwards, opened her hand and then made it into a fist as if she'd caught my word. And the pyramid wobbled and her muscles strained and she called out 'Stories!' and opened her hand as if to let the word fly towards the audience, and then she bent down and took three coloured batons from the hands of the men below her and juggled them.

The human pyramid juggled batons and balls and words. They called out that there would be stories about magic and stories about beasts. Stories about beauty and stories about feasts. Stories of loss and hunger and defeat; stories of love and good things to eat. And one by one, as they called out the stories and the names of the storytellers, they jumped and somersaulted down onto the grass in a shower of colour and musical instruments, hats and firesticks, batons and balls.

When they landed each one stood in precisely the right place to catch the ball, the baton, the instrument, the hat or the firestick that was his, or hers. And then all was still and the almost-sea of the Bristol Channel glinted and the sun shone and the sky was a luminous blue, and the coasts of Devon and Somerset were as clear as the stripes on the acrobats' tights.

And the acrobats turned, in unison, and their leader, the woman from the top of the pyramid, called to the audience to follow them and they began to play their instruments. The leader played her wooden pipe and the others played a drum, a flute, two fiddles and a tambourine that trailed ribbons. They played copper hand-cymbals, a mouth organ, a pair of maracas, a thumb piano and the man who brought up the rear played a comb wrapped in grease-proof paper with enough energy for a trumpet.

The members of the audience stood and brushed grass from

their thighs and then they began to sway and clap and follow the acrobats. The line of people snaked away across Rose Lawn and the sound of the acrobats' music was eventually muffled by the pines as the people disappeared through the wrought iron gate and down the flint steps to the jousting field and the storytelling tents below.

I watched until the last person had disappeared between the pines, and then I turned and saw a figure beneath the stone arch in the red brick wall. The figure was dressed from head to toe in green. Its long green coat reached the ground and even the face of the figure was painted green which made the pink of its lips garish, almost bloody. He, or she, raised a hand to me and I saw that even its hands were painted green. I smiled at the figure, uncertainly, and raised my hand.

The figure began to walk. It trailed green gauze from its shoulders and it wore a green top hat. Its legs, which I saw when its green tunic flapped open, were encased in tight green-striped trousers and it had green Robin-Hood boots on its feet. It was a thin figure and its legs were long. Leaves and twigs were sewn into the green gauze train that dragged behind it and a couple of children ran through the arch behind the figure. One of them, a girl, pulled at the figure's train and then she giggled and ran away. The other, a boy, ran past the green figure and stood on the gravel, hands on brave little hips, in its path.

I ran down the spiral stone steps as fast as I could. I had to ask a question. I had to be sure. I ran through the wooden door and out onto the gravel path. The figure stood still in front of the boy.

'Why are you dressed like that?' said the boy, in a small voice, as he looked up.

'I am the Green Man,' said a male voice through the pink lips.

'I can see you're green,' said the boy. 'Why?'

'Some people call me Jack-in-the-Green and some the Green Man.' As he spoke the leaves attached to his cheeks and forehead moved. 'And some,' he looked up at me, 'think of me as a symbol of fertility.' I went to sit beside the girl, on the wall. She swung her legs.

Iris's story

'Can you see him too?' I said to her.

She stared at me. 'Of course I can see him,' she said. 'I just don't want to talk to him.' She gave me a quizzical look but I smiled and the Green Man took the boy's hand. He told the boy that if he looked closely at the carvings in cathedrals and churches he would see the Green Man. The boy asked him if he was a storyteller and he said he was. When they'd discovered when and where he would tell his stories, the children ran down the stone steps and disappeared through the iron gate.

The Green Man turned to me. 'That was an odd question,' he said.

'It's a habit,' I said, smiling.

'A habit?'

'I used to see people who weren't there,' I said. 'So these days I ask ... just to make sure.'

The Green Man said 'I see,' as if he didn't, and we walked down through the pines to the jousting lawn. I inhaled their resinous smell and I felt wonderfully well.

The Green Man strode onto the jousting lawn while I walked towards the beach. I passed a woman who'd set up a face-painting stall opposite a stone sundial. There were several bright pots of paint on her table beside sponges and brushes, and an excited queue of children who waited and talked about what they wanted painted on their faces.

A child whose head of red hair curled and shone just like Vivie's, laughed. I had to stop to catch my breath. And even though her face was not at all like Vivie's young face, I had to hurry past, my fingers involuntarily curled around the letter in my pocket. When I reached the beach I sat and stared out at the almost-sea. I wished I didn't long for my daughter so, but I do, and I cried for my loss. And as I cried I sensed Vivie crying too. Her presence was so strong that I half-expected to see her walking along the beach towards me. I knew something was wrong. I fought the impulse to go back to the castle and ring her; I simply sent her my love, silently, and then I walked to the little stone stage that I'd discovered. It is sheltered by a rock that juts out overhead and it is worn smooth by the soles of many feet. I closed my eyes and waited for the pictures in the story that comes from the sea, Murmurina's story, and I thought that I would tell my stories for Vivie tomorrow because it is her birthday. And if the sun shines the way it has shone all morning – and the weathermen say that it will – people might be tempted to come and listen to my stories, if only for a chance to sit in the sun.

Vivie's story

Vivie had hardly slept. Charles had not come home, as he'd said he wouldn't, but Vivie had half-expected that he might and she'd veered between drinking, promising herself not to have another one and remembering things that she would have preferred to forget. Lately she'd noticed that when she drank, memories of what she'd done when she'd been drunk before came back. It was as if she had two memories, and the one that was fuelled by alcohol was gaining the upper hand.

With several drinks inside her she'd remembered more than she wanted to about the way she'd encouraged the man in the corner of the bar to kiss her. She'd liked his mouth and his laugh and the way his beard neatly outlined his jaw but when he'd leaned forward to kiss her she'd thrown her glass of wine at him and left. And now that same man had been sitting on the low wall in front of the house opposite and Vivie – drunk or sober – couldn't remember telling him where she lived.

She lay in bed with a sheet tangled round her body. She was hot and sticky and dry-mouthed. The memory of the way she and Charles had met, just after Dick had rung to say that her mother had had another breakdown, filled her mind. She tried to will it away, but it wouldn't go.

She had smoked her last cigarette and all she could think about was how much she needed another. She'd dropped the receiver; she couldn't listen to what Dick had to say, and then she'd grabbed her coat and run downstairs and across the street into the off-licence. On the way out she'd bumped into a man and his dog and tripped over the dog's lead. She'd apologised to the man and heard his sane, sensible voice asking her if he could buy her a bottle of wine to replace the one that had smashed. He'd said, politely, that he was so sorry, and that it was all his fault and would she please let him buy her some cigarettes too, because, couldn't she see, hers had been soaked by the wine.

Vivie had watched the man and been reassured by the ordinary things he'd said. She'd noticed his large capable-looking hands and she'd felt better, felt somehow anchored back into a world that was safe and ordinary, a world that had nothing to do with her mother's madness. She'd wanted him to go on and on talking about ordinary, everyday things.

When she got back to her flat she lay in the bath repeating everything he'd said, over and over again. And then the man began to leave ordinary notes at the off-licence for her. He signed the notes 'Charles Stukeley,' and she'd been reassured by his solid-sounding, ordinary name and when, one day over a drink, she'd told him that it was her mother's birthday, it was he who'd thought of the cake and the candles and the flowers that they took to her mother in The Abbey. It was he who'd said that, apart from the bandage on her mother's hand, he couldn't see anything wrong with her at all.

But Vivie's heart had jolted when her mother said, 'I knew a story about a tree, once.' She'd longed to leave the room but she'd managed not to. She'd managed to listen to Charles and her mother talking about geese and then her mother said that when her hands shook less she would start her millinery business again, and it did sound normal, Vivie knew that, but it didn't feel normal. Not on the inside.

She wondered how long her mother would manage to stay sane in front of Charles. How long she'd manage to prevent her insides from spilling out. She waited, anxiously. She watched her mother's hands flutter as if they didn't belong to her.

She stood picking at the skin on her fingers while Charles had a conversation with her mother's doctor because she couldn't. The doctor, a woman, said it was a good thing for Iris to have visitors, now. She said she needed people who knew her. She said it would be good if Vivie came regularly, and neither Vivie nor Charles admitted that Charles had never met Iris before.

The doctor said that Iris had transferred all her attention, all her affection, to things and that she needed people who loved her to help her through, to help her back. She said it would be particularly good if Vivie came to see her mother on her own, but Vivie knew she couldn't. She'd only just managed to stay in the room with Charles by her side, she knew she'd never be able to stay with her mother without him.

The sound of a telephone brought Vivie back. She leaned from the bed and scrabbled for the receiver. She hoped it would be Dick and dreaded that it might be Charles.

It was Charles.

He told her that he was going to spend another night with Robert, that he was coming to collect some things, later, and then he hung up.

Iris's story

Kit didn't come home when Vivie was born. And when I did manage to catch him on the telephone he wouldn't say when he would be back. He just said he was free, wasn't anyone's, that he would come and go.

Joan told me she thought he'd cried when she rang to tell him about Vivie, but despite that he didn't come back and I was miserable.

If there is a moment that triggered the start of my long journey into the dark, it was then, when Vivie was born and Kit didn't come home. Despair took hold of me because Kit would not be mine, just as he'd always said in his fish poem, and he obviously did not care that he had a daughter. He told Joan that I should have talked to him about my desire for a child, and I knew I should have. He said he wasn't sure he could do what he called 'the responsibility thing.'

I tried to make a cocoon for Vivie and for me, a place where we could live away from my sadness, my darkness, and sometimes I succeeded, but more often it found its damp, stealthy way in. And when I was still ambushed by the darkness and my tears three months after Vivie was born, I clung to Joan's words.

'It's quite normal,' she said, in her brisk Edinburgh accent. 'There's absolutely nothing to worry yourself about. You've just got a great big dose of the baby blues.'

Joan was a nurse, so I trusted her, but still I travelled further and further away from everything I knew, everything and everyone I loved. I travelled against my will but I could not stop. I travelled further and further into a grey, misty country where sadness and fear reigned and my bright expression disappeared. I learned how to put on brightness. I did it for other people. I became an adept at pretence; I became an actor. But the length of time I could stay bright diminished as the days and months went by, and behind my bright mask the grey fog swirled, collected and lodged. I was terrified that there would come a day when it would overwhelm me altogether.

There were days when my jaw ached from my determination to hold on to my bright face. There were days when I dropped dishes and glasses onto the red quarry tiles in the kitchen and heard a sarcastic voice say, 'Fumble fingers, fumble fingers.' There were days when I knew where I'd heard those words before, and days when I didn't. There were days, or parts of days when I caught sight of something, or someone, for a moment, someone who strolled across the garden in the rain. There were days when I looked into the bathroom mirror and could hardly see myself. There were days when I knew myself watched from the other side of the mirror.

There were days and days of despair.

Kit did come back, but he never said when he would come and always he left without a promise to return. He ended up in Spain and, as far as I know, he's still there. I know there were some sunny times, but the ECT has long since claimed most of them.

I know that we painted the laburnum tree onto the kitchen door, because it is still there. But I cannot remember when we did it. The ECT has left me with only one memory of Kit in the cottage after Vivie was born. He burst into the kitchen and Vivie jumped up and flew into his arms and asked him where he'd been. Matthew stood, shyly, not sure if he was also eligible for a hug. Joan could not hide her disapproval but Dick, who never judged anyone, welcomed Kit back.

Kit took off his black peaked cap and put it over Vivie's red curls and she would not take it off all day. He told us he'd brought something for us and he led Vivie and me into the room where I made my hats. He threw his battered suitcase onto the floor and said we should sit down beside it. He made a flourish with his hands, clicked the brass locks up and waited for our reaction.

The suitcase was filled with small dirty rags that curled up at the edges.

'Can't you see what it is?' he said.

But we couldn't, so Kit plunged his hands into the suitcase and when he started to pull elastic bands off the bundles of rags and throw them into the air, I saw what they were.

'They paid cash,' he said, with a grin. He'd been employed in Canada, he said, in a logging camp. He said it was good, hard, honest work. And then he stood up, stood inside the suitcase, undid all the bundles of money and threw them into the air.

Vivie caught a handful and asked if we were rich now, and Kit said we were and he took us to Brancaster Beach and Vivie ran about and her hair flew up from beneath her father's black cap, and we ate fish and chips and it was very cold and grey and my hands went numb, and then he left.

Kit left us with one thousand ragged Canadian dollars and took himself away. He strode across the green on his long, thin legs and we watched from the window of the room where I made my hats.

Vivie said he'd given her his black cap to keep forever. She was only nine and it was much too big for her, it covered her bright eyes. And I had a bleak, black sense, as black as the black of Kit's cap, that he would not be back.

Matthew's story

Dad are I are drinking coffee in a rectangular red brick courtyard behind a tea shop near Malmesbury Cross. We're the only ones here and Dad's eaten two home-made scones.

I say, 'We should get going,' but Dad says there are such things as motorways if, as he puts it, 'We are really pushed.'

I say, 'You hate motorways, and anyway what about your map … and all your plans for this journey? The darning?'

He shrugs and says, 'This is more important,' orders more coffee and tells me the name of the pink rose, Bantry Bay, that's climbing up the wall beside our table. When the coffee comes he says, 'Isn't it something to think that you and I lived under the same roof for all those years and yet we never really talked about it?'

I say, 'I never wanted to talk about it, it was all too difficult, and anyway I wanted to be a hero, Vivie's gallant knight, but I fell off my charger.'

He says, 'You did all you could.'

I say, 'Vivie was braver than me, she did everything she could to stop Iris being taken away and her courage spurred me on. When she failed, I knew what I had to do. Vivie convinced me that bringing Iris home would solve everything.'

Dad pours the coffee and says, 'Solving everything is a pretty tall order … even for a knight.'

I say, 'My plan made her so happy.'

Dad says, 'To make someone happy is an honourable thing.'

I say, 'But, as you well know, my plan didn't work. It just made everything worse.'

Dad spreads his arms and says, 'Our world would be a pitiful place if we only attempted things that we were certain would work, and besides, you were very young.'

Speaking of Love

I say, 'As you keep saying, but it was so obvious Iris was ill ... I don't know why I ever thought my idea would work.'

Dad says, 'You believed it because Vivie believed it.' He looks at me. 'That's her trouble. She still believes she should be able to help her mother, do *something* to chase away the madness, and that's why she still can't see her. She feels guilty. And Iris did, once, make her promise all kinds of impossible things. But there was nothing more Vivie could have done. Iris was very ill. She needed the specialists.'

He waves a wasp away from the crumbs on his plate.

I say, 'I think the doctor did a noble thing, dancing with Iris. I couldn't understand it then, I thought he'd gone mad, too. I thought everyone had gone mad, but now I think it was noble.'

Dad says, 'It was.'

I say, 'I went for a long, furious walk by the river with the dogs after Iris was taken away. I stamped along and hoped the dogs would get themselves tangled up in the fishermen's lines and steal the fish lying by them on the bank.'

Dad laughs and I say, 'I kicked everything. I kicked the bluebell seedheads and the trunks of the beech trees, I kicked up clods of earth. I yanked the heads off buttercups and I tore a branch off a beech and thwacked the ground with it. I was furious with my tears and I stomped on through the wood hoping no one would come the other way. The dogs were in the river and I never called them back. I walked all the way to the wooden bridge and over it and along the edge of the field on the other side of the river, over the stile and across Jepson's farthest field. You always said he took pot-shots at people who walked across his fields and we should keep to the edges, so I walked straight across his field hoping he'd take a pot-shot at me. I ended up at the top of Church Lane.

'I wouldn't have known Vivie was there if it hadn't been for the dogs who'd already found her. She was sitting on the verge hidden in the tall grass and cow parsley, but they found her. She was almost in the hedge where the dog roses grow. I could see she'd been crying too and then she said she was sorry she'd been so, as she put it, "thing", and I could have kissed her, but I didn't. It was

172

the first time she'd spoken to me since the day Iris was taken away. We sat surrounded by the bitter-smelling cow parsley and shared one of your apples and she said Mum had told her she wouldn't be able to see Iris for a long time.

'She said, "Everyone keeps telling me she needs a rest and she needs time on her own. But what do *they* know? I know she's frightened of being alone. I know she wants to see someone she knows, like me".'

Dad says, 'See what I mean? She took the whole thing upon herself.'

I say, 'I told Vivie Iris wasn't alone but she glared at me through the cow parsley and said, "She IS," and then she said, "I mean she's with people she doesn't know," and that's when I said, "We could go and see her, if you like. We could go by ourselves."

'I said, "We could write to her and say we want to come and see her and ask where's a good place to meet her."

'And so Vivie wrote that letter to Iris and I spent most of the night with an old *A to Z* of yours, working out how to get across London. By three o'clock in the morning I'd made a list of all the stations and streets between Liverpool Street and Paradise Park.'

The waitress comes and asks us if we want anything else. Dad asks for a jug of water and I look at my watch; it's two o'clock.

I say, 'Dad, we really should get going.'

He says, 'Not until you've finished, and that's an order.'

I smile at Dad and I feel a sense of release, as if a tight band round my chest has been eased. And I am relieved that he thinks none of what I am telling him foolish. I realise I am filled with love for him. I look at him and I hope he knows how I feel.

I say, 'Vivie read me Iris's letter on our way through the Forest. Iris said she was waiting for the people who minded her to find her mind. She said she would wait for us underneath a big oak tree and she said its branches were full of people. She said they'd all like to see us. She said you could see the oak tree from the road, and she said Vivie would be able to walk through the railings, if she turned sideways. She signed the letter "Iris R" and there were looped lines under her name.

'We both behaved as if the things Iris said in the letter weren't odd.'

Dad says, 'There were many more letters. We kept them from Vivie.'

I say, 'What did they say?'

Dad says, 'We never opened them.'

I say, 'Have you still got them?' Dad shakes his head and says, 'When I finally faced the task of clearing out your mother's desk I found them and, when I judged it a good time, I gave them back to Iris.'

He says, 'She was grateful we'd kept them from Vivie.'

He says, 'She made a bonfire and burned the lot.'

Vivie's story

Vivie heard the metallic clack of Charles's shoes on the pavement. His brisk walk used to fill her with pleasure, but now it filled her with dread. She didn't know what to expect, even from dependable, reliable Charles.

She jumped up from his bed and, as she pulled on a skirt, she heard his voice in the street and, half-dressed, she peered out from behind the cupboard door. She saw him talking to the man in the pale linen suit. The man ground his cigarette into the pavement and Vivie's heart missed a beat as she watched Charles give the man some money which the man counted. Then the man turned and walked away down the street.

Vivie flung on a shirt, tried to brush her hair but it was too tangled to brush quickly, ran downstairs and sat at the kitchen table. She opened a magazine, leapt up again to fill the kettle, took a dirty mug from the sink and put it on the table, sat back down and hoped Charles would think she'd been up and dressed all morning.

She heard his key in the lock. She stood up. Charles walked towards her and Vivie asked him if he'd like a cup of coffee. He didn't answer her, so she asked, because she could not stop herself, 'Who was that man, Charles?'

'What man?'

'The man you've just … paid. I saw you.' Her voice shook. 'The man who's been watching this house, watching me. Who is he?'

'I – he's – '

Vivie waited, her heart hammering in her chest.

'I decided to find out exactly what you were up to,' said Charles.

He sat down at the kitchen table. He seemed smaller, less substantial than Vivie had ever thought him. She sat down too.

She was breathless with shock.

'You mean – ?'

' – I mean I paid him to follow you. And now I know all I need to know.'

Vivie forced herself to breathe. Her whole world was disintegrating. She felt the sweat on her temples and she knew her hands were shaking. She made herself ask a normal question, a question that would not betray on the outside the turmoil she felt on the inside. She said, 'What has he told you?'

'That you've been going to St George's. Maternity wing.'

'That's where I went to have – '

' – and that you've been with Matthew – most significant time at the Prom. Monday.'

Vivie registered that Charles's blue eyes were filled with hatred.

'Oh, and by the way,' he said, 'I lied. It wasn't me who saw you. I was still in Harrogate.'

He said this as if he was admitting to something that didn't matter at all. Vivie was speechless. Charles stood up and began to pace about the kitchen; the metal toecaps on his shoes clacking on the floor.

'I know you're having an affair with Matthew, Vivienne, and the child, obviously, is his.'

Vivie stared at the magazine on the table. She saw a smiling woman standing beside fridges and washing machines. She read the words in the advertisement, trying with all her might to hang on to something, anything, normal. But the words read, 'Your world will be trouble-free when you buy Zanussi'. So, even advertisements were mad.

Vivie realised she hadn't heard what Charles had just said. Now he was saying, 'Do you think I never noticed how awkward Matthew was when you asked him to give you away? Do you think I never wondered why he refused? But, stupidly, I let you convince me. You kept saying you loved the way I made you feel. You said I made you feel safe and anchored and not afraid of your mother. You said you would love that to your dying day. But you never said you loved *me* and now, Vivienne, I don't think you've ever loved me. You were always thinking about him. When you started coming home late and stopped listening to me and we stopped making love, except very occasionally when you felt guilty, I had to know what was going on.'

When Vivie looked up she saw that he was leaning over the sink. She wondered, distractedly, if he was going to be sick, but she didn't get up, or speak. She felt as if she might break open at any moment.

'You began to behave as if I were just some old doorstop. Some old rock who kept the bloody door open so that you could come and go whenever you liked. You've stopped needing me, Vivienne,' he said. 'Haven't you?'

Charles faced the kitchen window. Vivie saw his shoulders lift and she managed to say, 'You've got it all wrong, Charles,' but the words sounded stilted, as if she didn't mean them.

Charles made no sign that he'd heard her, and Vivie didn't attempt to say anything else because she was terrified that some terrible madness would spill from her if she said one more word.

Iris's story

The last time I saw Kit was in London, but we never spoke. For one bleak week I watched for him; one bleak week in which my already anguished heart broke and my fragile world disintegrated utterly.

★ ★ ★

Every night for seven nights I stood under the plane tree opposite the blue door to Kit's flat, opposite the Troubadour. I watched and waited and hoped I'd see him.

There was a cherry tree whose branches were heavy with cotton-wool clumps of blossom on the corner where the Old Brompton Road meets the Earls Court Road, but the wind was a cold, vicious wind. It tore through the blossom clumps and ripped them apart so that hundreds of fragile white petals swirled in flurries across the street towards me, like snow, and the wind cut through me. I had to wrap myself in the grey blankets from my hotel bed, for my nightly vigil.

I never once went into the Troubadour. Nor did I ring Kit's doorbell. I wanted him to see me and change his mind. I wanted him to see me and love me. And then I saw him with a dark-haired woman in the Troubadour. They sat at our table, the table in the window, the table behind the rows of coloured coffee pots on their narrow wooden shelves.

I saw Kit stretch his hand across the table and take her hand.

I saw him push their red enamel coffee mugs out of the way.

I saw his lips move and I heard his voice in my head. It said, 'Go on. Tell me. I want to know what happens next.'

And I ran out from under my plane tree. I tripped over my blankets and tears streamed down my face. The only thing in my head was to get across the road and shake Kit. Make him see me.

Ask him what the hell had happened. Tear him away from her. Make him be mine. Not hers. Make him come home.

But I ran straight into John Dexter who stood in front of the studded wooden door, the Troubadour's wooden door. I heard a rattle, something on the pavement. I looked down, saw John Dexter's pipe spin round on its bowl. I must have knocked it from his hand. He put his arms round me. I collapsed into them and sobbed.

We bent, awkwardly, together, so that he could pick up his pipe. I said I was sorry.

'I am also sorry,' he said, 'about this.' And he inclined his head towards Kit who talked, gesticulated, his hair red and springy, his back to us, oblivious. 'But it was bound to happen, old girl,' said John Dexter. 'It is in the nature of the beast.'

'How the hell do you know?' I said, determined, once more, to get to Kit. I tried to push past John Dexter.

'I think it would be wiser not to,' he said.

I stared at him. He held my arms. His grip was firm.

'He does not love you. He does not love anyone ... enough. You deserve better. He will only humiliate you.'

I remembered the ticket girl as she left the Troubadour the night I met Kit. He never once looked up at her, he just kept hold of my hand when she left. I remembered myself, at home without Kit. I felt sorry for the ticket girl and sorry for me and I collapsed against John Dexter.

'Anyway where have you been?' I said, and I sniffed against his tweed jacket. 'I thought you said you were my friend.'

'I could ask the same of you,' he said. 'I have attended countless poetry readings at which you have not been. You no longer live where you used to live. You no longer work where you used to work. Where else should I have found you?'

His voice comforted me, calmed me, and his hug made me realise how much I longed to be hugged.

'His poem said he was no one's and no one was his,' I sobbed into John Dexter's shoulder. 'But I thought it would be different with me.'

Speaking of Love

'The perennial mistake of the species,' said John Dexter and he pulled away, knocked out his pipe against the wall and began to refill it. When it was lit he held it up under the street light, examined the bowl and said, 'No damage done.'

'I'm glad,' I said, and we turned and walked along the Old Brompton Road. He had his arm round my shoulders, I held up my blanket-skirts so that I would not trip.

'You may think it precipitate of me to say so,' said John Dexter, and he looked at me, his pipe between his teeth, 'but the heart does mend.'

I looked up at his dark eyes, his crooked smile, his snaggle tooth. 'I feel better already,' I said. 'I was just about to make a fool of myself. I'm glad you stopped me.'

'I am glad we met tonight,' said John Dexter. 'Because I think otherwise we might never have met again. I leave London in a few days' time. A new job.'

I slept that night in my bed in the miserable little room in Earls Court where dust-laden cobwebs drooped from the dirty cornice that disappeared through the partition wall into the next room. My vigil was over, and the next morning I was at Liverpool Street station before the first train left.

I stared through the sleet that slithered down the train window, and I listened to the train's clickety-clock, clickety-clock. I heard my mother's voice sing me a lullaby, in French, and I heard Vivie's voice tell me not to worry. She told me she liked it when we were all by ourselves. I heard John Dexter's voice say that I had made the perennial mistake of the species. And I heard Kit's voice perform his fish poem.

When I got home the laurel hedge had been cut back. It made the east side of my garden much lighter, less overhung, and when the clouds cleared away and a warm April sun shone it made the raindrops glisten on the yellow-flecked laurel leaves, on the pale green lambs' tails of my almost-flowering laburnum, on the green of my lavender bushes, on the grass. And I saw the iron gate that had been hidden by the laurel for years. It shone with a coat of fresh black paint.

Iris's story

Joan brought me endless cups of tea.

Matthew was disappointed that he might never see Kit again, and Vivie brought me spring flowers, buttercups mostly, which she arranged in the glass Kit had used for his beloved Amaretto. I didn't know what to say to her. I didn't know what to say to anyone.

I tried hard to concentrate on Mrs Villaine's hat. I sat outside. But the leaves on the beech hedge distracted me. They were such an expectant, luminous green that it hurt to look at them.

I went inside.

I heard a cuckoo. The first cuckoo of spring.

I drank a glass of water.

I told myself I must finish the hats for the wedding.

I heard a cough.

I looked though the kitchen window.

And then I saw him. He leaned on the newly painted gate in the middle of the newly cut-back laurel hedge. He smiled, straight at me.

I flew through the kitchen door, flew to the gate.

'Good morning, Iris,' he said. 'And what a very auspicious, bright spring morning it has turned out to be.'

I couldn't believe my eyes. John Dexter. Here.

He held out a letter. 'This was delivered to me, by mistake, this morning and I thought,' he looked down at the letter, 'I thought I should deliver it in person. Make sure it really was you.'

I smiled back at his crooked, snaggle-toothed smile. I was ecstatic. I hugged him over the gate and as he disentangled himself he said, 'My new job, by the way, is that of schoolmaster.' He inclined his head backwards towards the Old School House behind the laurel hedge. He held out the letter, his forearms rested on the top of the newly-painted black gate. He'd rolled back the sleeves of his viyella shirt.

I took the letter, looked at it, saw my father's handwriting, felt my heart somersault. Put the letter in the pocket of my dress. Took a deep breath. I hadn't written to my father for at least a year, so it surely wasn't a letter of mine, returned, unopened.

'I didn't know the school was re-opening,' I said. 'I thought there were plans for a village hall.'

John Dexter shrugged. 'Plans change,' he said. 'And then they change again. At least that is what I have always found.'

He pushed the gate a little way towards me.

'May I ... ?' he said.

'I'm sorry, of course,' I said. 'How rude of me. Would you like a cup of tea?'

We sat in the sunshine and talked. John Dexter pulled his leather tobacco pouch from the pocket of his tweed jacket and filled the bowl of his pipe.

I breathed in the sweet smell of his tobacco.

I fetched Mrs Villaine's hat and worked on it while we talked but the net behaved disobediently. It wanted to be sewn onto another hat, only I didn't know which other hat.

'Fumble fingers, fumble fingers,' hissed a voice in my ear.

I looked at John Dexter. He smiled at me so I didn't ask him if he'd heard the whisper. I didn't want him to say he hadn't heard it. I didn't want to appear stupid in front of him.

'I like people who are good with their hands,' he said. 'And you are very good with your hands, Iris Marchwood,' he said, his pipe held between his teeth, his snaggle tooth obvious. 'Very good indeed.'

But it seemed to me that my hands were clumsy. They dropped Mrs Villaine's hat.

John Dexter picked it up and handed it back to me.

I blushed.

Joan came through the beech hedge. She held two mugs of tea.

I introduced her to John Dexter and Joan put the tea down very carefully on the kitchen window-sill, so that it wouldn't spill.

She looked at John Dexter and then she left. She forgot to drink her own tea and she didn't talk to him, which wasn't like her at all. In fact it was quite rude. But I realised she was as bowled over by his old-fashioned good looks as I was.

John Dexter leaned close to me. I handed him the cup of tea that Joan had brought.

Iris's story

'I would love to hear your latest story,' he said. 'Will you tell it me?'

I pricked myself with the needle.

'I've had trouble with my stories lately,' I said, in a whisper. 'I seem to have lost them, somehow. I don't know why. Don't know what's happened. But they seem to have leaked from my head.'

I felt a lump grow in my throat. I looked away.

John Dexter took Mrs Villaine's hat from my hands and put it down on the flagstones by my feet. Then he took my hands in his and I felt my fingers tingle.

'Let me help you remember,' he said. 'Let me give you a hand. Let me be your storyhand, Iris Marchwood.'

I couldn't look at him. And I knew I should tell him that my name wasn't legally Iris Marchwood. That Kit and I had never married. That I'd just taken his name. So I tried to explain.

'Iris,' he said. 'Names cannot be "taken".' He put his finger under my chin and lifted it. 'But,' he said, 'it would be a great privilege to help you with your stories. You will allow me, won't you?'

My fingers tingled so much that they hurt. I cried and I smiled and I nodded. 'Sorry about the tears,' I said, and I looked into his dark eyes. He patted my hands.

'Everything will be fine,' he said. 'Just fine. You'll see.'

In the middle of the night I was wide awake and I felt strong, so I came down to finish the hats.

I started with the yellow net but it wouldn't obey. I danced round the kitchen table with Mrs Villaine's hat on my head when I remembered that John Dexter had moved in next door. The tip of my sewing finger tingled. I sat down, looked at the hat, tried to make the netting sit the way it should.

But I couldn't pin it down.

It danced out of my hands.

It really did want to be on a different hat.

I went outside into the garden and I held the yellow hat high.

I saw the gate in the laurel hedge. Its new black paint shone in the moonlight and I heard John Dexter's voice again. I heard him say that he would be my storyhand. And I felt so relieved, so much better. I was filled with an aching desire to see him.

Perhaps he wouldn't mind if we made a start on the stories straight away.

I opened the gate.

And then, suddenly, Joan was in front of me. She smiled. She said she had come to take me back inside. Did I realise I was outside? Well of course I did. That's where my next-door neighbour lived.

She hugged me.

Obviously she could see how happy I was.

Matthew's story

We order a third pot of coffee and the waitress says, 'It's all right. You don't have to keep ordering things to stay. We've only just opened and not many people know about us yet.'

So we drink water and I take our chairs out of the sun and put them down under the lime at the far end of the courtyard. The waitress brings cushions for Dad and a low slatted wooden table for our water jug and glasses, and even though it is getting later and later Dad insists that we're not going to leave until he's heard the whole story.

He says, 'You've kept all this bottled up for far too long. So tell me.'

I say, 'You know it all, Dad.'

He says, 'Not in your words, I don't. Not from the horse's mouth.'

I stare at his battered straw hat on the table beside the water jug and say, 'The jam jar full of change weighed my satchel down, and I was sure Mum would notice its bulk, but she didn't.'

Dad laughs and says, 'She did, but she didn't know it was money you'd taken, she thought it was food.'

I say, 'When we got far enough away along the road through the Forest, we changed into the clothes we'd hidden under the bracken the day before. And we recited the names of the stations to each other as we walked. There were only a few of them, but we felt so sophisticated knowing their names.'

I say, 'I thought of everything. I faked the notes from Mum to our schools. I saved – and stole – the right amount of money. I knew how long it would take. We left the empty jam jar with our school uniforms under the bracken, and it wasn't until the man in the ticket office at Brandon asked us where our parents were that

I realised how odd we must look: two children on their own, with money in silver coins for their fares.

'But Vivie, quick as ever, said, "We're going to see our mother. She's in hospital in London. That's what these are for. Dad's working." She held up the dog roses she'd picked on the way and the train pulled in and the people in the queue behind us became impatient – it was rush hour – and Vivie said, "She's expecting us," and he gave us our tickets. If it hadn't been rush-hour I think he would have stopped us.'

I say, 'There were so many people on the platform, all wearing shades of black or grey or blue and not one of them paid any attention to us. We stood all the way, between carriages, and we watched the fields rushing past and I wondered if we'd find our way across London but Vivie wasn't worried, she just held onto her flowers and chattered all the way. She was so happy, so like the self she had been before Iris broke down, and she believed unquestioningly in me and my plan and I felt better than I'd felt for a long time. It was working, everything was going to be all right again, I just knew it was.

'At Liverpool Street I held onto Vivie's hand as if I was saving her from drowning and I jumped to see over people's shoulders. Vivie tried to see round the people, and then she asked a man who was hurrying along beside us if this was the right way to the underground. He didn't answer, no one paid any attention to us, it was extraordinary, so we half-ran, half-walked inside the pushing crowd of people. We just went where they went. My hair stuck to my head in the heat, and the underground was so full that people could have licked the sweat off each other's faces, but each person behaved as if they were the only person in the carriage. It was stiflingly hot and the damp patches under people's arms were exactly my head height and they smelled, and they all seemed to be blue.

'Vivie kept her nose in her flowers and her arm round her mother's book of fairy tales. She said Iris had been carrying them round with her all the time before she was taken away to Salem, so she'd brought them for her. When the train stopped we were expelled from the carriage in a tidal wave of humanity. Vivie saw the sign for the Northern Line but there were so many people moving towards it that we were carried along with them anyway. Vivie said, "So this is the rush-hour," and started imitating the way people were walking fast, not quite running, holding her arms stiffly by her sides and making a serious face. I told her to stop because I didn't want her to draw attention to us, but still no one paid any attention to us, they just hurried on.'

Dad says, 'That's Londoners for you.'

I say, 'But by the time we got to London Bridge and found the train to Paradise Park all the people had disappeared. No one was going the way we were going by then, and I was relieved. We'd done it. My plan had worked and we were very nearly there; Vivie would soon see Iris and we would bring her home and everything would be all right.

'The road was lined with flowering chestnuts, some pink and some white, but no yellow buckeyes like yours, and it was the kind of hot day when all you want to do is be very still, but we were in a hurry. We had to get all the way back home and catch the school bus. It never occurred to me to think how we would persuade the driver to take Iris on the school bus. I'd worked out that we could spend two hours with her and that would give her time to collect her things and leave with us. And it never occurred to me that the schools would ring you. I thought I'd faked Mum's writing so well.'

I say, 'Vivie saw the sign first. She said, "We're here. This is the road it's on," and she hugged me and told me I was completely brilliant and the best friend she'd ever had in all the world, and we walked up Painswick Gardens and we didn't see a single person. There was just one green, wheezing bus and apart from that the silence made our footsteps seem very loud. There was a park on our right, all overgrown with stinging nettles and fallen branches and there were beeches and ashes and I wondered if that was the park Iris meant, but there wasn't an oak.'

I say, 'There were red brick houses on the other side of the road with neatly mown lawns and from our side of the road you could only see the top halves of the houses, their rooves and their chimneys and their upstairs windows, because the lawns sloped steeply down to the houses and their lower floors were hidden. I thought how I'd hate to live somewhere where there was no light downstairs.'

Dad says, 'A budding architect, even then.'

I drink another glass of water and then I say, 'There were black railings with arrowhead finials on our side of the road which I thought looked like spears, and then we came to a pair of tall, black, wrought iron gates with the word "Salem" worked in iron in the middle of each gate and Vivie said she was going in. I said I thought we should wait until we found the oak tree, but Vivie said that the railings were too close together and she'd never squeeze through them, even sideways. She said Iris must have forgotten what size she was. So we ran on, with the railings between us, and I remember there was grass on her side and pavement on mine, and I remember her hair streaming out behind her and wisps of it sticking to her forehead in the heat as she pounded along on the grass.

'We passed several large red brick buildings set back on Vivie's side of the railings, and a car park, and then we were running along the edge of a park, just as Iris had said in her letter. We'd agreed I would say hello to Iris after Vivie had had some time with her by herself. Then I would tell Iris we'd come to take her home, but first Vivie wanted to tell her mother a story she'd been practising especially for her, she wouldn't tell me what it was.

We both saw the oak tree and Iris sitting under it at the same time. We knew it was Iris because she waved at us. Vivie waved back and called out to her mother and there was a woman in a pale blue uniform, a nurse I supposed, with Iris. Vivie ran towards them and away from me, calling out while I tried to catch my breath by the railings. My lips tasted of salt and I was standing under a copper beech, I remember, while Vivie ran with her arms stretched out, the heavy book in one hand and the heads of her dog roses bouncing from the other. She called out "Mummy, it's me!" as she ran, but Iris didn't get up or run towards her and when Vivie reached the oak tree she flopped down beside Iris.

'I realised I was very thirsty as I squinted through the leaves into the bright garden.

'I had to screw up my eyelids against the sun, but I saw Iris standing up, and then I saw her fling Vivie's dog roses to the ground. I saw Vivie back away and I heard a harsh sound, like a rook or a crow, and I saw Iris stagger slightly. I saw the nurse catch hold of Iris's arms from behind and I saw Vivie stretching out her arms towards her mother. I saw the book fall from Vivie's hand and I saw Iris kicking out and struggling against the nurse and I kept hearing the rook, or the crow. I was suddenly very cold in all that heat.'

I say, 'I saw Vivie stumble and back away from her mother. I saw Iris's mouth, wide open, and I saw Vivie turn and run. I saw her hair flying out behind her and her shadow flying diagonally in front of her. I saw Vivie's eyes, wide open and terrified. When she reached me she clung to the arrowhead finials, panting.

'She said, "She doesn't know who I am, Matthew. I said it was me and she just ... she just sort of shouted and stared at me. She doesn't know who I am, Matthew. She didn't recognise me. She didn't even call me Lily."'

I say, 'I remember Vivie's knuckles were white and her arms were rigid and she was hanging on to the railings as if they were some kind of life belt and I saw the nurse, behind her, holding onto Iris's bent body. One of Iris's arms hung down and swung backwards and forwards like a gorilla's.'

I stop, pour some more water and Dad puts his hand on my arm. I feel the papery texture of his skin and stare at the liver spots. He says, 'Go on. Keep right on going until you reach the end.'

I take a deep breath and say, 'And Vivie said, "She threw my flowers away, Matthew," and I didn't know what to say to her and then she started to cry and we walked away on either side of the arrowhead finials. When she came through the tall Salem gates I put my arm round her and all the way home she kept saying, "Don't lose me, Matthew. Don't lose me."'

I say, 'The journey home was awful. Vivie panicked on the underground and we had to get off and I didn't know how to find our way back to Liverpool Street by bus, so by the time we caught the train we were both exhausted and Vivie just sat and stared through the window and wouldn't talk. And I knew we'd missed the school bus and I couldn't think what I was going to say to you to explain where we'd been. And Vivie's silence was terrible. She'd stopped crying but she didn't say a word, she just sat with her arms folded in front of her and she didn't move until I had to go to the lavatory and even then she wouldn't let me go unless she came too, right into the lavatory.'

I look up and say, 'And you know the rest. She's never spoken about it since and I've never forgiven myself.'

Dad says, 'I know.'

I say, 'I was responsible for Vivie seeing her mother when she was out of her mind.'

Dad says, 'Iris was out of her mind before she was admitted to Salem. Vivie saw all that, too.'

I say, 'I know. But what we did that day was supposed to help. To make things better. Iris was supposed to be getting well. And Vivie just wanted to comfort her. She didn't want Iris to be alone.' I look at Dad. 'I still dream about it, sometimes,' I say.

Dad says, 'Tell me.'

I look at him, drink some more water and say, 'That's enough for now, Dad.'

A bee buzzes among the Bantry Bay roses beside the wooden table on the other side of the courtyard and a church bell begins to ring. Of course, it's Saturday, someone must be getting married.

Dad says, 'How often do you dream about it?'

I shake my head, I feel tired and although I sense that Dad is looking at me I don't look back at him.

I feel Dad's hand on my back and I say, 'Often enough.'

He says, 'Tell me,' again and so, still not looking at him but staring down at the stone flags, and despite my tiredness, I begin to tell him. I say, 'There are several dreams, but in the most persistent one Vivie cries, even though she didn't on our way home that day. We are the only children on a train, all the other seats are taken by adults, but for some reason I am in charge and when the ticket collector arrives I try to avoid his eyes, but he keeps staring at me and he says, in a nasal voice, that the track will divide soon and I must tell the driver which way to go before it does. This is my responsibility and I know, the way you do in dreams, that it is urgent. I know that no one else can tell the driver which track to take. But I also know that I don't know how to find out which track the train should take. Vivie seems to sense all this and she kicks me in the shins when I stand up, and glares at me for being so hopelessly ignorant.

'The train sways and rattles over the tracks and Vivie says, "The driver needs to know. Why don't you go and tell him?" And I know that I must go and tell the driver and that it is urgent. But I also know that I don't know what to tell him. Vivie crosses her arms and thumps them down against her body and turns her back on me and then I see the water. She says, without turning round, "I should never ever have trusted you," and she bangs her forehead against the window. She says, "I hate you," and the water spills over the crook of her elbow and splashes onto the floor and I realise that the water is her tears. It slides over the wooden window-sill and down the wall underneath the window. It starts to swirl around our feet and it begins to rise and I know it will flood the train. I also know that if I don't hurry the water will make it impossible for me to get to the driver, and then I know what it is that I must tell the driver. I must tell him that one of the tracks is flooded, so I wade towards the door but when I open it a wall of water looms above me, and somehow I know that other people are crying in carriages further up the train, other people are making the water that's looming above me. And then the water crashes down but, miraculously, it divides around me and doesn't push me under, but I know I must hurry before a tidal wave of tears drowns us all. I see the ticket collector, out of the corner of my eye, crouched high up in the luggage rack.

'I take a deep breath and plunge forwards and I swim against the water and it isn't difficult, and even though the water is rushing against me I manage to swim along the corridors, past the doors of all the carriages towards the front of the train. The doors between the carriages open for me all by themselves, but the adults just sit still in their seats in their carriages while I swim past them and the water rises up under their chins. Sometimes the water surges against me and goes up my nostrils but sometimes it swirls past me and changes direction and helps me, pushing me on, and all the time I hear the ticket collector's nasal voice in my head, telling me to tell the driver which way to go, which track to take, before the track divides.

'When I am completely exhausted a woman's yellow hat floats towards me down the corridor and I know this is the last corridor before I will reach the driver. The hat turns on an eddy in front of me and I recognise it, but I can't remember why, then it bobs along beside me, and I know that I must save the hat from drowning. I catch hold of it when the last carriage door opens and my ears pop and suddenly there is no sound and no resistance. The door closes behind me and there is no more water. I am swimming through thin air and when I realise this I land with a thud on the floor behind the driver, the way people do in cartoons when they realise they've just jumped off a cliff.

'I have arrived and I am quite dry and the driver signals frantically with his arm and I try to catch my breath, try to tell the back of his head that I know there is a flood up ahead. But I still don't know which is the flooded track and which is the one we should take so I stand behind the driver and I see the rails racing towards us, racing underneath us, and then, very slowly, the driver turns to look at me and his face is Mum's. I can't hear the words that come out of her mouth but I realise that I know them by heart. I watch her lips move and I know she is saying, "I want you to tell me everything you know, Matthew Aldwater. I want you to tell me everything you know."

'I shout, "I don't know which track! I don't know which track!" and I hold up the yellow hat which drips drops of water onto the grey carpet of the driver's compartment and my mother takes off her driver's peaked cap and holds it under the yellow hat to catch the drops of water, and then I realise that she is facing the wrong way, that she can't see the track, and I try to turn her round but she is immovable and there is a terrible roaring rattling sound and I see, under her arm, that the train is ploughing through trees, breaking branches and grazing tree trunks but the driver, my mother, is oblivious. And then, in all the noise and wild rocking of the driver's compartment, I remember that I've left Vivie all by herself in the rising water, miles away down the train, all on her own.

'I always wake up from the dream with the effort of trying to make my feet move, the effort of trying to turn round to get back to Vivie before she drowns in all that water. Because I know I must save her before we all die in the train that no one is driving any more.'

Iris's story

I had to shut Lily up. I shouted at her because John Dexter was on the radio. But she shouted back, 'I need help with my homework.' And she said her name wasn't her name.

But John Dexter said, on the radio, that he knew how to catch stories and I must listen because then I'd find my stories again. So I took the radio up to my room and tied my purple silk scarf round him. Radiohim. I tied the ends under his radiochin. Purple for royalty. My hands and my fingers tingled.

Joan took me to the doctor because I told her I couldn't feel my hands. I knew I shouldn't have told her.

'Fumble fingers, fumble fingers,' hissed a voice.

'There really is no need for a doctor,' said John Dexter.

But when I turned round to ask him why he wasn't there.

I told the doctor my hats behaved in a difficult way and I had lost all my stories. He gave me some pills. In rows. Little silver coffins on a silver sheet.

Joan said I should swallow one, but I couldn't swallow.

Swallows fly.

John Dexter leaned against my laburnum tree.

I thought he'd gone. Thought I'd lost him. I was so glad he hadn't gone. I ran towards him. He stood in the golden sun-shine.

'Set the dead free,' he said and looked at my hands. They held the pills in their silver coffin rows.

John Dexter freed the pills, pressed them out of their silver coffins, one by one, and they fell down onto the grass all round the laburnum tree.

John Dexter said the pills would take my wings. He knew about swallows.

And we laughed.

Laughed.

Laughed.

And I cried and told him that my fingers tingled.

'Fumble fingers.'

John Dexter didn't say that, he said. But I think he did. Behind his beautiful hand.

And he said, 'Iris, be wary of doctors. Be very wary. Things are safe. People are not. Walls will keep you safe. People will not.'

I wanted to say that he was a person. That I was a person. But I couldn't seem to find the words.

Matthew's story

The waitress brings us egg and watercress sandwiches and I realise how hungry I am; the mayonnaise is lemony, the bread is crumbly brown soda bread and the egg and watercress mixture is delicious. We have a sorrel and tomato salad too: Dad saw the sorrel growing in pots by the courtyard wall and asked for it.

I say, 'This is the best lunch I've ever had.'

The waitress looks slightly surprised but she says, 'Thank you,' and, 'Tell everyone you know about us, won't you.' I say we will. I don't say that neither of us lives anywhere near Malmesbury.

Dad thanks her, and when she's gone I say, 'That's it, Dad, that's all there is to tell.' I am exhausted.

Dad says, 'Why is it that we humans don't talk about the things that mean the most to us?' He picks up his sandwich. 'We English humans, I mean,' but he is smiling broadly. 'We English male humans in particular.'

I spear some sorrel with my fork; Dad takes a bite of his sandwich and I say, 'Because we don't want to admit that we don't know what we're doing, don't know where we're going.' Dad looks at me over the rims of his half-glasses and I say, 'Because we don't want to risk saying what we really want, what we really feel, in case ... in case.'

Dad says, 'But all this not saying makes everything worse ... because we never discover what happens next,' he laughs, 'as Iris might say.'

He puts down his sandwich and picks up his battered straw hat and turns it round in his hands.

He says, 'The real risk, it seems to me, lies in not talking about the things that matter the most. That's what made Iris ill. What we don't say doesn't go away. It stays inside and after a while of not being spoken about it turns against us.' He puts his hat back on his head. 'That's how it gets its revenge. The things we don't talk about fester and then they infect us. They eat away at us, like a cancer.'

The waitress brings out a fresh jug of cold water and two clean, cold glasses. Dad pours the water and we both drink and when we put the glasses down, drops of water slide down the sides from the marks our fingers have made in the condensation. We finish the salad and our sandwiches and I know Dad is waiting, as patiently as he has all day, to see if there is anything else I want to say.

I say, 'Then I must've just talked myself into remission. Thank you.' And then I say, very softly, 'Dad, you do know I love you, don't you?'

Iris's story

John Dexter was in the kitchen. He held out the letter and I saw the rise and fall of the heart inside the blue envelope. The heart under my name.

And then he came. My father. He came here. And he brought his silence with him. I wanted to say things. I wanted to break his silence. But all my words flew away in the face of his silence. In the face of the wall of his newspaper.

Vivie wanted to tell him a story. I said that stories were forbidden. I tried to explain when she asked, but I couldn't remember why stories were forbidden and then I heard a sound, stone on stone, and I saw John Dexter. He knocked his pipe out on the iron gate and I thought perhaps he would be able to tell Vivie why stories were forbidden. But he was not interested. He did not want to talk about stories.

He said I should wear my white protecting veil.

He said white gloves were good for hands that tingled. White satin ribbons tied round my wrists. He said I knew where the white things were. He said I should hide my hands. He said they were ugly, clumsy hands.

I asked him what he'd done with my stories. 'Where have they gone?' I asked him.

But he just stared over my shoulder.

'A little strong, I should say,' he said. 'A little more than she deserves, despite the marks she bears, despite all the classic signs.'

He shouted at me. '*Look*, Iris.'

And I ran back. I fought my father with my clumsy hands that could not feel a thing. I felt a paralysing pain in my heart. And then everything inside me burst out of me and fell to the ground in a terrible tangle.

Matthew's story

As we drive out of Malmesbury the church bell strikes four and Dad says, 'There's one last piece of darning I'd like to do, just for the symmetry of the thing. Then we'll join the M4, otherwise we shall miss supper.'

I say, 'But you said you'd never travel on a motorway again, as long as you lived.'

He says, 'Time to get back on the horse, Matthew, don't you think? Probably should have done it years ago ... and anyway I'm looking forward to a good supper. Iris says the local pub serves wonderful food.'

So we cross the M4 on the road to Pucklechurch and Dad makes a spidery tick on his map, and then he folds it slowly and with difficulty, and looks at me. He pats the map on his knee and says, 'But it was worth it, wasn't it? All that darning? All the time it took?'

I say, 'It was, Dad, yes it was. Well worth it,' and as we turn west into the sun and drive along beside the motorway heading for the next junction, we both know we don't mean the roads and I have a sudden memory of him teaching Vivie and me to climb trees. He always went first to tie a white handkerchief at the highest point, and then it was our turn. He was a good teacher, but neither of us was ever able to reach the handkerchief, although Vivie always got closer than I did.

I tell him this and he laughs. 'Couldn't do that these days,' he says. 'Incredible to think I did, so often, then.'

We see the new Severn Bridge from a mile or so away, and the angle of the sun's rays to the steel cables makes the great triangular shapes they form shimmer, pale green, floating without apparent support, like pairs of gigantic sails against the sky.

They take my breath away.

Vivie's story

Vivie had walked, unsteadily, along Prince of Wales Drive until she stood outside the block where Robert lived. But Charles told her, through the intercom, that he had no desire to hear what she had to say.

She had shouted up at the window that he'd got it all wrong, that she wasn't having an affair with anyone, let alone with Matthew, and that she wasn't having *anybody's* baby. But when several other people leaned over their balconies and stared, and when, at last, Charles leaned over Robert's balcony and told her she was drunk and should be ashamed of herself, her vodka-fuelled courage deserted her and she turned away, fumbled for her cigarettes and began to walk unsteadily home.

Vivie breathed in the smell of new-mown grass as she waited at the traffic lights beside Battersea Park, and suddenly she found herself in tears because the smell of new-mown grass belonged with good things, belonged with times of hope and new beginnings, times of happiness and long-forgotten times when her mother had been well, before childhood had become a time she only wanted to forget. A spiteful judgement ruled that Vivie had never deserved a good childhood and that she knew why.

Vivie ran across the road, ran to get away from the smell of new-mown grass, ran with her head down, ran straight into a lamppost. When she stopped swearing she realised she was in Cambridge Road not Prince of Wales Drive. When she focused properly she realised, with a shock, that she was outside Matthew's house.

She stood and stared at his house and lit another cigarette. She'd only ever been inside Matthew's house once, when he had a house-warming party, but she'd never forgotten it. He'd built it. It wasn't like any other house in the street.

Vivie inhaled deeply and thought that although Charles had

got all the reasons wrong, he was right. She *had* been unfaithful to him. Not loving him, even if she didn't love anyone else, was being unfaithful to him. It was a terrible thing, worse than he would ever know, not to want his child and to have got so close to telling Matthew all about it when it had absolutely nothing to do with him.

Iris's story

I am to be tested.

All the great ones, the prophets, the seers, the men, the women, the milliners and the martyrs. They have all been tested through the ages.

'To fend for yourself is a test,' John Dexter said, but he refused the cabbage I held out to him. He said it smelled. My clumsy hands dropped it.

Vivie fed me. She was my angel but John Dexter said be careful, be vigilant, watch her because she would poison the food one day.

'And remember,' he said, 'her name is Lily. Lily is a species of Iris. Why is it that you refuse to remember that?'

He said she had the marks on her face, all the classic marks.

I wore white in the garden, white wrapped round me, my protecting veil, because John Dexter said my time to be tested had come. My time to eat from the tree of knowledge. My time to tell good from evil. The smoke from his pipe was blue and the fruit from the tree was delicious. And we danced together.

'If I Loved You,' he sang to me, into my ear.

And I felt more alive than I have ever, ever felt. And all the words flooded back. 'If I loved you, Words wouldn't come in an easy way, Round in circles I'd go.' It was music to dance to, music to sing to. Beautiful music.

I breathed in the perfumed brilliantine in his hair.

And then I wore yellow because it was the colour of life.

And then I was not alive. Then I was filled with something that wanted to drown me from the inside. It was difficult to think and difficult to speak, difficult not to dribble, difficult to be me with John Dexter, who was my only friend.

He was in the big oak tree. He'd had branch meetings, he said, and he smoked his pipe. He smiled down at me as I sat beneath him, his legs dangled above me. He began to speak to me and I knew it was important but then he was very angry, because he had been interrupted. He said, 'Look at the marks on her face, Iris. Look carefully at the species of Lily, the marks of the betrayer. Refuse to talk to her. And do not accept what she brings for she brings poison.'

But when I watched her run away her red hair flew and there was an ache in the very middle of me and I had to hit myself where it ached to stop the pain. I had made a mistake. I heard a terrible croak, a howl, and I wanted to tell John Dexter that I had done a wrong thing. I wanted to say she didn't look like a betrayer or a poisoner. But I could not find the words and I was afraid to tell him he was wrong because he was my only friend and if I told him he was wrong I might lose him and then I'd have lost everything. And everyone.

He laughed, a terrible, ugly laugh when she ran away but the ache inside me told me I knew her. Told me she was familiar. And I tried to explain that to John Dexter but he said the betrayers always had red hair and she had red hair, and then he turned away, went back to his branch meeting, behaved as if I wasn't there.

I heard a bird sob.

I heard the heart that beat inside the oak tree.

I knew I was broken. I couldn't feel my own heart.

The nurse said we had to go in. She said, 'This won't hurt.'

It hurt.

She said, 'Count backwards, from ten.'

But I couldn't remember what came after seven.

Something shoved between my teeth and then everything was black.

I was beside a nurse in pale blue who held me up, but I just wanted to sink into her. I was weak and my head hurt. I wanted to be sick.

The nurse spoke but her words flew around. I just couldn't pin them down.

Speaking of Love

Six something. Mondays. Fridays.

A bowl of cornflakes.

But my hands couldn't make the spoon reach my mouth.

They brought the tea in one great big brown pot. They plonked it on the table in the dayroom and you didn't have to worry about milk or sugar because it was all in there, in the pot. Which was good because I couldn't remember if I liked milk or sugar in my tea, and that way it was one less thing to worry about.

When we were in OT we made sacks but I started to cry because my hands couldn't manage them.

Annie helped me. She said, 'You're just a mad hatter, Iris, aren't you?' And that made me laugh. But I laughed too much. They didn't like it. They gave me more ECT.

A man in the dayroom asked the ward doctor if he could tell him where his mind was. His mind, mind, not his brain.

We all waited for the answer.

But the ward doctor didn't answer which meant, we all knew, that he didn't know the answer. And the man who asked the question said, 'If you cannot tell me where my mind is, doctor, then how can you cure it?'

The man walked over to me.

I was on the window-seat.

He said, 'Keep that under your hat, Iris,' and tapped the side of his nose. And we laughed. But not too much. For fear of ECT.

Everybody smoked. Everybody.

And nobody bothered with ashtrays. Nobody.

The man whose bed was next to mine in the ward sat beside me in the dayroom. He was in a chair that was so broken all I could see was his head above the brown arms. But he told me important things and I listened. He did not talk about the lost souls.

'It helps,' he said, 'if you just answer the questions.'

'They're stupid questions,' I said.

'I know,' he said. 'But you have to play the game.'

He leaned over and put a cigarette into my mouth and I sucked on it. He took it out again. My hands were numb, so I couldn't do it for myself.

Iris's story

'How many birthdays does the Queen have?'

'Two,' I said.

'Remember that,' he said, 'because it's important, in here.'

There was a cigarette on the brown lino which burned itself out. Burned a hole.

I promised that I would remember.

John Dexter disappeared. He abandoned me even though I did everything he said. And I knew he'd taken all my stories with him.

I played Scrabble with the nurse called Ruth.

I made C-H-A-R-M on top of her M-O-U-T-H and then I put my finger over the C. I looked around to make sure I was right about John Dexter, to make sure he wasn't there, and then I said, 'He is this,' and I pointed to my eye, and to the 'C'. And then I pointed to the rest of the word, with my finger over the 'C'.

'Let's go for a walk,' said Ruth. 'And you can tell me about him.'

There were so many keys, so many locks and there was chicken wire that ran right up to the ceiling in the stairwell. But outside it was green and sunny and fresh and there was a fountain to stare at and a rose bed, yellow roses, and I breathed in their scent, breathed deeply. And I knew that I wanted to cry, and I knew that I could not cry.

Ruth said we should sit under the oak tree because the meds would make my skin burn in the sun.

I had to make sure John Dexter was not there first.

'He was my friend,' I said, 'he was. But he is a selfish friend. He's only with me when he wants to be with me. And I don't think he told me the truth.'

'About what, Iris?'

'About the marks on her face.'

'What do you mean?'

'They're just freckles,' I said. 'Harmless freckles on her face.' Ruth's eyes showed she understood. 'It was a terrible thing that he said. Not what a friend would say. And he said her name was Lily and it isn't.'

Ruth just waited.

'But I have got a friend,' I said. 'He planted a tree for me. He is my real friend.'

'Would you like to see him?' said Ruth.

'Yes,' I said.

We sat there, silently, and then I said, 'Could he bring her, too? My daughter?'

Ruth looked at me. Her eyes were blue-green and the whites were very white. They shone, Ruth's eyes. I'd never noticed that before.

'Perhaps not just yet,' she said.

And I said, 'My mother used to tell me stories.'

'I would like to hear them,' said Ruth.

'That's the trouble,' I said. 'There aren't any more stories. They've gone. They were too heavy, you see. They weighed the branches down and broke them. The storytree is dead.'

Vivie's story

Vivie had been walking by the Thames.

She'd watched couples walking hand in hand on the warm summer's night and she'd hated them. She'd got into a vicious argument with a man on a bicycle who'd almost ridden into her. He'd shouted that it was his right of way. She'd shouted back and he'd told her he had no idea what her problem was but, he'd said, it obviously had nothing to do with the Thames-side cycle ways. She'd told him that he and his fucking poncy cycle-ways could fuck right off and then she'd laughed a hysterical laugh, felt a rush of adrenalin and danced wildly beneath Albert Bridge.

But now she was back in Charles's house and the only thing she felt was fear. Her world had collapsed and there was nothing left to hold on to. Images of her mother in the full flood of her madness kept forcing themselves into her mind. Vivie yelled, 'No!' at the images, but she knew she was lost. She knew that, however different she might seem on the outside, she was just like her mother on the inside. She was mad.

She poured vodka into a tumbler and then she saw that the green light on the answering machine was blinking. The message, obviously, would be from Charles and Vivie said, to the machine, 'I agree to whatever. You decide grounds. I agree. I haven't got a leg to stand on.'

Vivie stumbled forwards and the hand she put out to save herself hit the answering machine. The tape began to rewind. Vivie collapsed back into the chair beside the bookcase where the machine sat. She felt for the button to turn the machine off, but before she found it the machine gave a little click and the message began.

It was her mother's voice.

She sat bolt upright.

'Vivie, it's me. I had an intuition, a strong feeling about you this morning. It was so strong that I thought for a moment you were in the room with me.'

Vivie's heart began to beat too quickly. She sat frozen in her chair. She whispered to the machine, 'Don't say those spooky-mad intuition things to me. I'm not there.'

'I don't want to upset you, Vivie, darling,' said her mother's voice from the machine, 'but the feeling was so very strong that I had to ring and see if you were all right. If there's anything I can do ... anything at all ... I know I'm not the first person you would turn to but I would do anything for you, Vivie, anything at all. Please let me know if – ' Vivie heard a sound like a gasp.

'I'm sorry, darling,' said her mother's voice, 'I didn't mean to cry, but I was thinking about you, thinking about your birthday, and then this feeling overwhelmed me so completely ... but I expect you're fine. I expect Charles will do something wonderful for your birthday, he's so good at that kind of thing, isn't he? I hope it will be a happy birthday, Vivie, and ... what I really want to say is this ...'

At last Vivie managed to move. She reached out to turn the machine off, but then she heard her mother say, 'I want to say I love you, Vivie. I love you very much,' and Vivie froze again, her hand poised above the machine. 'I have always loved you,' said her mother's voice, 'and I have never said so. I've never even written it down ... but it's the only important thing to say. I love you, Vivie darling. I love you.'

Her mother had stopped crying, but Vivie began. She collapsed back into the chair and tears slid out from the corners of her eyes and gathered in the hollows above her collarbone.

'If life was a story, Vivie,' said her mother, 'I could retell it. But it isn't and I can't. I just wish that what happened to me had never happened in front of you. I wish that you hadn't had to do what you did and I wish that you hadn't been so very frightened by it all. That's what I wish.'

A great sob burst from Vivie.

Vivie's story

'But if my feeling is right,' said her mother, 'and it's so very strong that I think, perhaps, it is ... if something is wrong, Vivie, at least know this, know that I love you and know that I know what a wonderful, brave and beautiful person you are. What a kind and thoughtful daughter you are and always have been.'

Vivie's tears streamed down her face. She bit her lip until it bled.

'I love you, Vivie,' said her mother, 'and I will be thinking of you tomorrow. Happy birthday.'

The machine clicked and the tape whirred as it rewound. Vivie sat without moving. Her heart hammered in her chest but, instead of feeling as if she was about to disintegrate, instead of the familiar feelings of panic, instead of feeling as if she was being propelled helplessly towards an unknown destination, all she felt was the reassuring solidity of the chair against her back and under her legs, the floor beneath her feet and the solid arms of the chair beneath her own arms.

After a while she rewound the tape and listened to her mother's message again and, as she did so, she closed her eyes and saw her child self, digging. She smelled the damp earth and she saw the small green, blue and red enamel box on the ground beside her. It had been her father's box. He'd brought it back from India and she'd loved it. He'd kept cigarettes in it and every time she'd opened it she'd breathed in the sweet smell of his tobacco. She'd always hoped cigarettes would taste the way they smelled in that box, but they never had.

Vivie watched her child self open the box and she saw the inside of the lid. It was the deepest, bluest, shiniest enamel and she remembered how she'd loved it but how, after her mother's breakdown, she'd emptied out her father's cigarettes and put everything that she loved into the box and buried it. She saw the folded pieces of paper she'd chosen so carefully to go into the box: the letter from her grandfather saying he'd like to meet her; the poem her father had written for her when she was five; the piece of paper with her name and Matthew's name linked together in her childish hand. They had all gone into the box. And then she'd put some flowers from her storytree, some yellow laburnum flowers, on top of the pieces of paper and she'd taken the box up to St Agnes Redemere churchyard and buried it.

She thought that the beautiful enamel box would be ruined, now. She imagined it rusty and without colour or pattern. It had been in the earth for twenty years. She wondered if anything inside it had survived.

And then she reached out and rewound the tape and listened to her mother's message for the third time, without once feeling frightened or panicked. Even her heartbeat had resumed its steady pace.

And there were no judgements as she listened, just the sound of her mother's voice.

Iris's story

Ruth walked beside me down the long corridor.

'Wish me luck,' I said, as I went in.

I sat opposite them. Some wore white coats.

'How are we?' said one, from behind a table. Another wrote something down with a beautiful, shiny, gold and black pen.

'Just me,' I said, 'for three months now, it's just been me,' but he didn't seem to hear me.

Three blank walls surrounded me. A picture hung behind the white coats. A mountain. Underneath the picture it said 'Shap Fell'. I wondered where he had fallen but I didn't say a word.

A beam of wintry sunlight made one man's hair golden, just on one side. He had thin lips.

'Now,' said another man, as he looked up and put down another shiny pen, red this time, 'how have we been managing?'

'*I* have been managing well,' I said.

'That's good,' he said, and looked down at his notes.

'What day of the week is it, Iris?' said another.

'Tuesday,' I said, obediently.

'And when is the Queen's birthday?' said another. He put his fingertips together in a tent shape under his chin.

'The Queen has two birthdays,' I said, and I sat forward in my chair, alert and ready for their questions. 'She has one birthday on the twenty-first of April and one in June. The one in June is not always on the same day.'

They all looked down at their papers and scribbled. The youngest one's face was red. But I didn't say a word although I fought back a desperate desire to laugh. The Queen's birthdays were my passport. I wondered if she knew. And I wanted to ask them to sit where I sat and I would sit where they sat and ask them what it was like to be me. But, of course, I didn't. They would have thought me mad.

'Where do you plan to live when you leave Salem, Iris?' said the one who'd been the first to speak.

My hands tingled more than they'd done for days. I could really feel them. I grasped them together tightly, nails in my palms. I hoped I wouldn't draw blood. They must not see it if I did. But I could feel them, I could feel them, I could feel them.

I looked down to hide the smile that threatened to spread right across my face.

'Iris,' he said again, 'where will you go when you leave here?'

'Home,' I said. I couldn't say too much, for fear that the laughter might escape.

He looked at me. He wanted more.

'My next-door neighbours,' I said, 'Dick and Joan Aldwater ... they are good friends. They live next door. They've been here to see me.' I didn't know if I'd be able to keep the laughter inside.

The first doctor's lips made a half smile. He closed his folder and pushed it away from him. So did all the others. Some folded their hands on the table. And some snapped the lids onto their expensive pens.

The thin-lipped one stood up. 'I wish you well,' he said and I thought I would explode. I couldn't keep it in. A laugh burst out.

Ruth came through the door and took hold of both my arms and said, 'Is Mrs Marchwood discharged?' She looked fierce.

The first doctor opened his folder again.

Please please please please please let me leave.

'Her exuberance would be quite appropriate if she *is* discharged,' said Ruth and the thin-lipped one looked at her, rubbed the bridge of his nose with his forefinger and thumb and nodded.

Ruth led me from the room. I shook badly. I looked back and saw the thin-lipped one. He leaned on the table. I suddenly thought he was old, and tired, not young and golden-haired at all.

I wanted to skip. I wanted to run. I wanted to dance. When we were in the garden, Ruth and me, I did do a kind of a dance, even though the drugs didn't want me to move quickly. And I told Ruth over and over again that I could feel my hands, really feel them, properly.

Iris's story

Ruth said she had put some blankets under the oak tree. It was cold and the sun was weak and wintry. We wrapped ourselves in the blankets and sat under the oak tree and Ruth gave me my precious broken-backed book, my mother's book of French fairy tales. I hugged it to me under my blanket and Ruth looked at me. 'Promise me one thing, Iris?' she said.

I nodded.

'You must never come off the meds,' she said. 'Never.'

I nodded again and we sat still for a bit. Then I pushed the blanket back and looked at my hands. I could feel them and they could feel the cold and my book, and Ruth pushed her blanket back and put her hands on top of my hands. There was blood on my left palm, in the middle.

'The thing is,' I said, 'I don't know what to do about Vivie. It's been so long. I won't know where to start. I won't know her.'

Ruth said she understood. She said just to take things one step at a time.

I put my hand on my heart. 'She is this tall,' I said. 'She is as tall as my heart.'

Ruth nodded and said she would find some disinfectant and a plaster for my hand. She walked with her arm around me all the way back to the ward and I sank sideways into her.

And then I cried.

And we stood still in the corridor and I cried and I cried and I cried and Ruth said it was good to cry because sometimes the meds took away everything you felt.

Matthew's story

Dad says, 'Drive past the shops and head for Beach Road.' He is reading from a piece of paper covered with his erratic, spidery writing. 'It's obvious, apparently, although it's not called Beach Road.'

I laugh and he says, 'It's called Colhugh Road but everyone around here calls it Beach Road, apparently.'

I slow down and almost miss a small iron sign painted with a white arrow and black lettering, high up on the side of a house. It says, 'Beach, 1¼,' and above it is an arched metalwork sign that says Colhugh Road. Both signs look as if they've been there for ever.

Dad says, 'There are lots of humps in it.'

'What?'

'In the road.'

The MG's low-slung undercarriage doesn't like the humps at all.

Dad says, 'Go along Colhugh Road; turn right into Flanders Road.' And then he says, 'The White House is at the end of the wall on the right.'

And so we find what must be the most comfortable B&B in these islands. Dad's room is palatial with an enormous white bathroom, mine is smaller with no bath, but both our rooms look out over a terrace packed with pots that overflow with petunias and fuchsias, and there are white wooden trellises covered with sweet peas whose scent fills my room.

I have a bath in Dad's bath while he rings Iris; he is planning to ask her to join us for supper but when I come out he says, 'I can't get through, it's constantly engaged. She did warn me that the only telephone at the castle is a public one. She said the Atlantic College students use it all the time.'

He tries one more time after he's had a bath, but it is still engaged and he says, 'Perhaps it's for the best. She'll want to get to bed early tonight, anyway. She's not expecting to see us until tomorrow.'

We walk back up the hill into the village, to the pub that Iris told Dad about. It is late and the whitewashed stone buildings are bathed in the red-gold of the setting sun, but inside the oak-beamed pub it is cool and dark.

I go to the bar and order a bottle of wine. Dad has insisted on more of the banned red, and I try to memorise the menu which covers several blackboards, but I soon give up because one whole blackboard is devoted to different kinds of mashed potato: there's mustard mash, olive mash, sun-dried tomato mash, chilli mash, pea mash, anchovy mash, broad bean mash, too many mashes to remember, and then there's the fish blackboard, and then the pie blackboard, and more. So I take the wine back to Dad and say, 'You're going to have to come and look at the menu yourself, the choice is a bit of a challenge to the memory.'

He smiles, puts his hands on the table and pushes himself up and when we're standing side by side in front of the blackboards, he says, 'Funny things memories,' and he pushes his glasses up onto his forehead and peers at the fish board. 'You'd think that a man who managed to remember so much, today,' he is smiling so broadly that he should have been laughing, 'you'd think that that man would be able to remember the names of a few bits of fish, and a few kinds of mashed potato now, wouldn't you?'

I put my hand on his shoulder and say, 'You would, but it could be that that man's memory is exhausted, or on strike, at least for the rest of the day.'

Iris's story

Dick and Joan and I sat on the train.

The sky was grey and miserable and the ploughed fields looked as if they'd been carved from wood.

My walk was weird, and my right hand shook, but I was on my way home. And I could feel my hands, properly, as they held on to my mother's book.

When the taxi drove us along the lane at the top of the green I saw Dick's yellow buckeyes, stripped bare for the winter. But the thick trunks of the ordinary chestnuts that supported them, that they grew from, comforted me. They looked so solid. They made the lives of the yellow buckeyes possible, the yellow buckeyes that Kit and I'd seen together, with their glowing red-pink leaves. The elegant yellow buckeyes that were held safe on the strong shoulders of the ordinary chestnuts.

I put my hand on my heart and I said to myself, 'Vivie stands as tall as my heart. That's all I need to remember. She stands as tall as my heart.'

EARTH AND SEA

*B*eside the sea, in a hut that stood between the high and the low watermarks, a fisherman lived with his wife and their daughter, Murmurina.

When the spring tides came their hut was completely flooded.

When the ebb tides came the fisherman's wife swept sand and seaweed from their hut, the fisherman returned stranded sea creatures to the sea and the hut was completely dry.

But there were, of course, many other times when the sea found its way into the fisherman's hut, and Murmurina was the only one who welcomed the sea when it flooded, or trickled over the threshold. For Murmurina had been born with a fat fishtail that glistened where she should have had legs, she made 'O' shapes with her mouth when she should have had a voice, and when the spring tides brought creatures into their hut which were more like her than she was like her father and her mother, Murmurina felt at home.

But all was not well with the fisherman and his family for it is difficult for those with legs to live within water, and it is difficult for those with fishtails to live without water, and so the fisherman and his wife argued about where they should live until one night, while the fisherman fished at sea, a strange thing happened.

A fish spoke to the fisherman from his nets.

The fish said, 'Go inland.'

The fish leapt in the nets and said, 'All will be well with your daughter if you go inland.'

And the fish said to the amazed fisherman, 'Do not

stop your walk inland until you find an empty hut in a clearing in a forest where no one else lives.'

The fish leapt high in the air once more and said, 'And never ever accept any thing from any one you can see.'

And then the fish leapt over the side of the fisherman's boat and was gone.

The fisherman told his wife and his daughter what the fish had said, and the fisherman's wife said, 'Our daughter, Murmurina, who cannot walk and who cannot talk, and whose only joy is the sea ... how will all be well with her if we go inland?'

The fisherman looked up from the net he mended on his knee and said, 'I do not know. But the fish has leapt in my nets for three nights now. For three nights the fish has spoken the selfsame words. And on the third night, last night, when the fish struggled to repeat all the words, I knew that I must give my word that we would go inland. And so I did. And then I let the poor, tired fish swim away. We must go inland, wife,' said the fisherman. 'That is all I know.'

And so it was that the fisherman and his wife wrapped all that they owned in blankets which they slung across their backs, and they wrapped Murmurina in a blanket packed with damp seaweed so that her fishtail would glisten and remain fat, and they carried their daughter inland.

They walked for many many days but each evening, wherever they stopped for the night, a parcel of food wrapped in a chequered cloth, a large pewter jug full of fresh water and a wooden barrel filled with salt water and seaweed appeared close by. And not once did they see the person who brought these things.

On the evening of the two hundred and seventy-fifth day of their great walk inland the fisherman, his wife and their daughter, Murmurina, arrived in a clearing in a forest where an empty hut stood and no one else lived.

The hut was dilapidated but, mindful of the words the fish had spoken, they set out to make it habitable. And every evening a chequered cloth filled with food, a pewter jug filled with fresh water and a wooden barrel filled with salt water and seaweed appeared by the front door of their hut. And not once did they see the person who brought these things.

And so it was that a day came when the fisherman's wife swept the hearth, as usual, and Murmurina lay wrapped in her blanket filled with damp seaweed; but on this day the fisherman's wife saw a small door which she had not noticed before. When she opened that door Murmurina's heart began to beat faster than ever it had beaten before. And when she saw the broken pieces of wood that her mother pulled through that door Murmurina pressed her hand to her heart in an attempt to still its wild beat. When she saw the wooden hoop covered with cobwebs that her mother pulled through that door Murmurina shifted inside her blanket filled with damp seaweed. And when Murmurina saw her mother put up her knee to break the first piece of wood for the fire, she cried out, 'Do not break it, mother, for I know what it is.'

The fisherman's wife dropped the piece of wood and stared at Murmurina.

'Did you speak, my daughter?' said she.

Murmurina nodded. 'Please mother,' she said, 'bring me the broken pieces of wood and the wooden hoop covered with cobwebs for I know what they are.' And the fisherman's wife ran to her daughter and took her in her arms and said, 'So the fish spoke true.'

By the time the fisherman returned from the forest that evening, the outline of a spinning wheel was laid out flat on the grass in the clearing in front of the hut.

'Good evening, father,' said Murmurina, and she smiled up at her father. 'Will you help me make this

*wheel spin as it should?' The fisherman's eyes filled with
tears at the sound of his daughter's voice and he could not
speak for joy. His daughter touched his hand and said,
'For I must spin what I am given to spin.'*

*And so it was that when the spinning wheel was
made an extra parcel of striped cloth was left beside the
parcel of food wrapped in a chequered cloth, the large
pewter jug full of water and the wooden barrel filled with
salt water and seaweed, each evening. And inside that
extra parcel of striped cloth – which they came to call the
spinning parcel – was the stuff from which Murmurina
spun fine thread.*

*The thread that Murmurina spun grew finer and finer
and she hummed as she spun and she murmured as she
spun and very soon she could spin the finest threads from
raw silk and from wool, from cotton and from hemp and,
by the time she was fifteen, she could spin thread from
any thing. She could spin her own hair into fine thread.
She could spin grass into silky green satin threads. She
could spin cobwebs into iridescent threads and, when
Murmurina found lumps of coal in the striped-cloth
spinning parcel, she spun tough pale threads from the
sparks that flew from the coal as she held it against the top
of her spindle. The threads that she spun from the sparks
sparkled, and her mother said that, knotted together, they
would make a good pot scourer while her father said that,
singly strung through her hair, they would bring her good
fortune at new moon.*

*As word of Murmurina's spinning skill spread,
travellers from distant lands came to ask her to spin thread
from the gifts they brought. But Murmurina never spun
a single thread from their gifts because she and her family
remained mindful of the words that the fish had spoken,
and so the travellers took their gifts away and gave each
other puzzled looks as they left. But when one particular
traveller took his gift away he was filled with the powerful*

white heat of anger. He was angry that the gift he had brought had been rejected. He swore revenge.

And so it was that one morning, when the fisherman worked in the forest and the fisherman's wife delivered fine-spun thread to the weavers who lived on the far side of the forest, Murmurina sat in the clearing at her spinning wheel and she felt a chill in the air. She shivered, and when she looked up she saw that it was dark on the far side of the clearing.

Murmurina saw a Stranger break into the clearing.

Murmurina saw the dark cloak that flowed out behind the Stranger, the dark hood that was pulled low over the Stranger's face, and the pale mist that trailed from the Stranger's heels. And, as the Stranger strode towards her, Murmurina saw that the clouds above kept pace with the Stranger so that by the time he stood in front of her, the clearing was wreathed in shadow and large drops of rain had begun to fall.

In honeyed tones that belied his true nature, the Stranger commanded Murmurina to spin thread from an object that glittered, but Murmurina, mindful of the words the fish had spoken, said that she could not. The Stranger pushed the object that glittered towards Murmurina and it so dazzled her that she put up her hand to shield her eyes and, as she did so, she touched the object that glittered and the Stranger laughed a laugh that was more like a croak than a laugh.

'Now,' said the Stranger, 'you can refuse me no longer, for where I come from to touch a thing is to accept a thing.' And Murmurina trembled and she saw the hood of the Stranger's cloak fall back and the Stranger's smile was crooked and one of the Stranger's front teeth crossed over the other and the Stranger's face was a divided face: on one side the skin was smooth and bearded, on the other it was wrinkled, warty and hairless. On one side a black wet eye, on the other a dry white eye. On one side short

hair, on the other long straggly hair.

The Stranger commanded Murmurina to spin and she felt the treadle begin to rock of its own accord. And the Stranger said, 'Those who refuse me shall lose all that matters to them. Those who do my bidding shall be rewarded with all that they desire.'

But, as the Stranger spoke, the mist that trailed from his heels stole up through Murmurina's nostrils, stole into her veins and into her brain until it mystified all her senses and she no longer knew where she was, nor what it was that she did. And so she did not know that her fingers had closed over the hard, ridged edges of the object that glittered, and she did not feel how it juddered against her palm. She did not sense that the treadle rocked wildly, nor could she see that she had not spun one single thread.

Murmurina did not feel the Stranger snatch the object that glittered from her palm and she did not know that her hand fell onto the spindle and was pierced, and she did not hear the Stranger say, 'Word has spread that you can spin thread from any thing, and I brought you the most precious thing in my possession and not one thread have you spun from it!'

And the Stranger said, 'Those who refuse me shall lose all that matters to them!' and he snatched up the fisherman's axe from its place by the woodshed and brought it down onto the treadle as it rocked wildly, brought it down onto the madly spinning wheel.

Murmurina fell backwards and the pieces of her spinning wheel flew across the clearing, but as the Stranger lifted the axe to bring it down for the third time onto Murmurina's paralysed body, the fisherman and his wife ran into the clearing and flew at the Stranger and pulled the axe from the Stranger's hands. They slew the Stranger with great four-handed swings of the axe, and the Stranger's body crumpled to the ground and dissolved into a pool of black liquid that glittered. Sparks flew from an object in the middle of the liquid and the fisherman smashed the object into the smallest pieces with the back of his axe.

But when the fisherman and his wife turned to their daughter they felt their hearts would break, for Murmurina was out of her mind. Her body shivered and shook as if she would break into little pieces, and the sounds that she made made no sense. And it was then that a great storm raged through the clearing and when the fisherman and his wife picked up their daughter her paralysis left her and she struggled against them, and her blanket fell off in the struggle and they saw that her tailfin had been severed and they were sure that she would die.

And when the hungry and thirsty fisherman opened the door of their hut late in the evening of that terrible day, the chequered cloth lay empty on the ground, and the large pewter jug, the wooden barrel and the striped cloth were all empty. The fisherman held the pewter jug out under the rain and he and his wife argued bitterly about the other's stupidity: how could she, or he, have ever believed the words of a talking fish? And all the while the sounds that escaped from Murmurina's lips as she shook and shivered by the fire made no sense at all.

And so it was that, as the storm gave way to fine rain, the fisherman and his wife gathered up the pieces of Murmurina's broken spinning wheel and they saw that her tailfin was stuck to the treadle, and that her blood was on the spindle. And when, at last, the sun shone once more they saw a weaver on the opposite side of the clearing. She had come to request some thread, but when she saw how it was with the fisherman and his family she showed them what they could eat from the forest, and where there was water, and how to make poultices from leaves and from herbs for Murmurina's wounds. Gradually Murmurina's body ceased to shiver and the sounds that made no sense ceased, and the fisherman and his wife and his daughter lived in the clearing until the day came when, despite all the poultices, the fisherman's wife saw that Murmurina's injured tail was beyond repair for it had dried and shrivelled and, on that day, it came away from her body in her mother's hands. But as her mother bathed away the remnants of her daughter's shrivelled fishtail, she saw, there, at her daughter's hip joints, the pink buds of limbs, plain as day.

The fisherman's wife's eyes filled with tears and she showed her husband and he said, 'Even so, the fish spoke true,' and the fisherman's wife nodded. 'Our daughter shall have legs,' she said, and as she said these words, Murmurina opened her eyes and spoke.

'I should like to go home,' she said. 'I should like to go back to the sea.'

The sound of their daughter's voice made the fisherman and his wife smile through their tears, and they prepared to return to the sea. Murmurina asked her mother to grind the scales from her fishtail and to wrap them in the striped cloth of the spinning parcel. She asked her father to break the wood of her spinning wheel into the smallest pieces and to wrap them in the chequered cloth of the food parcel. And then she asked her father and her mother to carry her from the clearing, just as they had carried her into it.

On their journey back to the sea Murmurina's limbs grew until she had a perfectly formed pair of legs and so it was that, in exactly two hundred and seventy-five days, the fisherman and his family stood once more beside the sea by their hut, between the high and the low watermarks. And as Murmurina listened to the sound of the sea and the sound of the gulls and breathed in the salt air, she jumped for pure joy.

The fisherman and his family built a new hut above the high watermark and when, eventually, first the fisherman, and then his wife, died, Murmurina let the carrion birds pick their bones clean, as was the custom, and then she ground the bones down and sprinkled the ground bone onto the fish scales that she kept in the striped-cloth parcel and she let her tears fall onto them. And she sprinkled the ground bone onto the splinters of her spinning wheel that she kept in the chequered-cloth parcel and she let her tears fall onto them.

And one evening, as Murmurina sat at the water's edge, a fish looped up and out of the water in front of her.

The fish landed in Murmurina's lap and Murmurina clapped her hands together and laughed and the fish said, 'Now, my Murmurina, every thing is ready.'

Murmurina understood the fish perfectly and she carried the fish back to her hut in her skirt. She opened the parcel of striped cloth. She opened the parcel of chequered cloth. And she showed the fish what was inside and the fish said, 'As long as you spin there will always be things for you to sprinkle. And as long as you sprinkle there will always be things for you to spin. The one is born of the other. The other of the one.'

And that night, beneath a brilliant indigo star-studded sky where a crescent moon glowed, Murmurina took the fish back to the sea and she let that fish go.

And it is said that, each and every night, to this day, a woman sprinkles a little of what is in a striped-cloth parcel, or a little of what is in a chequered-cloth parcel onto the waves that lap onto the beach where she lives and that she hums, and that she murmurs, and then that she spins ... a story.

Part Four
Sunday, 30 July, 1996

Vivie's story

V ivie woke and, for a moment, wondered where she was. The chair reminded her. She stretched her stiff limbs and, wondering why on earth she didn't have the headache she deserved, she replayed her mother's message just to make sure she hadn't dreamt it. Then she dialled 1471 and wrote the number down on the nearest thing she could find.

She rang the number – she didn't recognise the code – but there was no answer. She rang again and again but no one answered, so she made herself a cup of coffee and only then did she notice the time. It was light, but it was still early, only six o'clock, and Vivie realised that she hadn't slept so well, without a sleeping pill – and in a chair, for goodness' sake – for as long as she could remember; nor had she woken so early.

She walked back into the sitting-room feeling light-headed and, she hardly dared think it, happy. But it made no sense. How could she be happy when she'd lost her job and, more than likely, her husband? And then she remembered, with a start, that it was her birthday, her thirtieth birthday and she was alone. She had no plans to celebrate her birthday, no one to celebrate it with and even that didn't seem so bad.

She sat down and, as she drank her coffee, she looked round Charles's sitting room and realised that there was nothing of hers in the room, except her CDs. Everything else was Charles's and she liked none of it.

She tried the number again, but this time it was engaged. She replayed her mother's message and cried, again, as she listened to it.

'It's the only important thing to say,' said her mother's voice, 'I love you, Vivie darling. I love you.'

Vivie felt as if something hard and metallic inside her was

dissolving, and then something between a sob and a laugh broke from her as she saw, when she reached for the telephone number again, that she'd scribbled it on the CD cover beside the text that read, 'Doctor Dahl told Rachmaninov that his cure lay in his music. And it proved to be so. Mental illness never troubled him again; the concerto received a rapturous reception.'

Vivie dialled the number and this time it was not engaged. Her heartbeat accelerated as she waited to hear her mother's voice, but instead she heard a male, American voice.

'Atlantic College,' he said.

'Um, can I speak to Iris Marchwood, please?'

'I don't know an Iris Marchwood,' said the American. 'But there are plenty of folks staying here this weekend. I could put a notice on the board?'

'Where is Atlantic College, please?'

'Well, ma'am, I'm standing in a public telephone booth in a mediaeval castle in Wales,' said the American.

'What?'

'St Donat's Castle. Part of Atlantic College, ma'am.' He drawled it all out. 'The craziest location for a college you ever saw.'

'Oh. I must have got the wrong number,' said Vivie. 'Sorry.'

'There's a festival going on here,' said the American. 'Is this Iris Marchwood a storyteller?'

Vivie gasped. 'Yes,' she said. 'Yes, she is.'

'So, I can put a notice on the board for you? Like I said?'

'No,' said Vivie. 'Don't worry. But ... um ... can you tell me how to get there?'

'That would depend upon where you're coming from, ma'am.'

'London.'

'Okay. Now, here's the thing ... you take the train from Paddington, London, to Bridgend, Wales. Then you catch the little bus, the one-four-five. It'll bring you right to the castle gates. Takes about half an hour, but I should say there aren't that many buses on a Sunday.'

'Thanks,' said Vivie.

Vivie's story

'It's been a pleasure, ma'am,' said the American.

Vivie hung up and ran upstairs. As she stood under the shower she repeated over and over again, 'If I don't do it now, I never will. If I don't do it now, I never will. And,' she told herself as she reached for her towel, 'if she's still mad I can always leave. I can always leave. I can always leave.'

And still there was no judgement.

Matthew's story

It is a still morning and there's no breeze but I can hear water trickling somewhere, and the birds are singing. It's already hot, the sky is a cloudless blue and I'm lying in bed staring at it and remembering that yesterday, when we drove across the new Severn Bridge, I looked up and saw a single cloud scudding between the pylons hundreds of metres above us. It gave me a sudden, dizzying sense of our turning planet.

We think we live on stable ground because our streets don't move and neither do our structures, at least they don't here in the northern hemisphere. We live, every day, as if our planet was static. We pay only lip service to tectonics when we design buildings. But we live in a turning, shifting world while we hang on to the illusion of immobility. If we could actually *feel* the planet turning, if we lived each day conscious of gravitational forces and shifting tectonic plates we might develop a sense of urgency about our own lives.

Last night Dad and I agreed that he'd take a taxi to the festival and I would walk; I'm looking forward to it. Our landlord told us it would take about an hour to walk to the castle; he said the view was magnificent, he said the path runs along the cliffs that overlook the Bristol Channel.

I pull on some shorts and a t-shirt from my bag and as I shave I remember my dream. I dreamt about Vivie last night. We were in bed and her long red hair touched my face and my chest and her grey eyes, with that strange brown triangle in the left one, stared down into mine and the long dimple in her left cheek deepened as she smiled; her thighs were warm on either side of mine. I told her the freckles across the bridge of her nose looked as if she'd spilled some cocoa powder there and, as I shave, I realise that's exactly what they do look like.

Matthew's story

I've never dreamt about Vivie that way before, not once in all these years, but I might as well have because it seems to me now that her ghost, her presence, has come between me and every other woman I have ever known, just as if I dreamt about her that way every night.

Iris's story

People walked under the arch in the stone wall at the far end of the lawn. I could see them from my window, there were hundreds of them and there wasn't a single cloud in the sky. I pushed the window open and the warm air enveloped me the way it does when you step off a plane in climates far more temperate than ours.

'It won't rain on Rose Lawn today,' I told myself, and I lifted my face to the sun and, as I felt its warmth, I thanked my lucky stars that I could do that. Thanked my lucky stars that my system was no longer filled with drugs that made my skin so fragile it burned at the first touch of the sun.

Vivie has been on my mind since I woke up. I hope my message hasn't upset her, but I had such a strong sense of her unhappiness that I had to speak to her. And even though she wasn't there, perhaps because she wasn't there, I said the words I should have said so long ago, words I've never managed to say to her before, words that none of us say enough.

The morning before I left St Agnes Redemere to come here, last week, Dick and I sat in my garden drinking tea. I had just asked him the question I often asked him, and we'd talked about Vivie.

'There isn't anything she could be frightened of any more,' I said. 'I've explained everything in my letters. If she's read them she'll know I am well. I don't know what else to do.'

'Hmmm,' was all he said.

'I've unearthed so much, written so much about it all to her. She must know, now, that it's unlikely to happen again.'

'I think she needs to hear something more fundamental,' said Dick and his pale blue eyes twinkled. I stared at the cobwebby lines on his forehead, and the lines that fan out from the corners of his eyes. He waited for me to say something, but I didn't know what to say.

'You don't have to be a child to feel unmothered,' he said, and he squeezed my arm, 'do you?'

I stared at the flagstones.

'Sap rises in the oldest of trees ... the children we were remain within us.'

I couldn't look at him.

'Vivie was very young when you had your first breakdown,' he said. 'I think she needs to hear – '

' – what I have never told her,' I said. 'She needs to know how I feel about her.' I looked at him. 'That's what you were going to say, isn't it?'

Dick nodded, and a blackbird sang. He whistled back and then he smiled. 'That's what I was going to say,' he said.

'You're right,' I said. 'I know you're right. Ruth said more or less the same thing about me and my father. But the thing is I've always wanted to tell Vivie face to face. It looked false, written down. It looked as if I wanted to obliterate everything that happened with those three words. And ... I don't know,' I said, 'answering machines ... they're so impersonal. So she doesn't know. But I know how important it is to say the words ... and to hear them. I know how I felt when you said them to me.'

Dick kissed me then, and whispered that he still loved me. 'More than ever,' he said. And I told him I loved him.

They *are* the most important words in all the world, and if they are never said they become more and more difficult to say. Impossible, eventually.

But I told Vivie I loved her last night. At least I told her answering machine. I said it more than once. And now I'm worried that I might have made things worse. I don't know how she will react, now that the words are out.

The green figure, the Green Man, walked along the gravel path under my window. The green gauze covered with leaves and vines and twigs cascaded from his shoulders. Children looked up at him, pulled at his sleeves, giggled and ran away. And I thought about the stories he told, yesterday. Stories of trees, and longevity and fertility and mystery; stories of the love the trees have for the earth and for us.

I turned and tucked in the sheets on my bed, breathed in their lavender scent, the scent that was my mother's favourite, and pocketed some coins for the telephone. I walked down the spiral stone staircase. I planned to ring Vivie again to wish her happy birthday and, more truthfully, to find out how she felt. I couldn't bear the thought that she might hate me for what I'd said or, worse, just think me a sentimental old woman.

But when I got downstairs there was an Atlantic College student on the only telephone and his instructions about how to get to the festival were detailed, so I decided I was not meant to ring Vivie again, that I must leave whatever would happen to her. Dick would tell me not to ring her again if I asked him what he thought. I know he would.

So I walked down the flint steps through the pines and I breathed in their resinous smell. I walked on down to the beach to watch the pictures unfold in my mind for one last time before I tell my stories this afternoon.

I have a trick that reminds me to follow the pictures. I dig my thumbnail into the pad under my little finger whenever a new picture appears. I do it so that I won't give in and tell the story in words that I already know. I do it to calm my nerves because I am no longer on safe territory. I do it so that I will follow the unfamiliar path. And I do it when a different story altogether turns up, like a film on fast-forward in my head. I do it so that I will tell that story and not the one I'd planned to tell. And I know now that if I refuse to follow the pictures that turn up the story dies: its very heart stops beating.

And, as the pictures began to appear and I followed them with words, I realised that I have said all I can say to Vivie, now.

Now, I must leave it to her.

Vivie's story

Vivie knew she'd made a mistake.

She told herself so as she stared through the window of the speeding train. Just because her mother had told her she loved her was no reason to behave as if everything had changed.

People didn't recover from breakdowns, she knew that, and to think, to hope, that they might was as ridiculous as believing in fairy tales.

A judgement ruled Vivie correct in every particular.

She hoped it wasn't far to the next station.

She bit hard into the side of her hand.

Iris's story

I stood at the edge of the sea. I closed my eyes and I heard the sound it made and I breathed in the salt and seaweed smells. And, as I did so, I remembered how like a polluted sea I'd felt, once. How nothing flowed. How all was stopped up and dead. How I couldn't do the simplest things. How I spilled the coffee when I tried to put it into the cafetière. How I couldn't remember one single story. How I couldn't think straight, or crooked, even.

I felt as if I was full of brown effluent that bubbled and dribbled and sweated its way out of me. The Largactil was a prehistoric, deep-sea monster. It was slothful, it slithered inside me and leaked its poison into my body from its anus.

It made me sluggish, and heavy. It liked me that way.

It could not fly and it was glad that I couldn't because it couldn't.

It weighed me down, all year round.

When my laburnum tree was raggedy with its long empty seed pods, I sewed indigo velvet onto a hat. But my fingers were clumsy and I wore dark glasses to stop the glare. The Aldwaters lent me their yellow parasol so that my skin wouldn't burn, and Dick brought me tea in a yellow mug.

A bird flew low over our heads.

'Wood pigeon,' he said and sat beside me. I could see the lavender he'd planted for me in the stone urn behind him.

'Pests shouldn't be so beautiful, should they?' he said. 'But that sound is beautiful. If velvet could make a sound it would be the sound of a wood pigeon's wing as it pulls through the air.' He put his hand on my arm. 'Don't you think, Iris?'

I held the needle up. It glinted. What Dick had just said was unbearable.

'I can't go on like this, Dick,' I said. 'I cannot live with the

Largactil monster. It poisons me. It wants me dead.'

I looked at him, straight into his pale blue eyes. 'Will you help me?' I said. But he said he couldn't. He said I had to swallow the pills. And Joan agreed. They all agreed.

'It is the lesser of two evils,' said Joan, brightly, kindly. She meant well, but she wasn't me so how could she know? She was a nurse though, so when she handed me the little white pills I took them. And Vivie looked on, half-hidden behind Joan.

'It's for your own good, Mum,' said Vivie and my heart wanted to split open. 'They will make you well again. Auntie Joan says so.'

And I knew what Vivie meant, so I swallowed them. She meant *she* would feel better if I took the pills, and so I did.

But none of them understood, not even Dick. They didn't really understand about the Largactil monster and the poison it oozed from its anus. And they didn't know about John Dexter; John Dexter who had been my best friend in all the world; John Dexter who had become the devil; John Dexter who wasn't able to fight the slothful Largactil monster any more than I could.

But Dick was always there, and that helped. He even persuaded the Forestry Commission to let me go with him into Thetford Forest so that I could work for him, because I had no money to pay the rent. I never really did any work, I couldn't concentrate, but Dick said it didn't matter, and he said he would teach me the bird calls when we were in the Forest. But when he tried to teach me I couldn't learn them. My mind was too dulled.

And then, one day in the Forest, Dick said, 'It can't be any worse than this,' and he told me he'd talked to a man who worked at a different kind of clinic. And that that man was German and he brought new medicines, new ideas from Germany. He had told Dick what to expect when a person stopped their meds.

Dick said he would help if I promised not to leave my cottage except with him, or to stay inside and call only for him, not Vivie, not Matthew, not Joan, if things got bad. He said if I would let Vivie continue to stay with them and not expect her to move back in with me, he would help.

I nodded, hugged him with my clumsy hug that shook, clung to him and dribbled. I would have agreed to anything that meant I could eject the poison-leaking Largactil monster from my body, from my mind.

And then John Dexter turned up in Vivie's empty room and said that, because of me, he was ruined. He said it was my fault that the school funds had been stopped. I tried to say that I had never stopped any funds but the words came out muddled, backwards, senseless and useless.

John Dexter sat on Vivie's empty bed and smoked his pipe. He wanted me to do something, I knew he did, but he wouldn't say what it was and I couldn't guess, and that made him angry. I told him that I couldn't live with the deep-sea Largactil monster that leaked poison from its anus.

And I wanted to say that I didn't think I could live with him either, but his eyes were as dark and beautiful as they'd always been and his hair was just as shiny and I couldn't say it. He smiled his crooked smile that showed his snaggle tooth as he smoked his pipe and he said he was glad I'd stopped the Largactil. He said that that was very, very good. And then, encouraged by his approval, I summoned my courage. I said I'd always tried to do the right thing, and I thought the right thing was for us to end our friendship. The sudden fury in his dark eyes made me shake so much that I could barely say another word, and he stared at me and his stare was like an arctic wind. He said everything I did was wrong. Everything. He said that he would have to teach me, that I needed him to teach me. He said it was no time for a friend to leave when there were things to teach, no time at all.

He said he did not like me to walk into Thetford Forest with Dick. He said we had much more important work to do, together, he and I.

I tried to say that he had stolen the words to my stories and that was terrible. I tried to say he'd said he'd be my storyhand and he hadn't been. I did manage to say that I didn't know what the important work was we had to do together. But he just said, 'I think you do, Iris, old girl.'

And when I tried to say that Dick had been very good to me and I wanted to do what he asked, John Dexter said that that was not how he expected to be treated. He asked how I could expect him to be my friend if I didn't stop those walks into Thetford Forest with Dick. And his eyes were so sad then, so full of loss and sorrow and love, that I couldn't end our friendship. After all, he *had* been my only friend in the worst of times. He *had* saved me from Kit. I did know that. And so I did what he asked and I sat there, on the floor of Vivie's empty bedroom, and I watched him lock the door. And I did not go with Dick into the Forest.

I don't know how many days afterwards it was that Dick came into Vivie's room and said the door wasn't locked and took my hand. I don't know how long it had been since I had washed or eaten, but Dick said I should wash and eat, and come with him into the Forest.

I know I struggled against him but, eventually, I did go with him. And when we were there I tore through the Forest like a wild animal. I ran and I laughed and I broke branches and I screamed and then I cried at the foot of a pine tree. And then I swung round it and I cut my hands on its sharp bark. And Dick said I shouldn't let Vivie see me like that because it would frighten her. But he said he would stick by me if I didn't let anyone but him see me like that. And that made me think how much fear there is in the world.

And then there was a quiet day in Thetford Forest and the pines sent their resinous smell to me, and the sun gave my back its warmth, and Dick dug and planted and tended and sawed and wrote his labels while the geese flew overhead.

We saw them through the trees and Dick copied their calls, 'Wink-wink-wink,' and I laughed and Dick told me that the pink-feet, the ones he'd copied, moulted all their wing feathers in one go when they got here and then they couldn't fly for weeks.

'They go to sanctuaries,' Dick said, 'to places where they will not be disturbed.'

And I hugged him with all the strength that suddenly flooded through me, and my arms did not shake and I could string words and thoughts together, and I did not dribble and the deep-sea Largactil monster had taken its anus-venom and slithered out of my body, I knew it had. And Dick said, 'Steady on, there, Iris,' and that made me laugh and laugh and laugh.

And slowly, very very slowly, my life returned.

My hands were much less clumsy. I could do small things with them and I began to make my hats again and, eventually, I had some success: some new clients turned up and some old ones returned.

And one evening Dick told me about the shrapnel in his leg that the doctors couldn't get out, the shrapnel that they kept an eye on and that might come out all by itself, one day. And he told me how he got it and how, at Dunkirk, when he lay wounded on the beach, the bombers came over again and again and a soldier from his regiment threw himself on top of Dick to save him from any more hurt or injury when he should have run for cover for himself. And he told me how he died, that soldier, when he saved Dick's life. He told me how, on the fourth of June every year, he made a visit to that soldier's grave.

'I owe that young man my life,' Dick said. 'And so I try, each day, to do something worthy of his courage, something that acknowledges his great sacrifice.'

We went to a storytelling gathering in Swaffham, Dick and Joan, Matthew and Vivie and me. And Vivie sat next to me, bravely, but she held on tightly to Joan's hand, not mine. And a man with long grey hair tied back in a ponytail told the story of John Chapman, the Pedlar of Swaffham. John Chapman who was told, in a dream, to go to London Bridge because he would find his fortune there.

But John Chapman very nearly starved in London until he met a man, on London Bridge, who told him that he had been told, in a dream, about a pot of gold that was buried under a hawthorn tree in the garden of a pedlar who lived in Swaffham. The pedlar's name was John Chapman, said the man. But the man said he'd never believed in dreams so he knew it couldn't be true. But John Chapman ran from London Bridge with the man's words loud in his ears. John Chapman travelled as fast as he could back to

Iris's story

Swaffham because John Chapman did believe in dreams.

I began to go regularly to those storytelling gatherings and I'd walk home through the Forest in the twilight. The storytellers gave me the courage to try to put my own stories back together and then I began hesitantly, to tell my stories to them. I lived without the Largactil monster and, even, without John Dexter. He hadn't returned since I'd gone back into the Forest with Dick. And all seemed to be as well as it could be. Except that Vivie could not bear to be alone with me, nor could she live with me.

When she left to work in London I knew she was relieved to be old enough to live away from me. And I tried very hard not to mind. And I failed.

The way she looked when she left broke my heart. Her shoulders were rounded and her head was down. Her beautiful, wild red hair was pulled back severely from her face and she reminded me of a bird whose feathers have been coated with oil, a bird whose wings no longer work, a bird who is condemned never to fly again through no fault of its own.

I knew that my madness was the oil-slick that had done that damage and I hoped that she would manage to free her wings from the oil when she lived away from it, away from me.

That afternoon, when it began to rain, I went out and stood in the rain and it was cool and I turned my face up to it and I pushed my hair back and the rain poured over me and I asked it to wash what I had done to my daughter away.

I began my first letter to her on that day, in a desperate attempt to explain.

Vivie's story

By the time Vivie's train reached Swindon she'd decided not to get off.

She'd touched her favourite black cap for luck and told herself that she had to stop letting her mother's behaviour rule her life; that she was beginning a new decade and that she'd never find out how her mother really was if she never saw her. And she had said she loved her, and she hadn't sounded mad. Well, not the old kind of mad anyway.

She stood up. She needed a cigarette and, as the connecting door sighed shut and she drew the smoke deep down into her lungs, she told herself everything she knew, everything she'd found out, about schizophrenia. She'd discovered that people could recover and never have another breakdown. And she knew that her mother was supposed to be one of the recovered kind.

Then she kicked the door. It was her birthday, for heaven's sake; she should be out enjoying herself, not worrying about all this. Everyone else in the carriage was, she was sure, on their way to see a lover, or to a reunion with a long-lost friend, or to a celebration. She was the only one travelling nervously to Wales to see a mother who terrified her, on her birthday.

The only one whose husband thought she was having an affair she wasn't having.

The only one who'd made such a mess of her life.

The train slowed down and Vivie stared through the window and saw great shaggy bushes of the plant that had grown from the window-sill of her flat. It threw itself up between the tracks, growing from the cinders. Its flowers were thick and long and heavy and purple and its abundant leaves were silvery-grey. There were bushes and bushes of it and Vivie wondered, not for the first time in her life, how on earth the plants thrived without water and earth. How they managed to be so healthy, beautiful, even, without the necessary food.

They were courageous plants, and stubborn. They flourished against all the odds.

Iris's story

I stood under my tree. I leaned against it and stared up through its branches that spread out like fingers. The leaves were still green, but it seemed wrong that they were and its seedpods hung down, split open and empty.

Small hailstones bounced off the grass and tears poured down my face because Joan Aldwater was dead.

All through that winter Dick came to sit in my kitchen and he told me how he missed Joan more than he could ever have guessed he would. He said he felt guilty because he'd never imagined life without her. He'd always known she would be there. She was so reliable and capable and so much younger than him. He said he hadn't told her that he loved her nearly often enough.

And now she was dead because a stupid driver on the M11 had driven too fast on the inside lane, pulled out in front of her dog van and she'd driven straight into him. 'Bloody, bloody motorways,' he said, his head in his hands, his elbows on the table. 'But it's my fault. I should have taken that old wreck of a van off the road years ago.'

Then he came and stood beside me at the stove – I'd made an omelette for us – and I told him that he was the kindest man I knew, and I said I was sure Joan knew it. I said I knew it because he'd done more for me than anyone else in the world. Even John Dexter. In the days when I thought John Dexter did good things for me.

And then I wondered if I'd said the wrong thing, until he smiled at me and the fan-shaped lines beside his eyes deepened and grew closer together and I saw that they were like miniature deltas at the mouths of two rivers, carrying water. And I touched the water with my fingertips.

And we lived like this, keeping each other company, sometimes eating in my cottage and sometimes in his, and we talked to each other and we listened to each other. But then the telephone call came, from the hospital in London. My father was very ill and I had to go, quickly. Dick came with me to the station, in the taxi. He said he would come to London with me.

'I'll be all right,' I said. 'Don't worry,' and I kissed his cheek.

But when I found a seat on the train John Dexter came down the aisle and sat opposite me. He travelled backwards. I travelled forwards. I felt very cold. I was not glad to see him and I didn't like the expression on his face. He reached towards me and took hold of my hand. My fingers tingled. I tried to take my hand away but he pinched it so tightly that he hurt me.

'Well, here we are again, old girl,' he said. But he did not say it kindly and the woman next to me got up and moved to a different seat.

John Dexter let go of my hand and I put my hands together to rub them, to warm them up, but when I looked down I saw that they banged into each other and I didn't know why they did that. And then I realised, with a terrible shock, that they were numb. I couldn't feel them. It had happened again.

Dick collected me from the hospital. I knew the sister was about to send me to Salem. I told Dick so on the telephone, and he came.

'People die every day,' the sister said. 'It is a common enough occurrence. I simply haven't the time to cope with hysterical relatives.'

But I had to struggle with John Dexter because he stood between me and Dick on the street. He dodged so quickly that whichever way I went, he was there between us. And when Dick grabbed hold of my wrists I was convinced that he was going to take me back to Salem, so I began to struggle with him, as well. I battered him on the shoulders. I said I must not, could not, go back there.

'I promise you, Iris,' said Dick, 'I give you my word that you will not go back to Salem. But I have rung the man, the German, you remember? The new German medicines. The new German ideas.'

'This is not a war,' I yelled.

'I think, perhaps, that it is,' said Dick and he gripped my upper arms. 'Or, at least, a crucial battle.'

But all I knew was that my father was dead and he'd cried in his hospital bed and I'd seen his tears, and I'd never seen my father cry before. And he said something to me about how like my mother I was and how he had been wrong and I had been right, but I did not hear everything he said because John Dexter's voice drowned him out from the other side of my father's bed.

'Drink this,' said a voice.

'It is poisoned,' said John Dexter.

There was a candle. John Dexter blew it out.

'Drink this.' I saw a mouth move in the gloom. 'It will help you.'

It was bitter. It dribbled down my chin. And then there was a hand with pills in it.

'And swallow these, Iris.'

No deep sea monster. No no no no no no no.

'We cannot help you, Iris, if you will not help yourself. These will help you.'

I knew that voice. But it disappeared, into the darkness.

I tried to keep hold of something. I tried so hard. I tried to remember. But everything, except John Dexter, slid from me.

'They will try to talk you out of me, old girl,' said John Dexter. 'Remain on your guard.' His voice was so beautiful that I wanted to cry.

And then there was a bright bright light.

'No ECT, no Largactil. No poisoned-anus monster.'

'We don't use ECT here, Iris,' said the voice that I knew I knew. 'Nor have I prescribed Largactil.'

The bright light was sunshine. It came in through a big window beyond my bed.

'You are at The Abbey, not Salem.'

A face looked down at me. I knew that face. 'I have prescribed

Stelazine, it is less retardive than Largactil. The dose will be reduced, Iris, as you recover. But, to begin with, you must take it.'

'Ruth?'

'Yes, Iris, it's Ruth.'

'Then I am at Salem and you've lied to me.'

'Sit up, Iris. Look around you. Does this look like Salem?'

She helped me sit up. Did the pillows. And I saw that I was in a bed in a room on my own. There was a balcony. French windows. A big lawn outside which was frosty.

'You're not at Salem, Iris. This is The Abbey. And I work here.'

'Have you become a German?' I said.

Ruth laughed and said she was still English, but she said the clinic was run by Germans and the ideas, and the way they worked at The Abbey all came from Germany. Different ideas. Gentle, good ideas, she said.

'We do things differently here, Iris,' she said. 'And if you want to, enough, you will get well here.'

I rested with a warm poultice tied round my stomach. It comforted me like a hotwater bottle, comforted me like love.

Ruth sat in a chair by my bed. 'It'll help you,' she said. 'It's got yarrow in it.'

But Ruth was cut off by John Dexter. He leaned against the French windows. His pipe was in his mouth. He did a slow hand clap.

'It will tie you down,' he said.

I sat up. Suddenly I wanted the poultice off me, but my hands were too clumsy.

'Trust me,' said Ruth, and she smoothed it back down. 'They take a while to get used to, but everyone here comes to love their cloths.' She looked at me. 'That's what people here call them. But really, it's a poultice.'

'Do not believe her,' said John Dexter. 'It has leaked poison into you all afternoon. It must come off.'

'Who is it?' said Ruth. 'Who's there, Iris?'

John Dexter put his finger to his lips and shook his head. The room filled with blue-grey smoke from his pipe, and I started to cough.

I made Ruth open the French windows, even though she said it was much too cold. But I had to escape from the smoke. The cloth thing stayed attached to me, round my stomach and Ruth asked me what it was that had made me cough.

'His smoke,' I said.

John Dexter knocked his pipe out on the iron rail of the balcony behind Ruth. He stared at me. 'Do not speak to them of me, old girl,' he said. 'This is a war zone. Germans everywhere. Remain silent at all times.' His dark eyes shone, his snaggle tooth showed.

'Who's there, Iris?' said Ruth as I scrambled out of bed.

John Dexter swung one leg over the balcony. 'I am your ally, old girl, remember?' he said. 'I would not lie to you. You can trust me. But you must leave this place. Come. Hold my hand. Jump.'

But Ruth held onto me, held onto the cloth thing round my middle.

'It's all right, Iris,' she said. 'I've got you. I've got you.'

But it wasn't all right, because I had to watch John Dexter land below me on the lawn and stride away.

I didn't know who to believe.

Vivie's story

Vivie gasped then tried to pretend that she hadn't. She didn't want to draw attention to herself. She bit her lip and gripped her forearms. The train had gone into a tunnel and she couldn't stand tunnels.

The train rushed from the tunnel into a deep cutting. Vivie saw a wall of trees and relaxed a little. She hoped there wouldn't be another tunnel, but the heedless train hurtled on, made a 'thrrrrp' sound and Vivie's ears popped.

She forced herself to imagine wide open blue skies. She thought about the sea. She crushed her lucky black cap in her hands and told herself it was only a tunnel. Only a tunnel.

Matthew's story

I order a taxi for Dad and then I set off. I expect to see the sea at every turn in the chipped limestone track through the fields; expect to be standing on a cliff edge with the sea below me before I've gone half a mile, but it's taking much longer than I thought it would.

There are larks singing high above me and there are seagulls wheeling and screeching close by, but at every bend in the uphill track there is yet more scrubby grassland, yet more yellow ragwort and thistle, yet more hawthorn and bramble. I must be much further inland than I realised and I'm impatient to see the sea, just as I used to be when I was a child and we drove to the coast and Vivie and I sat facing each other in the back of Mum's dog van, beside the dogs on their beanbags. There was always a prize for the person who saw the sea first, or who claimed they'd seen the sea first; it was the whole point of the journey. But, today, the sea is proving elusive.

Since yesterday, since admitting to Dad that I've always loved Vivie, I've felt relief and shame in just about equal measure. I'm relieved that he knows, I feel better for telling him, but I also feel a sharper sense of shame at my cowardice, at my failure to tell Vivie I loved her when I had the chance, when she gave me the chance, I think. Now he knows that as well and this morning I wish he didn't. My failure was Charles's triumph; speak now, or forever …

At last, here's the sea. A grassy valley opens out below me to the south and at the far end the Bristol Channel is glinting and sparkling. I stand and stare at it and persuade myself I can smell salt in the air, but I can't; I'm too far away.

That summer, after Iris came back from Salem, we drove to the coast and Iris said the prize for the person who saw the sea first would be a kiss. But when we should have been straining to see the sea through the chicken-wire that kept the dogs, and us, from clambering into the front seats, Vivie and I stayed resolutely where we were. We didn't look at each other and nor did we look for the sea, because a kiss from Iris in those days was always full of dribble and neither of us wanted one.

Then Vivie shot a look at me, quick as lightning, and shouted, 'I can see it, I can see it,' without even looking, and she put her fingers through the chicken-wire onto her mother's shoulder and I felt ashamed of myself. Vivie kept hold of Iris's hand all day that day; I remember because I got bored sliding down the dunes by myself with the cold wind blowing the sand back into my face. When we got home I said I was sorry, but Vivie just said, 'For what?' and slammed her bedroom door in my face.

Vivie's story

Vivie avoided the gaze of the woman with white hair who sat in a seat on the other side of the aisle. She wondered, extremely irritably, why women like that so often singled her out. She tucked her hair back up under her lucky cap to keep it off her face – it had become very hot in the carriage – and she stared down at her hands and tightly crossed her fingers.

She said to herself, 'Please God let that be the last of the tunnels and then I'm getting off.' She picked at the skin on her thumb.

And then, to her horror, she heard the woman address her.

'It's Vivie, isn't it? Iris Marchwood's daughter?'

Vivie's heart lurched. How the hell did this woman know her name?

'I'm Ruth,' said the woman and Vivie saw her hand stretching out, almost touching her own. 'Ruth Carpenter.'

Vivie neither shook the woman's hand nor looked up, but she knew exactly who the woman was. Ruth Carpenter was the doctor from The Abbey. The doctor who'd wanted her to see her mother on her own when she couldn't bear to.

Vivie stared resolutely, rudely, away from Ruth and out through the window. She made herself repeat what Charles had said when they'd driven to Lowestoft. He'd said that tunnels were just the connecting bits. He'd said, 'Just think of the Blackwall tunnel as the shortest route between where we are and where we want to get to. Nothing to it.'

And he'd said, 'Breathe deeply, Vivienne.'

But thinking about Charles brought a lump to Vivie's throat and she turned towards the window. She hated anyone to see her crying but she couldn't stop the tears. They fell for her aborted child and because she'd meant to love Charles, not to hurt him. They fell because it was her thirtieth birthday and she had nothing but failure to show for all those years. They fell for her childhood and for her mother's madness.

They fell for the sheer hopelessness of everything.

Iris's story

I stood on the balcony of my room.

A woman picked daffodils in the long grass at the end of the garden. She walked back across the lawn, a trug full of daffodils over her arm. She stopped underneath my balcony. She asked me if I liked daffodils. It was a brilliantly sunny day and I had to shade my eyes to see her properly.

'I like yellow,' I said and the woman smiled up at me.

'Then would you like some of these in your room?' she said.

I took a step forwards. I stumbled and reached for the iron railing. I thought I'd caught it but my hands were numb and I found I was grasping at thin air. I fell sideways.

'Wait there,' said the woman. 'Don't move.'

Moments later she ran into my room and Ruth followed her.

Ruth told me not to move while she checked my arms, legs, all of me. Then she said it was okay to stand and she helped me back from the balcony into my room. Ruth took my hand and I watched my fingers curl round her hand, but I couldn't feel a thing.

I sat in the chair by the table in my room. The door was open. There was a painted wooden plaque on the door. It was a tree. I knew what kind of tree it was even before I stood up to look at it closely. It was a laburnum, in flower and, printed in neat yellow letters underneath it were the words: 'Laburnum' and then 'Iris Marchwood'.

I'd never opened the door before. I'd never left the room. I didn't know I could. I'd never seen my name on a door before, anywhere.

I stared out into the passage.

I stared around my room. The daffodils on the table were such a beautiful, buttery yellow that I wanted to cry. But I couldn't even do that.

I walked down the stairs and out into the garden and no one, absolutely no one, tried to stop me. I sat on a stone bench surrounded by a yew hedge. It was safe there. Then I walked all round the garden.

When I went back inside I helped myself to tea, with other people, and there was only tea in the pot. No sugar and no milk. I asked if the house was ever locked.

'Only at night,' said the woman who sat down next to me. 'The same as you would with your own front door.'

A man came out of the kitchen and asked me if I would like to help them prepare the food sometimes. I lifted my hands and said they're too clumsy, and I couldn't feel anything with them but the man said, 'That's all right, we'll help you.'

I began to work with some clay in a room with a glass roof like a greenhouse and blinds you could pull, for shade. There were windows on three sides of the room and it was light and airy and I liked to watch the clay squidge and squash in my hands, even though I couldn't feel it.

There was a woman who helped me called Hanna, and I said that I thought the clay looked like solidified smoke, or a brain, and she asked me why, but I didn't know. But I loved the room because it was the kind of room that, if you had wings, you could have practised flying in. And then all you'd have to do would be to ask Hanna to open one of the windows, when you were ready.

I could see the gardens that stretched out below and I could see a stone birdbath on a pedestal, and the yew hedge that made a circle, and the long grass where the daffodils were. The grass was Granny-Smith apple green, and there were beech trees beyond and herbs grew, for our medicines, in the garden. They grew lavender in the garden too, I could see it from the room. I had crushed some and held it to my nose when I'd walked there.

Hanna said the clay hardened when you left it in the air, and you could make it soft again with water. She helped me make what I wanted to make when I asked her, because my hands were still clumsy but sometimes, in Hanna's room, my hands could feel the clay.

And I worked in the kitchen. I helped to prepare the food.

And I worked in the garden. I dug and I weeded and I loved the smell of the damp earth. It reminded me of home.

But John Dexter said that this was not his kind of work, so he kept his distance.

People helped me when my hands were clumsy, and when they started to tingle and could feel more Hanna helped me make a pair of hands from the clay. I loved those hands. They faced each other and touched at the fingertips and at the pad below the thumbs. Their sinews and veins and knuckles and nails, their palms and their fingers were beautiful. Hanna helped me make a gap between the palms and the fingers, carefully. We used delicate tools and it was difficult to mould the insides of the hands in the small space. But we succeeded.

It took many days' work in the light airy room. But they were a beautiful pair of hands when they were finished.

And then, one day, I could not bear to look at the hands because they made me want to cry, so I left the room quickly and I cried alone in my room. I told Ruth that it was the hands that had made me cry. And I told her that yellow makes me cry.

And then one day, when I was in the kitchen, I saw four thick black hairs that sprouted from the back of my right hand. But they were far too thick for hair; they were curved and pointed at the ends, like black crab claws. When I tried to pull one off I heard a slurp and then I held a sheath between my fingers. And I saw that from my hand an ugly, fleshy, pale pink hook, like the flesh of a crab's claw, grew. But it was covered with slime and, as it moved in the air, it glistened. Small whistles and whines came from it; it sounded like a radio tuned in to a distant station, and I realised it was a claw-antenna. I realised that it picked up signals through the short white cactus hairs that stuck out from its slimy sides. It was the ugliest thing I had ever seen.

But I knew the signals were for me, so I put my ear to it and I heard John Dexter's voice through the crackles and whistles and whines. He told me to pull the black sheaths off the other three antenna and when I did they glistened and swayed slightly on the back of my right hand, and I felt sick because they were so very ugly. And then I heard John Dexter's voice, very clearly.

He said that I must stop this servant's work in the kitchen. He said it was beneath me. It was then that I saw that the antennae were infected.

So I sliced them off with the kitchen knife.

Matthew's story

I am in a thicket of brambles that are catching and pulling at my ankles and the track is so narrow now that I'd have to flatten myself into the hawthorn if anyone came the other way.

I'm wishing I'd worn socks, or jeans, not shorts and deck shoes, but it's so hot and I'd just assumed I'd be walking over bluff, across clifftops. I thought it would be headland all the way. I never asked.

Perhaps there's another path that I've missed.

It will be hard going if it's thicket all the way to the castle.

Iris's story

I was in the light airy room. My right hand was bandaged.

John Dexter was in the room, too. But I couldn't see him clearly, although I could feel his anger. Blue-grey smoke billowed from his pipe.

I turned away from John Dexter. I held the hands I had made with Hanna.

I wanted to hide the hands from John Dexter. I knew I didn't want him to touch them but, without warning, he suddenly pushed me forwards and my clay hands flew across the room. They slid along the shiny wooden floor and splintered and smashed up against the wall.

My heart broke.

I watched John Dexter's shadowy feet walk all over my broken hands and crush them and make them into dust on the floor.

Dust rose from my bandaged hand and mingled with the blue-grey smoke from John Dexter's pipe.

I knew I had to leave the room otherwise I would choke to death.

Vivie's story

'It's a *long* tunnel, *this* one,' said a squeaky child's voice, 'isn't it?'

Vivie put her hand over her mouth as if the words had been her words. The lights in the train carriage flickered, dimmed and then they went out altogether.

The carriage was pitch black and no one spoke. All Vivie could hear was people breathing and shifting in their seats and the tunnel was endless. A blue light flashed past and Vivie wished there were more.

The squeaky child's voice said, 'It's a *really really* long tunnel, isn't it?'

An adult voice answered, 'Of course it is, darling. We're under the Severn. Here, hold my hand.'

Vivie dug her nails into her palms as she took this information in. They were under the Severn, under a massive crushing weight of water. She felt foolish as she thought about it. She should have known. You can't get to South Wales from London without crossing the Severn, somehow. Only she was underneath it.

She began to gasp and choke. She felt as if she was suffocating. She felt as if her throat was closing up.

She saw her mother's vacant expression as she sat under a large tree.

She heard a croaking, rasping voice saying, 'No deliveries expected today. No flowers. No books. Nothing expected, thank you.'

She stared into a pair of eyes that showed no sign of recognition; a pair of eyes that stared, unseeing.

She saw a pair of hands throw some small pink roses onto a lawn.

She watched, terrified, as a book thudded onto her feet. She stared down at the book.

And then she pulled her feet out from under the book and she ran for her life.

Iris's story

Ruth gave me a powder to swallow, in a spoon, mixed with honey. It was called Stibium. I liked its name because it sounded as though it would make me strong. And I drank more of the bitter drink and took my pills and I told Ruth how, the day before, in the garden, I'd helped Julian dig out a dead lilac.

'But when we got down to the root,' I said, 'Julian leaned on his spade and said we shouldn't dig any more because it wasn't dead but connected to the living lilacs further along the flower bed. He told me lilacs have sucker systems. He said that they survive even when the mother root dies. So he said we'd just pull off the dead bits and leave the rest.'

Ruth smiled at me and I told her how the dead root had crumbled in Julian's hands; how after that I didn't pull any more up myself because he'd said it was the mother root and I wanted it to stay, safe in the earth.

Then Ruth said something but I didn't hear her because John Dexter laughed from the balcony. It was a horrible sneer of a laugh and before I knew it I was on my feet.

'You crushed my hands,' I said, and I stood as close to him as I dared. 'You CRUSHED my HANDS! WHY? I loved them.'

John Dexter stared straight ahead and puffed on his pipe.

'I broke nothing,' he said.

'You trod all over them,' I said.

I steadied myself against the wooden frame of the French windows. My hands tingled. I could feel the wood and the roughness of the cracked paint. I gripped the frame and then I said, 'John Dexter, why haven't you got any grey hairs? You should have, by now. I have.'

'I hardly think so, old girl,' said John Dexter, but his voice was suddenly difficult to hear, so I had to lean towards him.

'Speak up,' I said.

'You can hear me,' he said. 'There's no need to pretend that you cannot.'

John Dexter took his pipe from his mouth but it seemed to hover before his face because his arm and his hand had become indistinct.

'I rather think you are stuck with me for life, old girl,' he said. But his body had become disjointed. I could only see parts of him clearly.

'I am not stuck with you,' I said. 'I can choose.'

'Oh come on now, Iris, old girl,' said John Dexter. 'You know that's not true.'

I took a deep breath. 'I'm not sure you are real,' I said. 'Not in the way that I am.'

'And precisely what do you mean by that, old girl?' said John Dexter.

I could see his mouth, his eyes and his shiny hair. I could see his chin and his jaw, and one arm, but they moved in odd juxtaposition to one another. I could see his beige corduroys, his brown brogues. 'You always wear the same clothes,' I said.

'Which is a perfectly practical thing to do,' said John Dexter.

'Shave!' I said. 'And leave the hairs in the sink for me to see.'

'I do not happen to have a razor on me, old girl.' His voice was a hoarse whisper. 'Sorry.'

'Then eat something! Drink something! Let me see it disappear inside you. Here,' I said, turning back to the table, 'eat this.' And I handed him an apple from the bowl on the table.

John Dexter knocked out his pipe on the iron rail of the balcony. I heard the familiar sound but I could no longer see the pipe. But I saw the apple move as he took it from my hand.

My own hands tingled.

I saw John Dexter's snaggle tooth, his narrow lips, his neat jaw, but all as if through a mist. But his lips moved, his teeth bit into the apple and I lost my nerve.

'Iris?'

It was Ruth's voice. I turned to her. I heard a faint thud as something fell and I felt a strong pressure against my back. I knew it was John Dexter, but when I turned to face him I couldn't see him at all.

But I could still hear him.

'Do not let her talk you out of me, Iris, old girl,' he rasped in my ear and I smelled his stale smoker's breath. I turned my head away. 'Do not let her come between us. I beg you.'

'You came between me and my father,' I said. 'You made it impossible for me to hear the last words my father spoke. And you don't want me to hear myself, John Dexter. I will not let you do this to me any more. I will not.'

The pressure stopped, and I stumbled and then I fell. Ruth caught me and helped me to a chair.

'Open the door, please Ruth,' I said, after a while.

She looked at me. Her blue-green eyes asked me a silent question.

'To let him out,' I said.

I slumped in the chair and, out of the corner of my eye, I saw the apple, uneaten on the floor, just as it had been when I took it out of the bowl. And although I couldn't see him at all by then, I knew John Dexter walked out through that door. And I was, suddenly, very sad because he came as my friend, once. My only friend in all the world, once. But he became my enemy, my persecutor.

He wanted to kill my stories and to take my life.

He did not want me to live as me.

The last thing I saw was a twist of smoke on the landing and, when I turned to the French windows, I saw a patch of grey mist above the lawn. I watched the sun burn it off. And then there was nothing.

Vivie's story

Vivie realised she was leaning against someone whose arms held her up, and that she was sobbing her heart out. She didn't resist when she felt herself guided forwards. She noticed rectangles of yellow sunlight on the floor as her feet moved with the other person's feet and she felt that the direction they were moving in was the only possible direction to take; an inevitable direction.

Vivie heard the sound of a window being opened and then she felt herself being turned. Cool air touched her face and she breathed deeply. Then she stared up at the bright blue sky, and she heard the trundling sound of the slow-moving train.

Vivie said, through her tears, 'I am mad, aren't I? I've gone mad, haven't I?' to no one in particular.

'I don't think so,' said a gentle voice behind her.

Vivie turned and found herself looking into a pair of eyes that were like green-blue pools. She thought, perhaps, that they had tears in them too.

'I think you had an attack of claustrophobia,' said the owner of the eyes. 'Would you like a kleenex?'

Vivie stared.

'I'm Ruth,' she said as she handed Vivie a kleenex. 'Ruth Carpenter. We met at The Abbey.'

Vivie took the kleenex without saying a word.

'I thought you needed some air,' said Ruth.

Vivie blew her nose, rubbed her eyelids and turned away from Ruth.

The train was moving slowly through an abandoned station which Vivie saw was called Severn Tunnel Junction and, as she breathed in and out as slowly as she could manage, she saw bushes and bushes of the purple flowering plant growing from the concrete platform. The bushes swayed gently as the train went by, as if they were greeting her, Vivie thought, and she took another long, deep breath and turned back to Ruth, who held out another kleenex.

'Why are you on this train?' said Vivie, trying to keep her voice from shaking.

'I'm going to the storytelling festival,' said Ruth. 'I meant to leave yesterday, but I ended up doing the night shift.' She looked at Vivie. 'Are you – '

' – It's just that I hate tunnels,' Vivie blurted out. 'That's all. I can't breathe in them.'

The train trundled on but Ruth didn't say anything else.

'I can't breathe on the underground either,' said Vivie and glanced at Ruth. 'I ... I ... when I was on the underground with Matthew ... after I saw Mum ... I thought I was going to die. I made him take us off.'

Still Ruth said nothing.

Vivie blew her nose, again. 'I remembered it just now ... how I felt ... what happened ... seeing Mum that day ... the underground ... everything ... Salem.'

'I was there,' said Ruth. 'I remember.'

'You were there?' Vivie bit into the side of her hand. 'What do you mean you were there?'

'I was a nurse at Salem,' said Ruth. 'I was with your mother that day. I shall never forget it. You spoke so gently to your mother. You were an extraordinarily brave, kind child.'

Vivie stared at Ruth. 'What did I say ... to Mum?'

'You said you loved her. You said you'd come to help her, come to take her home.'

Vivie smiled a shaky smile. 'Oh God,' she said. 'Did I?'

Ruth smiled and words began to pour from Vivie. 'Mum rang last night,' she said. 'I haven't spoken to her for so long. I don't really know what I'm doing. And now this ... and it's my birthday,' and she found herself in Ruth's arms again, crying, again.

'I tried to stop them taking Mum to Salem. I hid myself ... Matthew helped me ... under the dogs' beanbags but I couldn't breathe. I was squashed and it was dark and then Mum yelled and I threw the beanbags off, I just had to, and I saw the doctor inject her in the bum. And they saw me.'

The train began to pick up speed.

'I haven't remembered any of this until now. I forgot everything. Forgot how Mum was when Matthew and I went to see her. Forgot how I was in the back of the dog van. Forgot how I yelled at the doctor. Forgot about the underground. All I've remembered ... until just now ... is Mum going mad in the cottage ... and me trying to warn her that the doctor wasn't her dancing partner. I haven't ever been able to get all that out of my mind.'

Vivie stopped and looked into Ruth's green-blue eyes. She saw that the whites were startlingly white and she saw that Ruth really was crying. Vivie held out her soggy kleenex, and they both laughed. Then Ruth pulled another kleenex from the deep pocket of her indigo dress and without Ruth's stabilising hands Vivie almost overbalanced. She put her hand out behind her and steadied herself against the carriage door.

'How could I have forgotten so much?' she said.

'Would you really like to know?' said Ruth.

Vivie nodded.

'One of the ways we protect ourselves from terrifying experiences,' said Ruth, 'is to "forget" them. We bury them. But if you're alone with a person for as long as you were, when that person is as ill as Iris was, you're unlikely to forget her illness. And it can feel as if,' she stopped and looked at Vivie through eyes that Vivie felt could see to her very core, 'it can feel as if you will go mad too, as if you will catch the other person's madness, as if it's contagious.' She smiled. 'People who've seen what you saw sometimes feel like that for a long time afterwards. It's not at all unusual.'

The train was clackety-clacking over the rails. 'And sometimes,' said Ruth, finding yet another kleenex from the deep pocket of her flowing indigo dress, 'sometimes it's right to stay away and to keep everything else that happened buried until you find your own equilibrium. Because until you know that you can hold your own centre of gravity in the face of another's loss of it, you may very well be overwhelmed ... all over again.'

'I haven't been doing so well on the gravity thing recently,' said Vivie. 'But do you ... do you think she'll do it again?'

'I don't think so,' said Ruth. 'How long since you've seen her?'

'This is the first time for ... I mean I've never seen her well, I don't think. Not since I was a child ... and I'm terrified,' said Vivie.

'Until you see her well,' said Ruth, 'you will only remember her desperately ill. And those memories will go on horrifying you, contaminating you, you could say.'

'Do *you* think she's normal now?'

'Normal is a word I dislike,' said Ruth, smiling. 'But if you must use it, then yes. She is.'

'It's just that ... it's difficult to believe you can get well from ... what she's had.'

'It is,' said Ruth. 'But schizophrenia's an episodic illness, as I'm sure you know. And I don't think your mother would have been invited to tell her stories at a festival if she was in a psychotic state, do you?'

'I don't know,' said Vivie. 'Who knows what happens at story-telling festivals?'

'A person in a psychotic state can't hold the threads ... can't hold a narrative line,' said Ruth. 'That's the tragedy. That's what they lose.'

'I didn't mean that,' said Vivie, 'about storytelling festivals ... it's just ... it's just ...' but her tears overwhelmed her again.

'Feelings buried alive never die,' said Ruth.

'You said that to me at The Abbey,' said Vivie, sniffing. 'When you were trying to persuade me to see Mum on my own. Without Charles.'

'I tend to say it a lot,' said Ruth.

'I've always thought I never did anything to help Mum,' said Vivie. 'But I've just discovered ... remembered ... what I did try to do.'

'You were a courageous child,' said Ruth. 'I've never forgotten what I saw you try to do for your mother.'

'Mum said I was brave ... last night,' said Vivie.

Ruth looked at her.

'When she rang last night she said ... she said ... well I'm on this train because of what she said.'

Vivie stared down at the blackened, soggy kleenexes in her hand and suddenly remembered how, when she'd been working with Sara on a cosmetics account, Sara had shown her her cuttings board for the job. The only cutting that had stayed in Vivie's mind was one about mascara. It said that the word 'mascara' came from *maschera*, which meant mask.

Vivie turned back to the window. She opened her hand and let the kleenexes fly, soggy blackened piece after soggy blackened piece, backwards and away, out of the train window. And as she watched the kleenexes fly Vivie smiled. She realised that there hadn't been a single judgement in the whole conversation with Ruth.

Matthew's story

I'm out of the thicket, at last, and sitting on baked earth on a headland at the edge of a field of maize. Blue speedwell runs along beneath the maize stalks and there is heathland in front of me, and to the east and west of me. I'm staring at the sea and it's glittering under the sun. The coastline bows out to the south and then curves in and away to the west in a wide sweep, and the sun is beating down. I should have borrowed Dad's hat. I gulp some water, pour some over my head and rub some into my scratched ankles and calves and, as I stand up, some loose change spills from my shorts' pocket and I bend down to pick it up.

The jam jar full of silver coins lived on the table by the window that looked out onto the village green, onto Dad's yellow buckeyes. After I'd plundered it for our journey to Salem it stood there, accusingly empty, waiting for me to refill it. It took me more than two years to repay the money; but I'd always planned to pay it back, I just never imagined how long it would take, and I hadn't anticipated my pocket money being stopped. But I repaid the money, every single penny. I did an extra paper round and I cleaned people's windows almost before they asked me to, and I did as many extra odd jobs as I could fit in, as many as I could persuade people that they needed to have done.

Once Iris offered to give me some money but I refused. I wanted to pay every single penny back myself, but I was sure someone else kept putting money into the jam jar. And one day, when it looked far too full, I tipped the coins out and counted them and there was much more money than there should have been. So I started keeping a record in the back of my maths exercise book, one column for the money I had put into the jam jar, another column for the weekly totals and the final column for the difference, and there always was a difference.

Speaking of Love

Each week I took out the extra coins and left them beside the jam jar on the table by the window. But every week they were put back and I never saw anyone putting them back so, after a while, I stopped taking the extra coins out but I still kept my record because I wanted to pay back whoever it was who was helping me, and when the day came and I presented my mother with exactly the amount of money I had taken, twenty-five pounds in one full jam jar, I put the extra coins into a second jam jar and told my mother I had no idea where they'd come from. She suggested I ask Vivie and when I did, and Vivie hotly denied it, I knew it had been her. That was when I realised she wasn't nearly as cross with me as I'd thought.

After that the jam jars were kept in the kitchen, on the shelf above the dogs' beanbags. One was Vivie's and one was mine and we only ever put silver coins into them, we never took any out. I said we'd spend them on something we really wanted, one day. But we never did and they're still there, in Dad's kitchen.

Iris's story

I was wrapped tightly in layers of towel and blanket, as if I had been swaddled. There were even layers around my head, I could have been an Egyptian mummy. I had been shown how to free my arms if I wanted to.

I had just had what they called an oil dispersion bath. I could still smell the lavender and feel the way my skin tingled from the brushes. A man had brushed my skin all over and his brushes had looked just like old shoe brushes. They were floating in the big old bath when I got in. And there was a candle at the end of the bath and a single white rose in a vase.

They really did do things differently, there.

I had to rest for an hour, afterwards. Ruth sat beside me. She put her hand on my shoulder and I closed my eyes, breathed in the lavender smell and drifted inside my cocoon where it was warm and safe.

And then, suddenly, I was inside a nightmare.

I walked down the Gloucester Road to buy a ginger cake for my father, for his birthday, for a surprise. I was seven and a half years old. I held my mother's hand. She wore a yellow dress and a yellow jacket. She told me it was called the 'New Look'. And she wore a yellow hat with yellow netting that came down to the bridge of her nose. I thought she looked quite beautiful. And I could smell her lavender and vanilla smell.

We turned to cross the road, my mother and I.

My right hand held her left hand.

But then was a terrible noise, a cacophony of sounds, and my mother's hand flew from my hand. My mother was torn from my grasp and clouds of blue-grey smoke billowed out from behind a tall red London bus and the smoke made me choke, and my mother was not there.

Speaking of Love

I couldn't see her.

A single yellow shoe flew above the smoke, in an arc.

I had let go of my mother's hand. I hadn't kept hold of her.

And then the smoke cleared and my mother lay in the middle of the Gloucester Road. Dead.

'It's all right,' said Ruth's voice. 'It's all right, Iris. I am here. I am here. It's all right.'

Ruth and I sat in her office beside an open window. We drank lemon and ginger tea. It was warm and there was a big jug of water and two glasses on the table between us and I had just poured some water into my palm to see how it felt. It felt the way I imagined mercury might feel, cool and more solid than water looks.

I had touched everything I could get my hands on. I held things and didn't drop them. I told Ruth that the worn candlewick of my bedspread was soft, like an old but familiar thickly pelted animal. I told her that the broken pieces of my clay hand sculpture were softly crumbly, not craggy, the way they looked. I told her that the edge of the table was sharp, the carpet furry, the bowl of the glass vase that held yellow roses on the table was cool and fitted solidly, comfortingly between my palms. I told her that the china door handle was resistant, smooth, and that my own nails, when they pressed down hard into my palms, were like fine fiery steel. Ruth's hand was warm and dry, I told her.

A couple of blackbirds sang loudly just outside the window. It had been four months. And we had talked about so much. I had told her so much. I had unravelled some of the threads of my life and laid them out and looked at them. I had pulled the tangle apart. I had woven some of the threads back together, discarded others. My hands had recovered their ability to feel and I was, slowly, remembering my stories.

So much had been recovered; so much left behind.

And I knew I was on my way home.

Ruth pushed her white hair back and looked at me through her clear blue-green eyes. I asked her how long I'd have to stay on the

Stelazine. I said I felt cocooned, not yet truly alive.

'For a while, yet,' she said. 'But not for ever.'

'How will I know when I can stop?'

'We'll monitor you,' she said. 'Schizophrenia – we believe – is a crisis of the spirit and we know that drugs, even the most natural of remedies, cannot cure a crisis of the spirit. But we haven't yet found a way to begin the cure without them. So, we'll keep reducing the dose and, if all goes well, you could be off it within a year, maybe even six months.'

I was glad to know that there would come a time when I wouldn't have to take it. Not like the awful Largactil, before.

'In the hospital,' I said, 'when my father was dying, he told me he knew he'd made a terrible mistake. He said he should have let me talk about my mother, should have let me tell her stories. He said he remembered how well I told her story about the Eiffelene trolls. And he cried then. But John Dexter, who I thought was my right-hand man, my storyhand, he didn't want me to hear the things my father said. Or, more to the point, *I* couldn't bear to hear. It was too much, too late and too painful.'

Ruth reached forwards and put her hand on mine. 'When you know that love exists but it isn't spoken about,' she said, 'it can be very hard to bear. It's worse, I sometimes think, than a complete absence of love because it's so confusing. You sense it, but if it is never talked about you doubt what you sense.'

I listened to the blackbirds. They almost managed to make me smile, despite my tears. I told Ruth how Dick whistled to them and how they sang back. And I told her that I'd shaped a story that had been in my mind for a while. 'I thought I'd tell it at the evening gathering,' I said.

I told Ruth that the story was about geese, about the pinkfeet that moulted all their feathers in a safe place, in a sanctuary. I said I thought The Abbey was like that. A safe place to moult. To be naked. To unmask the naked truth.

'I look forward to hearing the story,' she said, smiling.

And when I asked her how I would know if I ever hallucinated again, she said, with a wry smile, 'When you're in the grip of a hallucination you don't know you're hallucinating. That's the trouble. You believe everything you see and everything you hear.' She looked at me and I nodded. 'But there are triggers, warning signs, and you know, now, what yours are.

'And there's one thing you can be sure of,' said Ruth, 'and it's this. If you ever wonder whether or not you are hallucinating then you can be confident that you are not. A schizophrenic in the grip of a crisis never questions a hallucination, never asks herself whether what she is seeing, or hearing, is real.'

'I hope I never see or hear John Dexter again,' I said.

'The trick for all of us,' said Ruth, and she smiled her wry smile, 'is to find a way of living that works. Somewhere between a leaf in the wind and a fossil in rock. That's the trick.'

We stood and she opened her arms and gathered me into them and gave me one of those hugs that only Ruth can give. One of those hugs that make it possible to believe that there is a life, a potential life, a possible life, a good life, a life that can be lived without disintegration, out there in the real world.

At home.

Matthew's story

I am standing as near to the cliff edge as I dare; there are great boulders strewn like giant's marbles on the beach below me, and the tide is out. The limestone beneath my feet is eroding and, on the beach, there is very little sand, just uniformly rectangular slabs of flat limestone spread out beyond the boulders and small pools of water between them. The slabs look as if an exacting stonemason has carved out a gigantic courtyard for a Welsh sea king and the striations in the cliffs above jut out southwards into the Bristol Channel; they look as if they've been cut particularly for the purpose and laid one on top of the other, very carefully.

I turn and walk along the curve of the cliff, northwards, and I come to a bay where a whitewashed, flint-tiled Victorian house stands proudly on a lush green lawn. It looks so neat, so tame and stands in such contrast to the boulder- and wrack-strewn bay. I walk down to the bay and scramble over small boulders, and then I climb back up the other side into a beech wood where it is cool, where the sun finds its way through the leaves in dazzling shafts and I stop to drink some more water. In the middle of the beech wood there is a fork in the path and instinctively I head to my right, uphill, because I am heading for a castle and castles aren't built beneath hills and then, as I round a bend in the path the trees thin out and through the branches, across several fields, I see the castle. The Welsh flag flies from a white pole in the keep, the Red Dragon flutters in the wind, and the crenellated limestone walls glow pale yellow-gold in the sun.

I find myself breathless for no particular reason, so I stand still in the wood and drink some more water. When I emerge I walk along beside a field where shorn sheep graze; then another where the skin of the cattle shines like ebony under the sun and then a third, fallow field. I hear voices and I see seven or eight pairs of coloured banners lazily flapping against vertical wooden poles on either side of a steep, wide avenue on the far side of the field. I see people walking up and down between the banners, and children running. The banners herald the storytelling festival and there is something mediaeval about them; they could just as easily herald a jousting tournament or a mediaeval fair.

I quicken my pace because it has taken me longer than I thought it would to get here, and Dad will be waiting. The path takes me away from the field and out onto more heathland and then I see, over the edge of the cliff in front of me, another bay and a cement causeway and more crenellated limestone walls above the causeway. There's another Welsh flag, another Red Dragon, flying proudly above what looks like a lifeboat station and when I look down onto the rocky, boulder-strewn beach I see a woman in yellow trousers and a long yellow tunic walking up and down on a slab of limestone. A yellow scarf hangs down her back and as she raises a hand to tuck her white hair behind her ear I realise it is Iris. I realise she is speaking, practising her stories, and it's such a familiar, heart-warming sight that I stand and watch her for a while. Then I skirt round the top of the cliff because I don't want to walk across the beach. It would disturb her.

Iris's story

'How are you, Iris?' said Dick, and he tipped his straw hat forwards to shade his eyes from the sun.

We sat on the stone bench in the garden surrounded by the circular yew hedge. There was a pool in the middle made of pieces of scalloped yellow stone. The water flowed in and out and around the hollows of the stones and it bubbled gently, smoothly, in the middle like a wide, flat upturned plate. We just sat and watched it.

And I borrowed Dick's hat and I shifted the cloth around my waist, under my clothes.

'I am on the mend,' I said. 'On the mend.'

And in answer to his unspoken question, and the way he shifted his gaze from the bulge under my clothes, I said, 'It's all right. It's called a cloth. We all wear them, on different parts of our bodies. It just depends which part needs the cloth. I call mine my cloth of gold because it's yellow. It's got yarrow in it. And lavender.'

Dick smiled and the lines that fan out around his eyes deepened. 'The heavens' embroidered cloths,' he said. 'The blue and the dim and the dark cloths, of night and light and the half-light.'

He put out his hand and I put my hand into his. His arthritis had bent his fingers. They looked like the branches of trees that have weathered many storms. He squeezed my hand gently and looked at me.

'I can feel things again,' I said, and I smiled. 'And the clumsiness has gone. And I've made another pair of hands, from clay.'

We both laughed at exactly the same time. 'A spare pair,' I said.

'And John Dexter?' said Dick.

'Has gone. I doubt he'll be back.'

We were quiet for a while. We just watched the water and listened to its music.

'You are the only person, Dick,' I said, 'the only person, apart from Ruth, who never looked at me with pity or as if you longed to get away from me.'

'I knew you were still in there, somewhere,' said Dick. 'But sometimes it was hard, waiting for you to come back out. Waiting for you to come home.'

'I was in prison,' I said. 'But I'm out now.'

'You are a remarkable woman, Iris,' said Dick. 'A very, very remarkable woman.'

We looked at each other for a long time. A long, quiet time that had a glow about it. And then Dick stood and put his hands on the small of his back and bent backwards, a little. When he turned towards me I stood, took off his hat and pulled at a piece of straw that had come loose. I put the straw into my mouth and chewed on it like a piece of grass. I put his hat back onto his head.

'When will you come home?' he said.

'Not long now,' I said. 'Not long now.'

I took a step closer to him.

And he took a step closer to me.

We stood very close to each other for a long time.

And then he kissed me and I kissed him and my heart soared and the piece of straw tickled my lips.

Matthew's story

I am walking along a path that curves upwards and away from several stone cottages; the Bristol Channel is behind me and my knapsack swings from my shoulder. The sound of the sea fades as I climb and I hear a burst of muffled laughter, followed by muffled clapping up ahead, and then I am standing at the end of a long lawn where several striped tents are pitched, two large ones and three or four smaller ones, and groups of people are walking between them.

Pennants flutter from the apexes of the tents and there is a limestone church standing on high ground at the far end of the long lawn. There are three tall palm trees below the church and when I look up, and to the right, I see the castle, high above the lawn, above some pines, and the whole place is alive with fiddles and pipes and laughter and conversation and colour. I think this must be how mediaeval fairs were. The flaps of the closest tent are tied back and I can see a stage with four women standing on it, one playing a fiddle, one some little cymbals that are attached to her fingers and one the pan pipes. There are raked benches facing the stage and the fourth woman stands gesticulating, obviously telling a story in front of the musicians, but I am too far away to catch all her words. I walk past a group of stilt-walkers and jugglers, practising, and people wearing flowing colourful clothes walk up and down, and there are stalls selling food, and stalls selling scarves and beads and people wearing jester's hats with bells, and people wearing tall striped hats and children on bicycles weaving in and out of the crowds, many of them with painted faces, some of them stopping to pull at the trailing coat of a tall figure who is dressed from head to toe in green and looks like a walking tree. He puts his fingers to his lips and points to a sign that says, 'Quiet, please. Storytelling in progress.'

Speaking of Love

I'm not sure where I will find Dad so I walk along the lawn looking into the tents and then I see a small tent called the 'Hodja tent' with a notice outside it saying that last night, in one and a half hours, sixty-nine Hodja stories were told and that this is a new record. I wish I'd been there, and I wonder if there were any children among the tellers. I wonder whether I would have had the courage to tell a Nasrudin story to an audience larger than my small audience of two. It makes me think how courageous storytellers are.

I walk to the far end of the lawn beneath the church but I have not found Dad, so I ask someone how to get up to the castle. She points back the way I have come and says there are steps through the pines; I thank her and just beside the steps I see a small striped tent with a banner that says, 'Information' looping down across its open front and as I pass it, something glints and catches my eye. I stop and turn and see, just behind the tied-back tent flap, a complete suit of armour standing as it might in a baronial hall with its helmet under one gauntlet and its lance held in the opposite one.

Beside the suit of armour a piece of paper is pinned to the canvas wall of the tent which tells me that this is an ancient jousting field where tournaments used to take place. I read on and I discover that this suit of armour belonged to a knight called Peredur Llawchwith, which means Perceval the Left-Handed. I read that when left-handed knights jousted they could not protect their hearts with their shields, unlike right-handed knights.

I think about this as I climb the flint steps through the pines, because I am left-handed; many architects are.

Vivie's story

Vivie and Ruth bounced along in the back of an empty, noisy, rattling country bus. They were nearly at their destination; they had been travelling for twenty-five minutes and, when Vivie caught a glimpse of the sea she began to hum the tune of the song her mother had loved, the song they'd both loved and sung so often on their way to the sea. And, to Vivie's surprise, Ruth knew the words too, so they sang it softly together, on the bus.

> *'If I loved you,*
> *Time and again I would try to say*
> *All I'd want you to know.*
>
> *If I loved you,*
> *Words wouldn't come in an easy way,*
> *Round in circles I'd go,*
> *Longin' to tell you, but afraid and shy*
> *I'd let my golden chances pass me by.*
>
> *Soon you'd leave me,*
> *Off you would go in the mist of day*
> *Never, never to know*
> *How I loved you,*
> *If I loved you.'*

It was very hot and they'd opened the windows so that the air could blow in as the bus shook its way along narrow lanes between high green hedges. And then, at last, they were in a shady lane overhung with trees. There was a stone wall to their right and they'd just passed a sign that read 'Sain Dunwyd'. They were going downhill and the driver had just called out, 'Next stop's yours, my ladies.' And Vivie's heart began to beat quickly.

She grabbed Ruth's hand and held on tight.

'Don't forget to breathe,' Ruth said, and put her other hand on top of Vivie's. 'Just don't forget to breathe.'

'I feel much better,' Vivie said. 'But I won't forget.'

Ruth looked at Vivie and smiled.

'Thanks, Ruth,' said Vivie. 'Thank you.'

Matthew's story

I find Dad sitting on a wooden bench overlooking terraced lawns that march down towards the Bristol Channel. He is wearing his collapsing straw hat and he sits with his back to a great stone hall with a watchtower at its west end. He says, 'Isn't this marvellous?'

'It is, Dad,' I say and I tell him I've just seen Iris practising her stories on the beach.

Dad holds up a programme and says that she's telling her stories at two o'clock, on the lawn below the one we are on. 'So,' he says, 'there's time to have something to eat, and to look round this magnificent place.'

We walk along a gravel path and out under a stone arch in a red brick wall. Dad says, 'Perfectly situated, wouldn't you say? I saw it on my way in.' He is looking at a small laburnum tree.

I say, 'I wonder if Iris has seen it?'

Dad says, 'Undoubtedly. How could she miss it?' and we turn towards the empty grass-filled castle moat and walk above and round it. The curtain wall must have been pulled down years ago but a magnificent limestone arch still stands and we walk under it. We stop by an ancient olive tree which Dad instantly falls in love with – and takes a photograph of – and then we cross a small bridge over the grassy moat, walk under the portcullis and see a group of people listening to a guide beneath the thick walls of the keep. The guide points out the shutes through which boiling oil was poured onto invading armies, and we follow the group into the inner courtyard where he says, 'And in that narrow window, high up there, Lady Ann Stradling stood with her child at her breast and the sight softened the Roundheads' hearts. They departed without taking the castle.'

He says, 'Occasionally people still catch glimpses of the ghost of Lady Ann. Some people see the train of her grey silk gown disappearing round a corner ahead of them; others smell her strong, almost overpowering scent of lavender. She loved lavender and you are most likely to smell it in the room in the watchtower where she often stood and kept watch over the Bristol Channel, looking out for the black sails of the marauding Breton pirates.'

I walk back down to the jousting field and buy garlic and vegetable noodles and cold, pale lager and Dad and I eat and drink on the wooden bench overlooking the terraced lawns.

Dad says that the lawn directly below us, the one where Iris will tell her stories, is called Rose Lawn. And he says that the red rose that covers the retaining wall is called 'Danse du Feu.'

He says, 'I wonder whether Iris knows that that's what it's called?'

Iris's story

I stood at the window of my room in the watchtower. I had Vivie's letter in my pocket and I watched as people gathered below me, on Rose Lawn. I saw Matthew open out a canvas chair for Dick, and I saw him sit on the lawn beside his father.

Dick wore his battered old straw hat, the one he wore when I realised I loved him. It was newer then, but I like it better now.

And I knew that I had done all I could to prepare myself to tell my stories.

I was left with nerves and nausea and the pictures from my stories, all in the wrong order in my head. And, from time to time, a completely dark void where there were no pictures at all.

But I had to trust.

I just had to trust that the stories would flow.

I can do no more now.

Vivie's story

Vivie was amazed to see that the bus really had dropped them outside a castle. She'd half-wondered if the American had been exaggerating.

She and Ruth followed luminous green arrows on a stone wall, away from the castle, paid at a desk under some trees and had green plastic admission bands strapped round their wrists. Then they walked through a wood and down a hill overlooking the Bristol Channel, between banners on tall poles from where they saw the castle again, with the Welsh flag fluttering from a tower.

It was so hot that Vivie had taken off most of her clothes and tied them round her waist.

Ruth read the programme as they hurried down the hill. On its cover an Arabian knight sat on a painted saddle on a white horse, and inside there was a painting of the festival grounds and a list of the names of the storytellers and where they were telling.

'Quickly,' said Ruth. 'She's on at two. She must be about to start.'

They looked at the painted map of the grounds, turned it upside down so that they could work out where they were, and decided that Rose Lawn must be just in front of the castle. They hurried on beside a banner with the words 'Beyond the Border' painted on it, and then they saw a stone arch in a red brick wall, and ran through it.

Then they both stopped, abruptly. They found themselves standing on a lawn above another lawn which was full of people, and Vivie heard her mother's voice introducing herself, but she couldn't see her. She felt as if she'd strayed onto a stage and forgotten her lines.

They walked quickly with their heads down towards the sound of Iris's voice, keeping close to a flower bed below a brick wall.

But it looked as if they were going to have to strike out and walk the length of the ledge above the lawn from where Iris's voice floated towards them, until Vivie saw, just ahead of them, some red brick steps that curved down inside an alcove to the lawn below. When they reached the bottom they sat behind some over-hanging creeper, both glad that they hadn't had to walk across the empty lawn with so many people watching them.

Vivie took a deep breath and pushed the creeper away. She leaned out from the bottom step, holding the creeper, and she stared at her mother. She thought she looked beautiful. She was dressed completely in yellow and she looked, Vivie thought, like an Asian princess.

Vivie's heart beat wildly as she listened to her mother. She hadn't heard her tell a story for as long as she could remember and she tried to concentrate on what her mother was saying, but her heart pounded as she wondered what on earth she would say to her, afterwards.

Vivie hitched the creeper up behind a protruding brick, took off her cap and leaned her elbows on her knees. Then she remembered that Matthew and Dick would be there, somewhere, too, and she turned and scanned the audience. Straight away she saw Dick, sitting higher than anyone else, on some kind of a seat, and then she saw Matthew, staring straight at her. He was sitting beside his father, below him, on the grass. And as Vivie shaded her eyes with her hand and looked at them both, she realised that their familiar faces were the two most precious faces in her whole world.

When she turned back to her mother Vivie had begun to rub her chest in a vain attempt to still her heart's wild beating.

Matthew's story

Iris has just begun, but I am distracted by a movement on the lawn above us. I see two women, and then I realise one of them is Vivie. They've just run through the stone arch in the red brick wall on the lawn above and I see Vivie stop, surprised, I think, to find herself in front of an audience, although she couldn't have been more surprised to see all of us than I am to see her.

She turns to the woman behind her, tucks her hair back up under her black cap, and then they walk towards the edge of the lawn above us. They disappear down some steps I hadn't noticed, on the east side, and now they're sitting on the bottom step. The woman is half hidden by some hanging Virginia creeper but Vivie is leaning out, hitching up the creeper, untying the clothes round her waist, pulling off her cap, shaking out her hair, leaning forwards, elbows on her knees, hair falling over her bare freckled arms, watching her mother.

Iris is talking about herself and her stories and I don't think she's seen Vivie. I'm sitting on the grass at Dad's feet; he's sitting on the canvas chair. He whistled softly when Vivie appeared and said, 'My word,' but now he's looking at Iris who still hasn't seen Vivie, as far as I can tell, although I can't take my eyes off her.

Iris's story

I stood with my back to the rose-covered retaining wall and the Bristol Channel, the almost-sea, sparkled in the distance. Rose Lawn was full. I was surprised and delighted that so many people had come to hear my stories and, at the same time, I had to work hard to control my nerves.

I waited for the people, and my nerves, to settle down.

'This,' I told myself, 'is it.'

When I have told my stories before, at the small gatherings in Norfolk, I have often said something about myself and something about my stories before I tell the first one. Sometimes I've said that I haven't had to take neuroleptic drugs for several years. Sometimes I've said something about my schizophrenic breakdowns, or I've talked about the havoc that breakdowns wreak on the people we love. Sometimes I've said that people like me should talk about their experiences, and do what we can to de-stigmatise madness, to show that recovery *is* possible.

But I've never planned what to say and, as the last few late-comers drifted up from the jousting field and found somewhere to sit, I saw the Green Man come through the iron gate. He sat on the low stone wall to my right. And I thought about trees, and I found that I wanted to talk about how madness can terrify a loved one. How, to the loved one, the person they thought they knew becomes an unrecognisable person, and how the loved one needs time to recover, just as the person who suffered the breakdown needs time to recover. And then I looked at Dick, perched high on his chair in the middle of the lawn and I smiled at him. He put his bent fingers together, kissed the tips of them and blew the kiss to me.

And then I began to talk about my stories.

'My stories are my own,' I said, 'they come from my life, not from any particular tradition or country, except the ones that I know and live in. And my stories are true in the way that dreams are true. I began to tell stories years ago. My mother told me stories and I learned from her, and I told the stories I invented to my daughter. But the ECT I was given snatched my memories of those times and so my stories have changed, and they continue to change. I would love to be able to remember what it was like to tell stories to my daughter, but in its crude and cruel way the ECT taught me that stories get better when they are re-invented and re-imagined.

'After my breakdowns,' I said, 'as I unearthed my old stories, I had to build new bridges to connect the parts I could remember, and that showed me that each story has many possible paths, many ways it can be told. In the end it didn't matter that I couldn't remember the whole story, all that mattered was that the story wasn't completely lost. I could find other ways to make it whole again. So, sometimes, I thank the ECT for that. Not that I recommend ECT. A straightforward memory lapse would have been a kinder path to such a discovery.'

A few people in the audience laughed.

'But I do wish I could remember what it was like to tell my stories to my daughter when she was small,' I said. 'Because it was her eagerness for my stories that spurred me on.'

As I said that a movement, to my left, caught my eye and I saw a flash of red-gold hair. I turned towards it and I saw Vivie.

I was sure it was Vivie.

The sun made her glorious head of red hair shimmer. It fell down over her bare shoulders, over her arms and she looked straight at me. Her eyes shone; she sat on the bottom step in the alcove of steps I discovered on Thursday. She had drawn her knees up in the way she always used to, her freckled arms hugged them into her body and her sweet freckled face smiled a little nervously at me. Her father's cap was in her hands, the one I made for him, the one that's been hers for years.

'Oh please,' I said to myself, 'please please don't let me be wrong. Don't let this be a hallucination.'

Iris's story

And then I heard Ruth's voice in my head.

'If you ever *wonder* whether or not you are hallucinating you can be confident that you are not.'

'The first story I shall tell,' I said, and I looked straight at Vivie and realised that I was about to tell a story that I hadn't practised these last few days, a story that I didn't know I would tell until that moment. 'The first story I shall tell is a story about a tree. I shall tell it for my daughter and for a childhood friend of hers, because they are both here, and because today is my daughter's birthday.'

I saw Dick rub his bent fingers under his eyes. He looked between me and Vivie.

I saw Matthew stare at her.

She was here. She had come. They could see her and I could see her.

Dick always said she would come. In her own time.

One day.

One fine, fine day.

I began to tell the story for Vivie under the brilliant sun. I dug my thumbnail into the pad under my little finger, hard, to remind me to find the words for the new pictures that had begun to form in my mind, to remind me to be brave and follow those pictures with new words. To remind me to follow the unfamiliar path and not just to tell the parts of the story I already knew. To remind me that if I followed the new pictures with new words, the heart of the story would blossom and grow.

'This first story,' I said, 'has its roots in a story I used to tell a long time ago. But it has changed much since then.' I smiled at Vivie and I felt my heart beat faster with happiness. And, as the story began to well up inside me and show me its pictures, I realised that the end of the story would change, today. Because it was the story of a mother, a daughter and a tree and, today, for the first time for so long, my daughter was with me.

The pictures filled my head as I looked at the tentative expression on my daughter's face. My daughter. The person I love more than anyone I have ever loved.

Speaking of Love

Then I closed my eyes and I waited. And I watched the pictures take their places, one after the other, in my mind.

I caught a misty glimpse of the last picture.

And I began.

THE TREE STORY

*T*here was, once, a remarkably beautiful tree.
It had a long, elegant, grey-green bole and branches that spread out like fingers towards the sky. In spring it grew abundant, luminous green leaves. In early summer it bore yellow flowers that hung from its branches in clusters like golden lanterns. In late summer the fruits of the tree grew long and green and were reminiscent of the succulent, sweet beans that also grow at that time of year. And when the bean pods dried and hardened and split open, little black seeds were revealed that shone as if they had been fashioned from the finest jet.

Everything about the tree was beautiful, and word of the tree's beauty spread as word of beauty will always spread. And as the word spread, people travelled from distant lands to see the tree, and as they travelled to the place where the tree grew they spoke about what they might find, and so it was that word began to spread that the beautiful tree possessed remarkable healing powers.

Word spread that those who heard nothing at all, and those who heard too much, these people would be healed if they sat beneath the tree. Word spread that those who saw nothing at all, and those who saw too much, these people would be healed if they sat beneath the tree. Word spread that those who spoke not one word, and those who spoke too much, these people would all be healed if they sat beneath the tree. And word spread that those who were heartsick, and those who had an ailment of the body or of the mind, these people would all be healed if they sat beneath the tree.

Speaking of Love

It was said that the beautiful tree required silence from those who sat beneath it. And it was also said that in the part of the world where the beautiful tree grew, thoughts alone were enough to convey matters of the heart and of the mind between all living beings. And so, by the time the travellers from distant lands had arrived in the place where the tree grew, they knew without question that all who sat beneath the beautiful tree would come away healed from whatever it was that ailed them. The travellers came in their hundreds and in their thousands to sit beneath the beautiful tree, in silent thought.

But the travellers found that the ground beneath the tree was hard and stony and uncomfortable, and they found that there was no food or water nearby. And, in their impatience, many of them began to speak and they cursed the tree because it was impossible to sit comfortably, and silently, beneath it. They cursed the beautiful tree for the lack of food and water nearby. They cursed the beautiful tree for its obvious inability to heal, and the air around the beautiful tree grew thick with the curses that the travellers uttered.

And then a woman came to the place where the beautiful tree grew, with her child. This woman had not heard all the words spoken by the thousands of people who came to sit as close as they could to the tree, for there were so many words and so many voices in her own head that she heard nothing else. There were so many sights before her own eyes, that she saw nothing else. But this woman, who found herself a place close to the tree with her child beside her, she said nothing because she knew nothing about the remarkably beautiful tree, nor did she expect anything from the tree. She simply sat beneath it because she was tired. But the impatience of the travellers from distant lands could not be contained, and word began to spread among them that to sit underneath the tree would never cure anyone of anything. Word spread that the beauty of the tree contained the cure.

And so it was that the travellers began to tear at the remarkably beautiful tree. They began to pull at the tree and they began to break the branches of the tree. The travellers ate the leaves of the tree and they ate the flowers of the tree, because they were so beautiful. And because they were convinced that the healing lay in the very beauty of the tree itself, the travellers ate the seeds of the tree and some of them even began to pull at the delicate bark of the tree. When they did so sap, which proved to be the finest, sweetest syrup, poured forth and the travellers drank it down for they knew now, without question, that if they had something of the beautiful tree inside them, then they would surely be healed. The travellers ate what they could of the tree until the insides of the beautiful tree were exposed to the elements, and when the travellers saw that there was nothing left for them to eat, and still they were not cured, they kicked the tree and pulled at the tree until the day came when the tree, broken and bent, began to ooze a sticky black liquid that trickled down its torn stump of a trunk. The sticky black liquid gave off a stench so terrible that the travellers could not breathe the foetid air that surrounded the tree and so, one by one, they turned from the tree and returned to the distant lands from whence they came.

But those who had heartsickness still had that sickness. Those who spoke, or heard, or saw too much, still spoke or heard or saw too much. Not one traveller among the travellers from distant lands was cured of anything that ailed them, and all went on their way and mumbled about false promises and trees that could not heal.

Not one of their number remembered that it had been they who had spread the word that the beautiful tree could heal in the first place. Not one of their number considered that they had punished the tree for a promise of their own invention.

Speaking of Love

Only the woman and her child remained at the foot of the tree because the woman was one of those who heard so much and saw so much that it was impossible for her to hear what other people heard or see what other people saw. And so she could not understand when her child told her that they must leave, for all the other voices that she heard drowned out the voice of her child. And the child was not strong enough to pull her mother forcibly from the tree. So the woman sat beneath the tree because her soul was exhausted by the sights and the sounds that crowded in upon her.

And the woman expected nothing from the tree.

But the beautiful tree fell into a state of disrepair, for without the beautiful flowers which give way to the abundant fruits which contained the seeds of new trees inside them, how was the tree to multiply? And without the sap, without that finest and sweetest of syrups, how was the tree to remain supple and grow? The sticky black liquid that oozed from the beautiful tree's broken stump of a trunk made such a terrible stench that not a soul came near to shelter beneath it, apart from the woman, who did not notice the stench, and her child, who did not want to leave her mother. Travellers now looked upon the tree with disgust and so, in its disrepair, the tree began to spit the sticky liquid that stank from its torn trunk and from its broken branches and when that liquid landed on human skin, it burned.

Eventually the child, just like the travellers, found that she could not tolerate the stench, nor the scorching burns that her fair skin suffered when the tree spat upon her. And so she left her mother at the foot of the tree because she could neither persuade her mother to come away with her, nor could she make her mother understand what it was that she knew must be done.

The child looked at the burn marks on her skin. She looked at her mother who stared blankly back at her.

The Tree Story

She looked at the broken tree that oozed and spat and stank and, with tears that streamed from her eyes, and a worn handkerchief that covered her nose, the child turned her back on her ailing mother and the broken tree, and she went in search of the only thing she knew about that might help.

The child went in search of water.

But when the child found water, when she found a wellspring and drank down the cool, sweet water and breathed in the sweet, fresh air, she was overcome with the desire to sleep and she could not fight that desire. And each time she woke and drank that water and breathed in that air she was overcome, again, with the desire to sleep, and so she slept, again. And, in the short spaces of time when the child was awake, when she drank that water and breathed that air, she thought of her mother and she was overcome with a terrible fear that if she once left this sanctuary, this place where the wellspring full of clear, sweet water was, this place where the sweet, fresh air was, she might never find it again. And so she did not leave the place. And the longer she stayed, the blacker grew her memory of the foetid air that surrounded the broken tree. The blacker grew her memory of her ailing mother. The blacker grew her memory of the waterless, soulless place that her mother and the tree inhabited. Until all she knew was that she could not leave the sanctuary she had discovered and so she stayed, and the burn marks on her skin began to heal.

The child built herself a makeshift hut beside the wellspring, and she built sturdy wooden pails to carry the water. And she told herself that what she did was just as it should be, and all that she could do. How could she help her mother if she would not be persuaded to come in search of water herself?

But all the while the child's mother remained beneath the tree in its terrible state of disrepair, and the few travellers who passed the once-beautiful tree gave it a wide berth because of the stench it gave off. And so they did not realise that, by its roots, there lay an ailing woman because that woman, in her ragged clothes, had begun to look much like the roots of that tree, and so she was not recognised for the woman she was.

The tree creaked and groaned when the cold winter winds blew onto its raw, exposed insides and the woman moaned as the cold crept into her bones. But as the winter cold froze the woman and the tree, the liquid that stank solidified and the stench was no more. The woman huddled as close to the tree's broken trunk as she could, and the tree's broken branches leaned down as close to the woman as they could and, unknown to either the tree or the woman, something of each entered the other while the snow fell and the winds whistled and howled all around them. And the woman and the tree hibernated, fitfully, through that cruel winter. But they remained alive.

When spring came at last and the woman uncurled and stretched her stiff limbs she saw that, in the places where the tree's stinking, burning black liquid had landed on her skin, there were hardened scabs and she found that she could rub them from her skin. And the woman realised that the sights and the sounds that had plagued her were no longer. She saw the tree, and the plain upon which it stood, and the hill to the south; she heard the birds and the sounds that all the other creatures, who began to venture near, made. But there was one sight and one sound that gladdened the woman's heart beyond all others. In her mind's eye the woman saw an image of her daughter, and in her mind's ear she heard her daughter's voice. And these sights and these sounds were ineffably sweet to her.

The woman stood and stretched her stiff body and, on an impulse, she wrapped the tree's exposed places in the rags that she wore; she kept just one rag for herself.

The Tree Story

And as the sun grew stronger the rags that the woman had wrapped around the tree mingled with the sticky, black liquid that rose in the tree and the heat from the sun bound the rags and the liquid together and the rags hardened and made new bark and covered the tree's exposed insides. And the sticky black liquid gave off a fragrant smell.

The tree flowered once more and the woman reached up to take a flower, for she was hungry and its scent enticed her, but the tree's branch lifted just out of her reach, so that she could only gaze at it. And the woman longed for water but she found that she could not bear to leave the tree, so she made herself do without water, and she found she could survive without it, just as she had survived the long winter without it. But when the time came for the tree to scatter its seed, the woman scooped up a handful and ate them in her hunger. And the ailments that had left her in the long, silent winter returned. The sights and the sounds that no one else saw, that no one else heard, returned, and the sight of her daughter and the sound of her voice left the woman.

The woman fell back against the bole of the tree as she struggled with too many sights and too many sounds, but the bark that had grown from the rags she had given the tree was strong by now, and the woman felt the tree behind her, felt it support her. The seasons followed one another and the tree supported the woman and the tree grew beautiful once more, and it was in this long time that a soft silence, a silence like cool, sweet water, began to enter the woman and the woman understood, at last, that the tree had drawn the sights and the sounds that no one else could see or hear from her, as poison is drawn from a wound, and she understood that this unaccustomed, soft silence, and this unaccustomed, clear vision had become hers because the tree, itself, had absorbed the poison that had caused all her ailments.

Speaking of Love

It was then that an image of the woman's daughter returned to her mind's eye, and the sound of her daughter's voice returned to her mind's ear, and the woman realised that if she never ate the fruits of the tree again, she would never again become ill. The woman understood that the tree had drawn the poisons from her body and poisoned itself with them. But the woman also understood that, in the case of this particularly beautiful tree, to possess poison was to possess peace.

As the woman stared up through the tree's new branches that stretched up to the sky like the fingers of a pair of strong, young hands, she flexed her own fingers and spoke. The woman promised the tree that she would tell the truth about what had happened. She promised that she would tell anyone who cared to listen that if any part of the beautiful tree should be eaten, that part would poison the eater and this, the woman promised the tree, would ensure that no one would attempt to eat any part of the tree, ever again. The tree would be free to grow and flower and fruit and spread its seeds so that other trees of its kind would flourish and grow.

And so it was that a day came when the woman leaned against the bole of the tree and thought about the exchange that had taken place between the beautiful tree and herself. She thought about how the tree had supported her and how she had understood the tree and made her promises. And it was on that day that the woman looked up and saw a much younger woman walk over the brow of the hill to the south. The woman saw that the younger woman carried two wooden pails and she knew, just by the way the younger woman walked, that that younger woman was her daughter.

And the woman knew that cool, sweet water filled the pails that her daughter carried. And suddenly she was filled with a great thirst. And she knew that, when her daughter arrived and sat beside her beneath the beautiful tree, she would greet her but she would not ask her where she had been, nor why she had been away for so long. And the woman knew that, when the time was right, she would tell her daughter about the mysterious exchange that had taken place between herself and the tree. And she would tell her daughter about the poison and she would tell her that there had been so many days when she had seen the image of her daughter in her mind's eye and heard the sound of her daughter's voice clearly in her mind's ear.

The woman knew that she would tell her daughter these things when the time was right, but for now all she knew was that she and her daughter would drink the cool, sweet water together underneath the tree.

The woman knew this just as surely as she knew why the poison that lived inside the beautiful tree brought it peace, and why that poison did not make the tree any the less beautiful.

And then the woman stood and opened her arms to greet her daughter and, as she did so, her daughter broke into a run.

THE END

Acknowledgements

These books helped while I was writing *Speaking of Love:*

This is Madness edited by Craig Newnes, Guy Holmes and Cailzie Dunn, PPCS Books, 1999
Complete Healing by Michael Evans, M.D., and Iain Rodger, Anthroposophic Press/Floris Books, 2000
Toxic Psychiatry by Peter Breggin, HarperCollins Publishers, 1993
Sanity, Madness and the Family by RD Laing and A Esterson, Penguin Books, 1964
Feelings Buried Alive Never Die by Karol Kuhn Truman, Olympus Distribution Corp, 1991
Women Who Run with the Wolves by Clarissa Pinkola Estés, Ballantine Books, 1992
The Female Malady by Elaine Showalter, Virago, 1987

This film helped:

A Beautiful Mind directed by Ron Howard, 2001

And these people variously read drafts of the book and made – thank you so much – suggestions that improved it; or they taught me, or took the time to answer my endless questions:

Phil Barker, Rachel Barnes, Julia Bell, Kate Beswick, Jenefer Coates, Emma Coats, Yoni Cohen, Nick Keith, Tessa Gibbs, Kay McCauley, Lucinda Mackworth-Young, Fatima Martin, my cousin, my Middlesex colleagues, my mother, Sean Rafferty, Brue Richardson, Alan St Clair, Antonia Till, Angie Titchen, Jess Wilder and Peter Wise. But most of all Julia Bell at TLC.

Sue Gee and Linda Leatherbarrow at Middlesex university.

All the storytellers I've ever heard, but especially Sally Pomme Clayton and Daniel Morden; Jenny Pearson and Michael Harvey; Jan Blake; Dovie Thomason and Alexander Mackenzie.

David Ambrose at Beyond the Border; Denise Bormann at the Raphael Centre; David Crepaz-Keay at Mental Health Media; Mandy Everett at Bethlem; Michael Evans at St Luke's Medical and Therapy Centre; the fisherman at Lowestoft; Clare Frankl-Bertram at Frankl + Luty; MIND and the NSF; Robin Nicholson at Edward Cullinan; Barbara Pollard at The Abbey House Gardens and Doug Pratt at Battersea Park.

Thank you

The largest possible, special thank you to Heather Holden-Brown for absolutely everything.

And thank you to Simon Petherick and Tamsin Griffiths at Beautiful Books for their boundless enthusiasm, and for taking the risk; and to Jonathan Wooding for saving me from seeing moons where moons cannot possibly be seen.

A note about schizophrenia

It is a sad fact that, as far as I know, there is no equivalent of my fictional Abbey (where Iris recovers from her second breakdown) for people diagnosed with schizophrenia. But perhaps one day such a place will exist.

As MIND's publication, *Understanding Schizophrenia*, 2005, states: 'There's considerable disagreement about the diagnosis of schizophrenia.'

At the moment MIND's advice on drugs for those diagnosed with schizophrenia is that, 'Some people get short-term help from medication, then come off it and remain well. Others may benefit from more long-term treatment. For these people, staying on the lowest effective dose of the drug may be the best way of dealing with symptoms, as well as lessening any side effect.'

Salem, where I set Iris's first breakdown in the 1970s, is based on an amalgamation of information about mental asylums in the bad old days. In those days, as far as I know, enlightened attitudes to drugs did not exist but I hope that, one fine day, there will be ways to help all those diagnosed with schizophrenia to manage their lives without drugs.

The author and publisher wish to thank the following for use of copyright material

pages 68-69
His Need is Greater than Mine
Reprinted by permission from '*The Exploits of the Incomparable Mulla Nasrudin*' by Idries Shah, Octagon Press Ltd, London, publishers of The Corpus of Nasrudin books by this author.

pages 78-79
'To Whom It May Concern' ('Tell me Lies about Vietnam') by Adrian Mitchell © Adrian Mitchell 1997 reproduced by permission of PFD (www.pfd.co.uk) on behalf of Adrian Mitchell. Adrian Mitchell Educational Health Warning! Adrian Mitchell asks that none of his poems be used in connection with any examinations whatsoever!

page 123
www.pantheon.org
Perdix by Martha Thompson

pages 134, 202 and 283
'If I Loved You' words by Oscar Hammerstein II and Music by Richard Rodgers © 1945, Williamson Music International, USA. Reproduced by permission of EMI Music Publishing Ltd, London WC2H 0QY.

pages 242-243
Hugh Lupton, storyteller, for permission to include a version of himself and for permission to include a summary of his telling of John Chapman, Pedlar of Swaffham.

page 279
AP Watt Ltd on behalf of Michael B Yeats for permission to reprint three lines from *He Wishes For The Cloths Of Heaven* by WB Yeats. From WB Yeats, Collected Poems, Vintage, 1992.

MIND, for permission to quote from *Understanding Schizophrenia*, 2005, in these pages.

Sally Pomme Clayton for permission to quote her at the end of the book.

'Your stories have relieved me of my madness.'

King Shahryār to Shahrazād
in a telling by Sally Pomme Clayton
of one of the stories from
The Thousand Nights And One Night

More fiction from Beautiful Books

The Last Good Man
Patience Swift

A man has lived on his own beside the sea for many years. From a choice made long ago, he keeps himself separate from the world of people, and is completely at one with his environment.

His solitude is broken by the discovery, one early morning on the flat sands of a low tide, of a child washed up on the beach. Somehow, she is still alive.

Down in the village, a woman reflects on a lifelong fascination with an ancient love story as she faces an unknown future.

The new arrival on the beach sets in chain a sequence of events that no-one can alter, and in this mystical and powerful novel, we witness a man experiencing our world as though for the first time.

Published 2007
ISBN 9781905636037
£14.99

www.beautiful-books.co.uk